HONOR BOUND

What Reviewers Say About BOLD STROKES Authors

❧

KIM BALDWIN

"*A riveting novel of suspense* seems to be a very overworked phrase. However, it is extremely apt when discussing Kim Baldwin's [*Hunter's Pursuit*]. An exciting page turner [features] Katarzyna Demetrious, a bounty hunter…with a million dollar price on her head. Look for this excellent novel of suspense…" – **R. Lynne Watson**, *MegaScene*

❧

ROSE BEECHAM

"…her characters seem fully capable of walking away from the particulars of whodunit and engaging the reader in other aspects of their lives." – *Lambda Book Report*

❧

GUN BROOKE

"*Course of Action* is a romance…populated with a host of captivating and amiable characters. The glimpses into the lifestyles of the rich and beautiful people are rather like guilty pleasures.…[A] most satisfying and entertaining reading experience." – **Arlene Germain**, reviewer for the *Lambda Book Report* and the *Midwest Book Review*

❧

JANE FLETCHER

"*The Walls of Westernfort* is not only a highly engaging and fast-paced adventure novel, it provides the reader with an interesting framework for examining the same questions of loyalty, faith, family and love that [the characters] must face." – **M. J. Lowe**, *Midwest Book Review*

❧

RADCLY*f*FE

"…well-honed storytelling skills…solid prose and sure-handedness of the narrative…" – **Elizabeth Flynn**, *Lambda Book Report*

"…well-plotted…lovely romance…I couldn't turn the pages fast enough!" – **Ann Bannon**, author of *The Beebo Brinker Chronicles*

HONOR BOUND

by

RADCLYfFE

2005

HONOR BOUND

ISBN 1-933110-20-1

THIS TRADE PAPERBACK ORIGINAL IS PUBLISHED BY
BOLD STROKES BOOKS, INC.,
PENNSYLVANIA, USA

FIRST EDITION: RENAISSANCE ALLIANCE PUBLISHING 2002
SECOND EDITION: BOLD STROKES BOOKS 2005

CREDITS
EDITORS: JENNIFER KNIGHT AND STACIA SEAMAN
PRODUCTION DESIGN: STACIA SEAMAN
COVER DESIGN BY SHERI (GRAPHICARTIST2020@HOTMAIL.COM)

By the Author

Romances

Safe Harbor

Beyond the Breakwater

Innocent Hearts

Love's Melody Lost

Love's Tender Warriors

Tomorrow's Promise

Passion's Bright Fury

Love's Masquerade

shadowland

Fated Love

Distant Shores, Silent Thunder

Honor Series

Above All, Honor

Honor Bound

Love & Honor

Honor Guards

Honor Reclaimed

Justice Series

A Matter of Trust (prequel)

Shield of Justice

In Pursuit of Justice

Justice in the Shadows

Justice Served

Change Of Pace: *Erotic Interludes*
(A Short Story Collection)
Stolen Moments: *Erotic Interludes 2*
Stacia Seaman and Radclyffe, eds.

Acknowledgments

My thanks to Jennifer Knight, who reviewed the first edition with an eye toward addressing the quirks and foibles in my early writing while kindly forgiving my idiosyncrasies. The second edition has benefited greatly from her keen eye.

Stacia Seaman has once again made the final edits painless—and that is no small feat where I am concerned.

Sheri has created a wonderful set of covers for this series, and I am very happy to be able to publish the complete set to date.

Most especially, Lee makes room without complaint for the characters who demand the time that should rightfully be hers. She makes our life a safe place for me to write. Thanks will never be enough.

Radclyffe 2005

Dedication

For Lee
For Every Day

CHAPTER ONE

M ac Phillips looked up from his seat at the main monitoring station as the door to Command Central opened at 0625. He tried to suppress a grin but failed as he recognized the tall, trim, dark-haired woman who strode purposefully toward him. He stood and extended his hand with a smile. "Welcome back, Commander."

Smiling warmly, United States Secret Service Agent Cameron Roberts shook the hand of the boyishly handsome blond agent. "It's good to be back, Mac." Despite the personal difficulties sure to come, she realized just how much she meant it.

She looked around the large open room that occupied the eighth floor of a brownstone apartment building overlooking Gramercy Park in Manhattan. It had been almost six months since she'd been in charge of the Secret Service security detail that worked out of this space, and she had not expected to return; at least, not in any official capacity.

Heading this unit was not a posting she had welcomed originally. She had spent most of her career in the investigative division of the Secret Service, tracking counterfeit funds used in illegal drug transactions. Working with members of the DEA, ATF, and Treasury Department in the field, she had considered the protective arm of the Secret Service a place for rookies and bureaucrats. Guarding diplomats, foreign visitors, and members of political families did not interest her.

Until now. Now, it mattered a great deal.

"Is Egret back on the ground yet?" Cam asked. She shrugged her shoulders, trying to work out the residual stiffness from her midnight flight. She'd been in Miami on a new assignment, pursuing a trail of treasury forgeries that the agency hoped would lead to a network of cocaine importers, when the call had come reassigning her.

This change in her orders was completely unexpected, and the fact that she had been instructed to report to New York City immediately, with no explanation and no interim briefing in DC, bothered her. No one had suggested that there was potential trouble on this end, but then that didn't mean anything. The federal government depended upon multiple security agencies with overlapping spheres of interest and influence, and there were never-ending turf struggles. Even those with a need to know often didn't get critical information until it was too late to be useful. She'd had personal experience with that kind of foul-up more than once. And once, it had nearly destroyed her.

"Long flight?" Mac couldn't help but notice the strain in her expression.

"The usual." Shaking off the cloud of fatigue, she dispelled the memories along with it. She wouldn't let that kind of screw-up happen here, not with something—someone—so important at stake. She would find out who, or what, was behind her transfer.

But first things first. She had work to do before her initial meeting with the woman she was charged to protect. A woman who, under the best of circumstances, was an unwilling participant in her own protection, and one who was certain to be even more resistant now.

Cam refocused on Mac. "I'll need to be briefed before I meet with her. I've been in the air most of the night and haven't been informed of her location."

"She's back in the nest," Mac affirmed, pointing toward the ceiling and the penthouse apartment above them that comprised the top floor of the building. "They returned from China late last night, but Egret didn't want to remain in Washington. They came up by car about 0300. That wasn't in the plans."

"I guess some things never change." Cam smiled to herself. *She always has to remind everyone who's really in charge of her life.*

Mac shook his head, but he wasn't smiling. He regarded his chief seriously for a moment and tried not to think about how close she had come to dying only months before. She looked fit and healthy now, but he knew that she had only been back on active duty for six weeks. As usual when on duty, she wore an impeccably tailored, understatedly expensive suit and appeared capable, competent, and cool—all the things he knew she was. He also knew from experience that it was hard to tell very much beyond that just by looking at her. She rarely revealed what she was feeling, but could always be counted on to say exactly what she was thinking.

"The team will be very happy to have you back," he said.

"What about you, Mac?" She leaned one hip against the edge of the desk, her dark gray eyes studying his. "I'm bumping you out of the commander's seat."

"You mean out of the hot seat?" He laughed, shook his head, and leaned back in the swivel chair, gesturing with one hand to the array of computer monitors, audiovisual equipment, and satellite feeds from the NYPD and New York Transit Authority on the long counter in front of him. "I'm an information man. This is what I want to be doing, and these last few months of doing your job proved it to me."

"Good," Cam said briskly. "I'm glad you're okay with it, because no one is more important than the communications coordinator, and I need the best."

"Thanks." Mac felt good about her confidence in him. "You're doing me a big favor, Commander. I'm no good at the VIP stuff, and with this kind of detail, that's key."

Cam didn't need him to tell her that knowing how to handle high-profile personalities was a requirement of the work. It was one of the reasons she was good at this particular assignment, and it was also the reason her next task was going to be so difficult. Blair Powell, code name Egret, had had Cam removed once as head of her security detail, and she was going to be very displeased to find she had returned.

She has every right to be angry, Cam thought. *This reassignment changes everything. Jesus, how am I going to explain this to her?*

Six weeks ago, they had spent five nights in one another's arms. If she had known then that she would be back heading Blair's security detail, she might have made a different choice. *Yeah, right.*

Blair's face briefly flickered into her mind, and the instant surge of heat that accompanied the image told her she was kidding herself. She had wanted her then, badly. Had wanted her for months—too much for procedure or protocol to have stopped her. She wasn't sure what she was going to do about those feelings now that circumstances had changed, but the one thing she did know was that she had a job to do.

Cam stood abruptly. "I'll see everyone at 0700 in the conference room. Bring what you have on her itinerary for the week, projected out-of-town events for the immediate future, all pertinent problematic field reports from the time I was gone, and anything else that you think needs my attention. I need to be up to speed by the time I meet with her this morning."

Mac nodded, then watched Cam walk toward the small glass-enclosed cubicle in one corner that served as their conference center. He saw her looking casually left and right toward the center of the room where several work areas were partitioned off by low dividers. He knew that she was assessing the monitoring equipment that the men and women assigned to her command utilized twenty-four hours a day to observe and protect the only child of the president of the United States.

At precisely 0700, Cam walked into the conference room carrying her second cup of coffee. She set it down at the end of the rectangular table and looked over the faces turned toward her. They were all familiar. No one had transferred out during her absence, and that pleased her because all of them were confirmed good agents. She had seen to that when she first took command almost a year before, demanding that anyone not one hundred percent committed to the task of guarding the president's daughter transfer out. Those who had chosen to stay had proven themselves under fire.

"Well," she began, allowing a faint grin to pull at one corner of her mouth. "At least I won't have to learn any new names. And we can skip all the introductory bull and get down to business." She looked down the room to where Mac sat with a pile of memoranda in front of him. "Mac?"

"Nothing new planned on the foreign front until the trip to Paris with the vice president and his wife next month."

"Right. " Cam settled into her chair with her PDA. "We'll need the routine advance information on motorcade routes, local hospitals, and transit lines for each day's events. That should all be in the database. I assume they'll be staying at the Hotel Marigny, as usual. That needs to be confirmed."

She turned to the collegiate-looking African-American man on her left, who happened to be fluent in nine languages with a working command of seven others. "Are you still doing the advance work on the foreign travel, Taylor?"

"Yes, ma'am."

"Good. Then you can contact the secretary at the Protocol Department in Paris to review the scheduled functions—charity dinners, museum outings—whatever they have planned. I want guest lists for any pre-announced gatherings and seating placements for theatre and dinner engagements." The French were notorious for changing itineraries at the last minute, and Paris was an international city where terrorism was a very real threat. "Keep after them. Make sure we're current by the time we're in the air. I don't want to be surprised."

"Got it."

"Fielding." She looked at a burly redhead two seats to her left.

"Ma'am?"

"Check with your buddies in intelligence and make sure we have the latest on any dissident activity in France, particularly active cells in Paris. I want photos and bios distributed to all team members before we depart. Mac will schedule a pre-flight briefing for sometime the week before we leave."

Taylor and Fielding nodded and made notes while Cam signaled Mac to continue. He shuffled some printouts and said, "Domestically, there's the opening of the Rodman Gallery in San Francisco in three weeks."

"Where's she staying?" Cam asked absently, her mind still on the Paris details. International travel placed any recognizable political figure at risk, and when that individual represented a country as widely hated as the USA, the risk escalated.

"We don't know yet." Mac sounded uncomfortable.

Cam looked up, narrowing her eyes. "You don't *know*? She must have reservations by now. Who's handling her itinerary?"

Mac blushed but kept his eyes on hers. He had forgotten how unforgiving she could be about any breach in protocol. He prepared himself to be dressed down. "She is, Commander."

"She is," Cam repeated in disgust. She knew damn well it wasn't Mac's fault. Struggling with her temper, she closed her electronic notebook and stood. "Is there anything pressing that the team needs to discuss this morning, Mac?"

"No, ma'am."

"Who's heading the day shift?" She looked over the team.

"I am, ma'am." The answer came from a smooth-featured, dark-haired woman in her late twenties. She might have been any one of the earnest, athletic, all-American types so often associated with government agents except for the surprising intensity in her voice.

"Fine," Cam acknowledged with a quick nod. After one nearly career-ending lapse in judgment, Paula Stark had proven herself to be cool and levelheaded. She was an invaluable asset as a member of the shift that spent the most time in direct contact with the first daughter. "Then go get your detail organized."

"Yes, ma'am," Stark replied, getting to her feet.

"Mac," Cam added crisply, "if I might speak with you, please."

Chairs scraped as agents hastened to get out of the conference room. They'd all seen Roberts take people apart if she felt they had been lax in guarding the president's daughter—no matter how difficult Blair Powell might make that job.

When they were alone, Cam looked at Mac and raised an eyebrow. "Okay. You want to tell me what the hell is going on? First, I get called back with no explanation and no notice. Then you say that Egret is bypassing normal security protocols. What else is happening that I don't know about? I can't work in the dark here."

"I'd tell you if I could, Commander, but I don't *know* why you've been recalled." He looked across the table into Cam's unreadable dark eyes and chose his words carefully. He liked her; he respected her; he was happy to serve under her. But they weren't friends. They didn't share personal confidences. He didn't know, for sure, what her past with the first daughter had been. "No one reported any problems to me, either about my command or anything else. As for Ms. Powell…" He shrugged, looking exasperated. "Ms. Powell is difficult."

Cam almost smiled at that enormous understatement but did not. She remained silent, watching him, waiting for the rest.

"She remains very reluctant to reveal her plans or destinations. She refuses to discuss personal...uh, relationships, so we have no intelligence regarding potential threats from that area. She slips our surveillance—" He halted at the soft curse from Cam, then added quickly, "Not very often, but it happens."

"You reported that?" Cam asked. Fighting fatigue, she rubbed her face briefly. *God, Blair is stubborn.* But she couldn't blame her, not really. Living under the constant scrutiny of strangers was wearing, even under ordinary circumstances. And Blair Powell's circumstances were far from ordinary.

Mac straightened. "No, ma'am, I did not."

"Reasons?" She stared at him hard. The kind of breakdown in security he was describing usually demanded reassignment of the agents involved, often with demotions. But she knew Mac Phillips, and she knew he wouldn't circumvent regulations just to save his own skin.

He met her gaze directly, and his voice was steady and sure. "Because she works with us most of the time, and I made the command decision that she was safer with *us* than with replacements she might not trust. Even if there were some problems."

Privately, Cam agreed. She had made similar choices herself where Blair was concerned. Had she been asked at the time, she wouldn't have been able to defend these, not according to regulations. But then, Blair Powell couldn't be dealt with by the book.

"I guess I'd better inform Egret that I'm here," Cam stated. She wondered just how much Mac knew. "I'll review the plans for the remainder of the week with you later."

He stood. "Yes, ma'am."

As he watched her walk out, he understood that the subject of his breach in protocol was closed. Whoever had made the call to bring Cameron Roberts back as commander of the first daughter's security detail knew what they were doing. Roberts understood what it took to guard Blair Powell. He wondered fleetingly what would happen upstairs when Egret learned of the change in command and decided there was some information he would rather not have. What he didn't know, he couldn't testify about.

Chapter Two

Blair Powell, in paint-spattered jeans and a T-shirt with the sleeves and lower half carelessly ripped away, stared at a five-foot square canvas. Totally engrossed, she was barely aware of the paintbrush in her hand. She walked slowly back and forth in front of the unfinished work, her mind as empty as she could make it. She let the color, the movement, and the depth of the images take form without conscious direction. Just as she reached to add a hint of red to one corner, her doorbell rang.

"Damn," she muttered, glancing at the clock at the far end of her loft. Just a little after eight a.m. It was much too early for a briefing with Mac, but it couldn't be anyone else. She didn't get unexpected visitors.

She set the brush aside and wiped her hands on a soft cloth. Pushing an errant strand of blond hair behind one ear, she crossed to the door. When, out of habit, she glanced through the peephole, she blinked in surprise and stopped with her hand on the doorknob. She looked again, her heart suddenly racing. Hurriedly, she pulled open the door.

"Cam!" She didn't try to hide her pleasure, an uncommon lapse in her usual reserve. Blair had learned not to allow her emotions to show, because her feelings were the only private things still left to her.

Since she was twelve years old, her father had been a public figure, and as a result, she had been as well. Strangers had photographed her, or written about her, or sought to be close to her, all because of her father. Bombarded with all that attention, she had never been sure if someone really cared for her or merely her reputation. Cameron had been different, and Blair had let her get close.

"I can't believe it. God, I've missed you."

Cam's pulse quickened. It had only been six weeks, but it had felt like months. Blair was every bit as beautiful as the last time Cam had seen her. Blond hair verging on gold, thick and wild with a hint of curl, fell around her face in an untamed mane. Blazing blue eyes and a smile that could melt the polar ice caps made an already attractive face stunning. A deceptively lithe body hid well-toned muscles. And underneath all that, seething sensuality coupled with an unbendable will. Astonishing.

"Hello, Blair." Cam wanted to touch her, but couldn't. She didn't want to hurt her and knew she was about to. Her face revealed little of her desire or her regret as she smiled softly.

Blair was too intent on how good it was to see her to notice the slight reservation in Cam's tone. She reached out, grabbed the agent's hand, and pulled her into the loft, slamming the door behind them. In the next instant, she had her hands in Cam's hair, her lips on Cam's mouth, and her body pressed hard against Cam's, pinning her to the wall. When she'd temporarily satisfied her need to taste her, she pulled away a fraction and gasped, "I've missed *that*, too. It feels like forever."

"Blair..." Cam made an enormous effort to get her body under control. The unexpected onslaught had gone straight to her head. And other places. Her stomach knotted with need and her blood burned. She felt herself swell and grow heavy with arousal.

Shaking her head, she tried to quiet her lust. She had to tell her, and quickly, because she wasn't strong enough to resist. Didn't want to resist. "I..."

"When did you get back?" Blair threaded her arms around Cam's waist and leaned her hips into her. "I thought you were still on that case in Florida. Did it wrap up already?"

As she spoke, Blair started working on the buttons on Cam's shirt with one hand. She had been planning on spending the day painting, but that was before. Her fingers shook she was so hot for her.

They'd had only a few days together, and that had been weeks ago. Five short days after almost a year of denying the attraction growing between them. A near tragedy had finally brought them together, then Cam had left for Florida and Blair had accompanied her father to Southeast Asia. Nothing about the future had been settled—there hadn't been time—but none of that mattered at this moment.

"God, I want you," Blair whispered, almost groaning the words. No one, no one had ever done this to her before. Made her *want* so badly, or ache so deeply. More than sex, more than intimacy. Cam created an explosive combination of the two that scorched through her, leaving her always hungry.

"Blair," Cam gasped, grabbing for the hand on her shirt. "Wait."

"Too late." Blair laughed, throaty and low, shifting to straddle Cam's thigh. The added pressure between her legs made her gasp again, her eyes closing momentarily with the rush of excitement. "Oh, God. Way too late, baby. I need your hands on me. Now. I'm so, so ready."

"I'm working, Blair," Cam said gently, feeling her shudder and hoping Blair couldn't sense her own urgent response. Trembling, suddenly light-headed, she swallowed a moan as Blair thrust into her again. "We can't."

"You can be a few hours late for wherever you need to be. You're a regional director now," Blair muttered. She wasn't really listening to anything except the need singing through her pelvis. "I can't wait."

She'll never forgive me. Cam moved her fingers to Blair's wrist, circling it softly. "I'm working *now*, Blair. Here."

Something in Cam's tone finally penetrated Blair's consciousness, a hint of sympathy that eclipsed the desire Blair could feel simmering in Cam's body. With effort, she took one step away so that their bodies were no longer in contact. Her hands shook. She shivered lightly but steadfastly ignored the rush of persistent arousal.

"What do you mean?" she asked, her voice unnaturally calm.

She searched Cam's eyes for the answer, because Cam's eyes never lied. Not to her. What she saw in them hurt, deeply. Hurt in a way she hadn't thought she could ever hurt again.

"Damn you," Blair whispered on a breath, not knowing which of them she meant. "What have you done?"

"I've been reassigned, Blair. To you." Cam watched Blair back away, forced to let her go. *Jesus, I had hoped it wouldn't be this hard. I just need a little time to find out what's going on. Then I can explain, make you understand.* "Blair—"

"When?" Blair interrupted coldly, retreating across the room. She needed space between them. She had to stop wanting her long enough to think. "When did you find out?"

"Yesterday."

"And you said *yes?* Without even talking to me?" *What about us? Didn't that mean anything to you? I thought...oh, what a fool I was to think—*

"Blair, please," Cam said quietly. "There was no time. I received a directive from my superiors informing me that the president of the United States requested me to assume responsibility for his daughter's security. I could hardly say no."

"Of course you could," Blair said bitterly, "if you'd wanted to. There are plenty of other people who can do that job. Mac is handling it just fine." *Don't do this; please don't do this!*

"It's not that simple," Cam said, knowing her words would not help. She wasn't sure how to explain that part of her didn't *want* anyone else to do the job. Couldn't explain that every day while she was somewhere else, doing something else, she worried about Blair. She couldn't forget that there was an UNSUB, an unidentified subject, who had stalked Blair, photographed her, left messages for her, and ultimately, shot at her—and he was still out there. She *wanted* to be with her. She needed to be with her. "It's not just *about* us."

"No. It never is." Blair turned away, struggling with disappointment and betrayal.

Clearly, whatever she thought had been developing between them was over. Cameron Roberts was not the kind of woman to compromise her professional ethics by carrying on a clandestine affair with someone she was supposed to be guarding. It would have been difficult for them to see each other under any circumstances; now it would be impossible. Blair swallowed her pride and made one last attempt to undo what had already been done. This decision had been made without regard for her feelings, like so many others in her life.

"I could speak to my father," Blair said, disguising the hope in her voice. "The security director can name someone else to command the detail."

"I'm sorry." Cam struggled not to go to her. No matter how hard Blair tried to hide it, Cam could hear her anguish. "There's a reason I've been recalled. I don't know what it is yet, and neither does Mac. Until I find out, I'd prefer you not say anything."

"This is what you want?"

"I didn't mean to hurt you, but your safety is more important than anything else."

"That's not an answer, that's an excuse. Answer me, Cam. Is heading my security detail more important than *us*?"

"Yes."

Blair's face was a careful blank. "Well, that's it then, isn't it?"

"I'm sorry," Cam said again, unwilling to offer further excuses that would only be insulting to them both.

For the time being, she didn't have any choice except to assume the responsibility that had been given to her. And in truth, she wouldn't want it any other way. She had to know what was happening. Still, watching Blair's eyes turn cold rocked her. She couldn't think about losing her, not and still do what she needed to do.

"No need to be sorry, Commander," Blair said dismissively. "We both know how important your job is to you. Now, if you don't mind, I'm busy."

Cam worked to keep her voice neutral. "I understand. I'll need to discuss plans for the rest of the week with you."

Blair walked past her, careful not to touch her, and opened the door. "Then you can come back this afternoon for the scheduled briefing."

"As you wish," Cam said resignedly, stepping out into the hall.

The silence that ensued when the door closed solidly behind her was lonelier than anything she could ever have imagined.

"Mac," Cam said into her transmitter as she keyed the penthouse elevator outside Blair's apartment.

"Go ahead, Commander." Mac automatically checked the monitor providing visual surveillance of the hallway in front of the elevator. His eyes switched to the adjoining screen showing the interior of the elevator as Cam stepped in.

"Sign me out to my apartment," she said tersely. "It's the same address as before. Someone pulled a few strings to get it back for me."

She wanted a shower, a change of clothes, and a few minutes to herself. She needed to banish the sound of Blair's disappointment and the image of the pain in her eyes. She had to meet with her later in the day to confirm the agenda for the upcoming weeks, and she needed to be in control of herself when she did.

The very first moment she had seen Blair Powell, she'd been attracted to her. Out of duty, she had ignored those feelings for months. But, as time passed, she had come to know her, and desire had turned to caring. She hadn't been able to withstand both the demands of her body and the yearning of her heart, and—finally—she had succumbed.

Finally, she had touched her.

But it had been different then—then she hadn't been charged with protecting her. For those five days, she hadn't been a Secret Service agent and Blair had not been the first daughter. Now, everything had changed—she was professionally responsible for Blair's safety again. Now, she would somehow have to learn to live with her need, because she wasn't going to be able to touch her again.

Already, she ached with the loss.

Mac studied Cam's face in the monitor, and even with the mild distortion of the transmitted image, he could make out the tense set of her jaw and the grim line of her mouth. *Uh-oh. Things must not have gone well with Egret.* He wasn't surprised. Cameron Roberts had been shot in the line of duty, shot while guarding Blair Powell. Shot *in place* of Blair Powell when she'd stepped in front of her and stopped a bullet from a sniper's rifle.

The commander didn't remember the nightmarish scene as she'd lain bleeding on the sidewalk while agents surrounded Egret and dragged her to cover. Mac remembered it very well.

He remembered the president's daughter screaming Cam's name as Cam went down, and her struggling to break free of the restraining arms—struggling to go to the dying agent, heedless of her own safety. He remembered her sitting by Cam's bedside for almost two days while Cam's life hung in the balance. And he knew, too, that Blair Powell had requested that Cam be removed from her security detail once she recovered. He couldn't imagine she would be happy about this new arrangement.

"You're scheduled for a briefing with Egret at 1300 hours," he said while glancing over the day's events printed out on a clipboard by his right hand. When in doubt, revert to procedure.

"I've got that," she snapped as she walked quickly through the lobby, nodding curtly to the doorman as he hastened to hold the double glass doors for her.

Once outside, she stopped under the short green awning and surveyed the rooftops, barely visible through the trees, of the buildings across the park. It was the first time she had been back since the shooting. She stared at the sidewalk and recalled seeing the fine red mist on her hands and the clear, blue sky overhead as she lay on her back, feeling life slip away. She shivered lightly, thinking that it might have been Blair that day and not her. Then she shrugged the memory away and crossed the street toward her apartment on the other side of the square.

When she'd stripped off her jacket and eased out of her weapon harness, she walked to the windows that overlooked Gramercy Park directly opposite the Aerie. Staring at Blair's penthouse, she thought about her up there now—in that space that should have been a haven. The windows facing the street in Blair's loft were bulletproof, the fire escape ended one level below her floor, and the skylights on the roof above were crisscrossed with woven titanium mesh that would require a blowtorch to cut. *A posh fortress, but a subtle prison nonetheless.*

Cam couldn't blame her for hating it. She couldn't even blame Blair for being angry with her. She wished she could change it, but the facts of Blair's life were beyond anyone's control.

She turned away from the image of Blair's smile and the memory of Blair in her arms. Wanting her would not help either of them now.

After Cam left, Blair waited motionless on the other side of the door, listening to the distant hum of the elevator climbing to the penthouse to carry Cam downstairs. Long after she knew Cam was gone, she hoped foolishly that the agent might return. By the time she finally turned back into her empty loft, she had managed to replace longing with anger, a familiar antidote to disappointment.

If only she could convince her body that she no longer cared. Cam's arrival that morning had been so unexpected that she hadn't done anything except react. Few women had ever been able to excite her the way Cameron Roberts did, with little more than a smile. It was one of the things that made her security chief so frightening. Blair made a point of keeping everyone at arm's distance, physically and emotionally, but she had failed miserably with Cam. She'd been ready in a heartbeat just at the sight of her standing outside in the hall.

Walking through the loft, she was still throbbing with the aftermath of unanswered arousal. She was so angry with herself for allowing this to happen that even her body's automatic response seemed like a betrayal.

"Shower," she muttered under her breath, shedding clothes as she crossed to the partitioned area in the corner that adjoined her sleeping alcove.

She twisted the dial and stepped under the still-cold spray, gasping at first contact. Her nipples were still full and tender from the recent stimulation, and the wetness between her legs was not from the rivulets of water running down her body. She leaned against the far wall and let the warming cascade engulf her. She closed her eyes, and that was a mistake.

As soon as she surrendered to the soothing beat of the water on her skin, she saw Cam's face. She felt Cam's body along the length of her own—remembered being pressed together against the door. She imagined Cam's hands on her, just as she had imagined them so many times during the weeks they had been apart. Ordinarily such remembrances produced just a pleasant hum of pleasure, but she was already aroused, painfully so. The pinpricks of heat on her skin seemed to streak directly between her legs, and the tingling pressure building there warred with her self-control.

I will not think about her.

She grabbed soap and began to lather her neck and chest, smoothing her palms over her breasts and stomach. The flicker of her fingers passing over her nipples made her breath catch. Without consciously meaning to, she caught one between her thumb and forefinger and squeezed, arching her back slightly into the warm spray as the sharp pinpoint of pleasure-pain seared down her spine. It was too good, too good not to lift her hands and cup both breasts, squeezing as she rhythmically twisted her erect nipples until all she could feel was a steady burning pleasure beneath her fingertips.

Legs trembling, she pressed her shoulders harder against the rear shower wall for support. She ached inside. Still massaging her breasts with one hand, she pressed the other to her stomach, running her fingers lightly over her skin, moving lower with each stroke. Her pulse beat between her legs like a second heart. She knew how hard she was, had felt the stiff swelling as she straddled Cam's thigh. If she touched herself, she would never be able to stop. She had been close the minute her lips had found Cam's mouth.

I am always so damn ready for her. She imagined Cam's fingers where her own brushed through the hair at the base of her belly, and her clitoris twitched.

"Ah, God," she whispered, shuddering at the memory. She needed to ease the pressure, couldn't think of anything else. Her fingers slid lower, one on either side of her distended clitoris. Her hips jerked as she squeezed lightly, and she had to brace herself with one arm against the wall to keep from falling.

Her mind was empty of everything except the exquisite sensation of her fingertips rubbing over her blood-engorged flesh. She was dimly conscious of her muscles quivering and the pounding pressure of her orgasm building. Faintly, she heard herself whimpering with each teasing stroke. Neck arched, she thrust her hips steadily back and forth as her hand moved faster between her legs, setting her nerves on fire. When the inferno roared from her pelvis and scorched along her veins, she choked back a cry, her fingers squeezing down with each spasm, milking each pulsation to the very end.

As the contractions finally ebbed, she leaned weakly forward into the spray, both arms outstretched, palms against the opposite wall, barely able to stand. Her body was satisfied, but she took no satisfaction from it. She still felt hollow.

"Damn you, Cameron," she whispered.

Chapter Three

At 1255, Cam approached Blair's building for their briefing. Two things occurred simultaneously. The earphone connected to her radio transmitter crackled to life, and she saw Blair Powell flag down a Checker cab, slide into the rear seat, and disappear as the vehicle pulled away into traffic.

"Commander, please be advised that Egret is flying solo," Mac's voice informed her. "Unit one has been dispatched but does not have visual."

Cam turned abruptly, stepped into the street, and hailed one of the many taxis passing by, practically walking in front of it to force it to stop. As she pulled open the front door, she extended a hand displaying her open badge folder. "I need you to follow that cab up ahead."

The taxi driver stared at her. "You're kidding, right?"

Cam shook her head and got in beside him, her eyes following Blair's vehicle around the square. "I wish I were. You're going to lose them if you don't get going."

It was something about the utter stillness in her face and the unnatural calm in her voice that made him face forward, sit up straight, and, with his hands gripping the wheel tightly, execute a performance of New York City driving that would have won him a trophy at Daytona. He pulled to a stop ten feet and twenty-five seconds behind the cab that had carried Blair to a small coffee shop deep in the heart of Greenwich Village.

"Thanks." Cam handed him a twenty as she stepped out.

He leaned across the seat to look up at her. Her sculpted features, ebony hair, and deep voice seemed familiar, and he thought he finally understood.

"You're making a movie, right?"

She didn't answer. She was already halfway across the sidewalk.

As soon as she entered the small storefront café, she located Blair seated with another woman at a small table for two in the rear. Blair looked up at the sound of the chime over the door, her eyes meeting Cam's, but she gave no sign of recognition. Cam threaded her way through the few tables to the counter and ordered a double espresso. While she waited, she glanced around the room, noting the location of the exits and the general position of the few patrons, mostly twenty-somethings reading newspapers or working on sleek laptops.

She paid and picked up the small espresso cup, moving to the opposite corner of the room from where Blair was seated. She chose a small circular table in the front corner, her back to the wall. From there, she could watch the front and rear doors as well as everyone in the room without infringing on Blair's conversation. She would have been happier to have a car out front in case they needed to leave quickly, and she hoped that unit one—Paula Stark and her partner—would arrive momentarily. They'd been scrambling into one of the unmarked Suburbans in front of Blair's apartment building as she went by in the cab.

Fortunately, most civilians didn't recognize Blair when she went out dressed casually, with her hair down and wearing little or no make-up. Today, in jeans, a navy cotton V-neck sweater over her white T-shirt, and scuffed boots, she looked like most of the young denizens of the neighborhood. The man-on-the-street usually recognized public figures only when they were attired formally and placed in the appropriate surroundings. That was the one thing that made Cam's job easier, because Blair Powell certainly didn't.

"Commander?" Paula Stark's voice asked in her ear.

"Yes," Cam murmured, tilting her head slightly as she listened to Stark relay her position. She gave Stark her exact location and informed her that she'd stay inside with Blair. "Just maintain in the vehicle outside."

"Roger that," Stark replied morosely, wondering just how pissed off her commander was going to be that they had let Blair Powell walk unescorted right out of the building. The president's daughter hadn't pulled one of her old tricks in so long that when she called for the elevator and announced she was going to the lobby to get her mail, they hadn't brought the car around front in anticipation. When they finally realized that she had exited the building and was hailing a cab, they'd lost two minutes mobilizing. Stark sighed, settling back to watch the door to the café and the people going in and out.

Forty minutes later, the statuesque blond with Blair stood up and crossed the room to Cam's table. She leaned down far enough to show more cleavage than could easily be ignored and said in her low throaty voice, "How nice to see you again, Commander. Blair tells me that you're back in charge of her."

Cam shifted slightly so that she could keep Blair in her sightline. "I'm not sure I'd phrase it precisely that way, Ms. Bleeker," she said with a faint smile, her eyes following Blair as she gathered her things.

"Actually, Blair didn't put it exactly that way either. The way she described it was quite a bit more...*colorful*," Diane Bleeker said provocatively. In fact, Diane had sensed that Blair was on the verge of tears through much of the conversation, although she wasn't certain if they were tears of anger or tears of pain. Even if she was right, she knew that Blair would never give in to them, particularly when the woman at the heart of her distress was sitting fifteen feet away.

No one who didn't know Blair very well would even have realized how distraught she was. Diane knew because she and Blair had been friends since they were teenagers together at prep school, and she knew because six weeks ago Blair had asked to use Diane's apartment while Diane was in Europe.

It had been a long time since Blair had brought a lover to Diane's, because Blair rarely slept with anyone more than once and rarely planned for it in advance. She didn't need to plan an anonymous liaison with a woman she met by chance in a dark bar or at a high-society fundraiser. When Diane had asked whom she was planning on seducing, Blair's silence had been telling. Whoever she was, she mattered. Now, Diane had a very good idea just who that woman had been.

During a brief moment of madness, she contemplated informing the strikingly handsome, dark-haired security agent that she was making the biggest mistake of her life. If she chose to be Blair's protector rather than her lover, no matter how noble her motives, Blair would never forgive her.

But Diane knew she wouldn't say anything, today or any other day, and she wasn't altogether proud of the reasons why. Despite her long friendship with Blair, they had always been attracted to the same women, and most of the time they had been good natured about the competition because it was all in fun—the chase, the seduction, the consummation. This time it was different. For Blair to admit any feelings at all for a woman, it had to be serious. Even knowing that, Diane couldn't deny the quick surge of attraction she felt every time she saw Cameron Roberts.

"It was nice to see you again," Cam said, rising, but her attention was on Blair, who was walking toward the front door. "If you would excuse me." She stepped away to follow Blair.

Out on the street, Blair had turned and was watching Cam come through the door. At the same time, Paula Stark stepped out of the car that had been idling across the street from the café. Cam waved Stark back and walked over to Blair.

"It makes it difficult when we don't know where you're going," Cam said quietly, although she knew very well that Blair was aware of that.

"Apparently, the rules of this engagement can change at any time." Blair shrugged slightly. She wasn't able to keep the edge of bitterness from her voice. "Fair is fair."

Cam nodded and met Blair's heated gaze. "I know it must seem that way, and I'm sorry. For the time being, we're both going to have to live with it."

"No, *we* don't. You made the decision—I'll deal with it any way I want." Blair shook her head dismissively and turned her back, moving quickly away down the sidewalk.

Damn it. Cam caught up with her and fell into step, automatically placing herself between Blair and the street. She knew without looking that Stark and her partner would follow slowly behind them in the unmarked vehicle.

"There's no point in putting yourself in danger because you're angry with me, Blair," Cam persisted gently. "If you'll just let us do what we need to do, I'll intrude on your private life as little as possible."

Blair stopped abruptly and faced Cam, heedless of the complaining people who had to suddenly step around them on the narrow sidewalk. In a low, seething tone, she asked, "Has it occurred to you, Commander, that I *wanted* you to intrude on my private life? *You*. Not strangers twenty-four hours a day. Just you."

Cam ran a hand through her hair, struggling with both frustration and temper. She wanted to explain to Blair that she *did* care, and that she didn't plan for this to happen, and that it was torture to see her and not be able to touch her.

"Blair..."

Someone jostled her shoulder as they passed, and she swore under her breath. A public sidewalk was no place to have this discussion. If she had only managed to keep her own emotions under control when she had first been assigned to Blair Powell's security detail, none of this would be happening now. She had allowed herself to give in first to physical attraction, and then to emotional attachment. Now she had entangled them both in a situation for which there were no rules and only potential disaster.

She grimaced because she could see the pain in Blair's eyes, and she didn't have the luxury of explaining herself at the moment. Not here, not now.

"Can we talk about this in a somewhat more secure location?"

Blair laughed darkly, unable to help herself. If there was one thing she could count on with Cameron Roberts, it was that no matter what was happening, Cam would never let it interfere with her duty. And she hated being Cameron Roberts's duty.

She started walking again. "I don't think there's anything left to talk about. You made your decision. I don't intend to adjust my life to make yours easier. Now, if you'll excuse me, I'm going to the gym and beat the crap out of someone."

"Ernie's?" Cam asked, remembering the third-floor hole-in-the-wall establishment that Blair had somehow managed to frequent for six months before anyone in the security detail realized that she was there and not at her massage therapist's around the corner.

"Ernie's is the one place I can go that no one knows me and no one cares where I come from or where I'll be going back to. The only thing they care about is what I do in the ring." She wasn't in the mood for company. "I'd like to keep it that way."

"Wait a minute..." Cam hurried to keep step with her through the narrow streets of the Village as they headed north toward Chelsea. She barely stopped herself from grabbing Blair's arm to slow her down. "Are you trying to say that no one has been inside with you?"

"Not upstairs. One look at the Junior G-men and half the guys up there would have jumped out the windows to get away."

"That's my point, God damn it." Blair should never be left unguarded, even in the most secure circumstances. Exceptions occasionally occurred, but they were rare, and Ernie's was not one of them. It was a tough, almost exclusively male crowd, and Cam was willing to bet there was more than one man there outside the law. "I can't believe Mac didn't put someone with you."

"It's happened before—if you remember."

The biting tone of Blair's voice told Cam what she meant. She and Blair had spent five nights together at Diane Bleeker's East Side apartment while Diane was in Europe. None of the team had actually been in the apartment with Blair, but there had been a car with two agents parked on the street in front of the building. If the people stationed outside knew that Blair was not alone, no one had ever given any indication.

Cam hadn't liked placing fellow agents in a situation that they might later have to lie about, but at the time, she hadn't been assigned to Blair's security detail. Their few hours together each evening were personal—personal and intimate and no one else's business. She wasn't hypocritical enough to deny, even to herself, that she and Blair had tried to keep their meetings a secret, but they had not purposely eluded the Secret Service agents either.

"I remember." Cam steeled herself, refusing to discuss their personal issues when there was a real threat to Blair's safety to deal with, and knowing how Blair would react. "But the gym is an entirely different situation. You're in unsecured surroundings with two dozen men who, even if they *don't* recognize you, might present threats. If you *were* recognized, absolutely anything could happen, from simple harassment to abduction."

Her words were met with stony silence, but she continued.

"I don't know how you've managed to keep the team away from here, and I'm not certain I want to know, but I can't let you go alone."

"I know that," Blair snapped, turning down the alley that led to the unmarked, unpainted door that was the street entrance to the third-floor gym. "Usually a car waits just at the end of the alley. That should be good enough. I've been coming here for years. No one will bother me."

"I'm coming up with you," Cam said grimly. It was too late to change plans now, and since she was the only one immediately available, the responsibility fell to her.

"You can come up if you want, Commander." Blair stopped with her hand on the door and glanced at Cam, her face completely unreadable—her eyes flat and expressionless. "But I would prefer that you stay away from me."

With that, she opened the door and took the stairs two at a time, leaving Cam to follow.

Minutes later, Cam leaned against one wall, her hands in the pockets of her blended silk trousers, watching two fighters prepare to spar in the ring opposite her. Automatically, she gave the entire room and its occupants a thorough examination, noting how many people were present and each individual's position.

The top floor of the warehouse was dimly lit by what little natural light managed to seep through dirty windows situated well above head level and augmented by fluorescent fixtures dangling from heavy chains in the cavernous ceiling. The combination cast the entire space in a harsh, flickering haze. Sparring rings stood in each of three corners. In the fourth, a space was partitioned off from the larger room by plywood and exposed two-by-fours and served as the business office and makeshift locker rooms.

When she and Blair had first entered, Blair had disappeared into the tiny women's dressing area, which was nothing more than a closet with a curtain strung across the door.

For several reasons, Cam did not follow.

She had wanted to give Blair as much privacy as possible, and following her into the dressing room would only call more attention to them both. Furthermore, she had been in that dressing room with Blair once before, and she knew just how small it was, and she knew exactly how Blair looked when she stripped off her clothes to put on her workout gear.

She did not want to be standing two feet away from her when Blair did that, because regardless of her intentions, she knew she would be tempted. It had been six weeks, and not a day—hell, barely an hour—

had passed that she didn't think about Blair. What she couldn't tell Blair, and what she didn't want to think about herself, was how many times in those six weeks she had imagined how Blair's skin would feel under her fingertips.

So now she stood in the shadows where she could see the entire room and still be as close to Blair as she could be without actually climbing into the ring with her.

Twenty feet away, Blair jogged lightly in place on the soiled canvas cover of the ten-foot square ring while she waited for her opponent to adjust his gloves and get his mouthpiece between his teeth. She had been free-sparring for almost three months with some of the men in her weight class. None of the other female kickboxers who frequented the gym were experienced enough to spar with her. The men accepted her as one of the regulars, and no one thought anything of working out with her. After the first few times she'd put one of them soundly on the mat with a roundhouse kick or a strong right cross, they'd forgotten she was a woman and had fought her with no holds barred.

The young guy opposite her approached, a little belligerence in his attitude. *Perfect.*

She needed an outlet for her physical frustration and her mental turmoil. Cam's abrupt return and the sudden change in their relationship had left her reeling. Nothing would test her or distract her as much as being in the ring with someone who could potentially hurt her. She would be forced to focus and she would need to burn. Still, she knew that somewhere nearby, Cam was watching. She couldn't see her, and she didn't *want* to see her. *I want to forget her.*

But she felt her.

And part of her wanted Cam there, even though she hated to admit how comforting she found the agent's presence. Cam was so very good at making her feel cared for, even when it was part of her job. From the very beginning, she'd made Blair feel that *she* was what mattered and not just the status reports or job-performance evaluations that seemed to motivate so many of the dozens of agents who had guarded her throughout her childhood and into adulthood.

God, I hate that I love every single thing about Cameron Roberts.

Blair lifted her gloved hands and tapped them against those of her opponent, eager for the first contact, wanting desperately to erase Cam's face from her mind.

Cam watched Blair dance lightly across the canvas.

She's even better than she used to be.

Unlike most male kickboxers, who relied primarily on their punches for knockouts, Blair had to depend more on her legs, which were—as for most women—more powerful weapons than her hands. This gave her the advantage of staying beyond the range of most other fighters' punches and, with a well-placed kick, she could render a man unconscious. On the other hand, she wouldn't be able to weather too many direct blows to the face from a man her size or even one smaller. As Cam watched, Blair effectively countered a volley of punches and pushed her opponent back with a nicely executed front kick to his thigh.

As she kept constant vigil of the people nearby in her peripheral vision, Cam allowed herself the luxury of simply looking at Blair. Her hair was pulled back away from her face and gathered at the nape of her neck, the few remaining wild curls secured with a rolled red bandanna tied around her forehead. She wore loose navy shorts and a cropped white T-shirt that left her midriff bare. The small gold ring in her navel glinted against the sweat sheen on her skin.

Watching the muscles ripple in her stomach, Cam stared at the ring and remembered how it felt to rub her palm over it. It was a memory she'd relived many times since that first night they'd shared in Diane's apartment, and the intensity of the image remained undiminished.

She'd been there close to an hour, waiting for Blair. She tried to kill time reading a magazine from a stack next to the sofa, but she couldn't concentrate. Too anxious. Too worried about Blair. She knew the agents who followed her to the apartment, and watched the building, would wonder what she was doing at Diane's. Blair didn't make a secret of her sexual preferences, at least as far as her security team was concerned, but it was never wise to give anyone too much information of a private nature. And rumors of Blair trysting with a Secret Service agent would make for powerful discussion around the water cooler.

Cam reminded herself that she knew these agents, and she believed in her heart that they could be trusted to be discreet, but the habit of a lifetime of guarding her own secrets was hard to change. And there was more than just their personal privacy involved—there was the little matter of Blair's very public image. When and if Blair decided to share her private life with the world—because that's what it would amount to for someone in her position—it should be her choice and not because she had no freedom to chose.

Despite the potential problems, she couldn't wait to see Blair again. After resisting her for so long, now all she could do was think about her. When she heard the key turn in the lock, she got to her feet and crossed the living room toward the tiny foyer just inside the front door.

Blair stepped through, breathless and smiling, and deposited a bag and a bottle of wine on the small table nearby. For just an instant, she looked shy. "Hi."

"Hi." Even that small word was hard to get out around a throat suddenly tight with desire. She thought that she had never seen Blair look quite so young. When Cam kissed her, she meant it only as a kiss of greeting. But they hadn't seen each other for almost twenty-four hours, and they'd only had one night together then. It had not been enough, and at that moment, it felt like it would never be enough.

One of them groaned, and each began frantically undressing the other right where they stood. Soon, they were pressed together half naked, unable to stop touching each other long enough to finish the job. Hungrily trading kisses and small bites, Cam found Blair's breasts. She lifted them, squeezing a little harder than she intended as the astonishing thrill of finally touching her drove caution from her mind.

"Oh yes," Blair gasped, pushing harder into Cam's hands, working desperately to loosen the buttons on Cam's jeans. They were both in danger of falling in their eagerness to consume one another.

Finally, Cam wrenched her head back, gasping. "Wait! There must be a bedroom here. I really need to do this lying down."

Eyes wild with urgency, Blair simply grasped the waistband of Cam's jeans where she had managed to get the top button open and tugged. "Come on," she ordered, her voice husky with want. "Guest room. This way."

Cam followed, slipping one hand around Blair's body from behind, smoothing her palm over the silky tautness of a bare abdomen. The small gold ring rubbed lightly against her skin, and she didn't think she'd ever felt anything quite so sexy. She stopped Blair just outside the door to the bedroom, pressing her bare chest to Blair's back, lifting both hands to cup Blair's breasts again.

With her lips close to Blair's ear, she moved her fingers to Blair's nipples and squeezed. "Yesterday, you made me beg."

Blair jerked in Cam's arms, arching into her hands as Cam continued the pressure on her nipples. "Do you have a point, Commander?" She reached back with one hand, searching for the rest of the buttons on Cam's fly.

"Could be it's your turn to beg," Cam whispered, biting lightly at the skin below Blair's earlobe. She was about to slide her palm down Blair's stomach when Blair succeeded in opening her jeans and pushed her hand down the front.

"Fuck," Cam gasped as Blair's fingers slid through the wet heat between her legs. Her knees nearly buckled as Blair tugged at her. Wrapping her arms around Blair's body, she pressed her face to Blair's neck, floating for a moment on a wave of pleasure. Then she stiffened as the persistent pull of Blair's fingers drew her suddenly to the brink of orgasm.

"Uh-uh. No," she murmured, stepping back unsteadily, head buzzing with the thunder of blood, forcing Blair to move her hand. Shaking her head, she cleared the mist of arousal from her brain. She took a deep breath, trying hard to ignore the throbbing that began in her belly and thundered through her limbs. "Not so fast."

"Says who?" Blair turned in her arms and pushed at her jeans, ready to take her on the spot.

"Me." Cam kissed her again, pulling Blair's lower lip between her teeth, biting her lightly all the while backing her step by step into the bedroom. She kept her lips firmly on Blair's and grasped Blair's *wrists, keeping them away. She'd never last if Blair touched her again. She was already twitching with the faint warning tremors of impending orgasm, and it wouldn't take more than a stroke to send her over.*

When they hit the bed and fell backward together, Cam rolled on top, pinning Blair's hands above her head with both of hers. "Not so fast," she whispered hoarsely again, just before she caught Blair's nipple in her teeth.

Blair moaned in surprise and struggled to free her hands, thrusting her hips against the thigh Cam had driven between her legs. "Let me touch you," she urged in Cam's ear. "Let me do it fast this time."

"Soon," Cam murmured against her breast. It had been so long since she'd touched a woman this way, and she'd wanted Blair so badly for months. She'd denied it when she'd been in charge of her security detail, but she didn't have to now. "I want you so much."

Blair's hands were in her hair when Cam slid between her legs and finally put her mouth on her. Those same fingers opened and closed erratically as Cam sucked and licked and tortured her with her tongue. When Blair pleaded, Cam slipped her fingers inside; and when she begged, Cam moved her hand slowly deeper; and when she cried, Cam let her come, stroking and thrusting and turning gently until every muscle clenched and relaxed a dozen times over.

Then she lay her cheek against the inside of Blair's thigh, exhausted and content—without a single ounce of regret. But even then, as she listened to Blair's breathing finally quiet, some part of her knew it was borrowed pleasure, because happiness, most of all, came with a price.

Cam flinched as Blair hit the canvas hard, the memory of that night dissolving in the demands of the moment. Fists clenched, she took one instinctive step forward, then forced herself to stop as she saw Blair get to her feet. Blair swayed unsteadily for an instant, but then seemed to shrug off the effect of the left jab that had caught her in the face, signaling her partner to come ahead again.

Cam watched her carefully for the rest of the bout, which mercifully lasted only another few minutes. She seemed all right as she regained her balance and moved quickly to counter punches, even managing a spectacular leg sweep that put her opponent flat on his back, winding him for a minute. Still, Cam was happy when she climbed out of the ring and disappeared into the back of the gym.

When she emerged in a dry T-shirt, ready to leave, Cam joined her. "Nice fight," she said, relieved to see that Blair's eyes were clear and her gait steady.

Blair shrugged, smiling faintly. "I didn't exactly beat the crap out of him, though."

"Close enough." Before she could stop herself, Cam raised her hand and brushed her thumb across a bruise beginning to form on Blair's cheek where his glove had landed. "Maybe you should wear a helmet next time, Ms. Powell," she said softly.

Blair's eyes widened at the gentle caress. The touch was so tender it reached deeper than desire. Unable to take her eyes from Cam's penetrating gaze, she whispered, "I'll take that under advisement, Commander."

"Good. Because I don't want anything to happen to you."

"Yes, I know. That's your job."

There was no resentment in her voice, and Cam smiled, unexpectedly comforted by the first moments without anger they had shared all day. "That's part of it."

"Let's not go there again." Blair regarded her steadily. "You can tell your team to relax. I'm going home."

Chapter Four

Shortly before seven that night, Cam stepped into Command Central and walked wearily toward her desk in the far corner of the room. She had finally finished the briefing with Blair that had been scheduled for earlier that day. The first daughter had been cordial but cool as they reviewed her official activities for the next ten days; when Cam asked her about any personal engagements, she merely smiled thinly and said she had none.

Cam admitted to herself that she had probably appeared more abrupt than she'd meant to be, too. It was hard seeing Blair after a six-week absence with everything between them suddenly in chaos. This wasn't what she'd had in mind when she had imagined their reunion.

Sighing, she looked at a stack of memos along with a binder filled with field reports that Mac had left for her covering the time that he had been in charge during her medical leave. Just as she sat down and pulled the pile of papers toward her, Paula Stark stepped up to the side of her desk.

"Excuse me, Commander," Stark said, her spine stiff and her tone formal. The only thing missing was a salute.

Cam looked up distractedly. "What is it, Stark? Problem?"

"No, ma'am. I want to apologize for the breakdown in security earlier this afternoon. I take full responsibility."

Cam leaned back in her chair, studying Paula Stark's serious countenance. Five months ago, Stark had made what might have been the biggest mistake of her career. She had allowed Blair Powell to seduce her. That one night compromised her professionally and should have led to her transfer or even her dismissal from the service. But

Stark had done something unusual.

She'd come to Cam immediately and accepted responsibility without excuse. She'd given her word that it would never happen again, and as far as Cam knew, it hadn't. Cam didn't think about whether Stark still had feelings for Blair. That was none of her business. What had happened today, however, was very much her business.

"Stark, with this kind of detail, apologies are neither acceptable nor sufficient. You are in charge of the day shift, and that means if something goes wrong, it's on you."

The agent's eyes widened slightly, but she merely said, "Yes, ma'am. I understand that."

"Then ask yourself what you missed today. Egret can be very difficult to predict. I told the team once before, and it bears repeating, that the safest course of action is to assume that she is an uncooperative subject. That means you have to plan for the unexpected movement. I'd say you got lazy today, and you got lucky. If I hadn't been walking across the street and seen her climb into that cab, you would have lost her."

Lost her. Stark's stomach clenched. "Yes, ma'am."

"Think about that, Stark. Go the next step."

Remembering the sick feeling she'd had that morning when she'd watched on the monitor as Egret walked right past the front desk and out the door, all Stark could do was nod. What if they *had* lost her, and then something had happened—a kidnapping, or assault, or something as simple as an overeager autograph seeker forcing her off the curb into traffic? *God. We've all been lulled into a false sense of security the past few months because it seemed as if Egret was calming down. She hasn't eluded us for so long, we* have *gotten lazy.*

Cam suppressed a smile. Stark looked as if she were headed for the guillotine. "You're a good agent," she told her. "And you're a valuable agent, because there are places that you can go with her that no one else can. Be careful, be vigilant, be alert. That's all."

Stark realized that the commander had already turned back to her paperwork as she replied, "Thank you very much."

An hour later, Cam had finished going over most of the documents and put aside the ones that needed more attention. She just couldn't read anymore. She'd left Florida the night before at midnight and had gotten no sleep for over thirty-six hours. Ordinarily, that wouldn't bother her nearly as much as it did at the moment, but the stress of seeing Blair again under such difficult circumstances had taken a toll.

She was tired, and she was lonely. She stood, stretched, and headed for the door. She wanted a drink and to go to bed.

Just as she was about to step out the door, Fielding, one of the agents assigned to the night shift, called out to her. "Phone call for you, Commander."

She turned, suppressing a sigh, and picked up the nearest phone. "Roberts," she said sharply, no hint of fatigue in her voice.

"This is Carlisle."

"Yes, sir?"

"Be in DC tomorrow for a briefing at 0800. We'll convene in the conference room at my office."

Cam was instantly alert, her exhaustion fleeing as her suspicions were aroused. This kind of request was unusual. The call came too close on the heels of the abrupt order reassigning her to Blair's security detail. She didn't believe in coincidences. Something serious was going on, and it had to involve Blair if her supervisor was summoning her to Washington.

"I need to know if I should institute heightened security in regards to Egret, sir."

A moment of silence confirmed her suspicions. There was an information blackout and it involved Blair. Out of habit, she checked the monitors, which revealed closed-circuit video images of the entire building—every entrance, the parking garage, the elevators, the hallway outside of Blair's apartment. She almost expected to see someone launching an assault.

"There's no need for any special action at your end," Carlisle said gruffly. "Just be at the meeting, Roberts."

At 0750, Cam walked down the deserted corridor outside Stewart Carlisle's office. Some of the rooms in the warren of offices that opened off the industrial-tiled hallway were already occupied, but many doors were still shut, awaiting secretaries and staff to arrive for the workday. She pushed open the door stenciled with the word "Conference" and stepped into another of the generic rooms that seemed common to all government buildings. She nodded to the redhead, a woman she had never seen before, already seated at the table.

A long rectangular conference table crowded the center of the room, surrounded by a number of straight-backed chairs. A coffee caddy stood in one corner. She moved around the end of the table, helped herself to coffee, and settled into a chair opposite the woman who was reading a stack of papers she appeared to have taken from the open briefcase beside her. Neither of them acknowledged the other beyond their first neutral nods, leaving the introductions to whoever would be running the meeting.

Over the course of the next ten minutes, the door opened three times, each time admitting a man dressed in the regulation garb of a government agent. Navy blue blazers, gray flannel trousers, white shirts, and rep ties abounded in the Department of the Treasury building as well as the headquarters of the Federal Bureau of Investigation and every other security agency on Capitol Hill.

The last person to enter was Cam's direct supervisor, Stewart Carlisle. They had known each other for over a decade and were probably as close to friends as it was possible to be in this kind of environment. Each understood that, regardless of personal feelings or individual considerations, the system they served had the ultimate power and, like all governments, was not immune to error. Error that sometimes destroyed careers and lives. They also both believed that, however flawed, it was probably the best model currently available.

Carlisle nodded to her briefly and proceeded to the head of the table. From the end opposite him, a mid-forties, iron-gray-haired man, thin and fit appearing, coolly appraised each individual in the room. Across from Cam, to the left of the redhead, a man about Cam's age who looked like he might have played football in college stared at her, something hard in his gaze.

Cam did not know any of the other people present, but she recognized the type. The woman—early thirties, short well-cut hair, understated make-up, conservative suit—had a look of self-contained confidence that suggested she didn't work for any of the men in the room. An independent consultant or perhaps a forensic analyst. She had apparently come to give an opinion, and she probably didn't care about interagency politics.

The men were a different matter altogether. The two unfamiliar men were FBI, CIA, or both. They were unsmiling, faintly belligerent looking, and plainly annoyed, probably because the meeting wasn't on their turf. That concerned Cam. Because if the meeting was here on her ground, it confirmed her suspicions that the meeting had to do with Blair, and *that* worried her more than she cared to admit.

At precisely 0800, Carlisle began to speak. "Let's get the introductions out of the way. Secret Service Agent Cameron Roberts, who commands Egret's security detail," he said, nodding at Cam, his eyes unreadable as they skimmed over hers. Indicating the gray-haired man at the far end of the table, he went on, "Robert Owens, National Security Agency. Special Agent Lindsey Ryan, from the behavioral science division of the FBI," signifying the redhead, "and," pointing to the man opposite Cam, "Patrick Doyle, Special Agent in Charge of the FBI task force investigating Loverboy."

Cam stiffened, but her expression remained carefully neutral. Loverboy was the code name assigned to the man who had stalked Blair Powell the previous year, leaving her messages, photographing her, and presumably making an assassination attempt that had left Cam critically wounded. This was the first she'd heard of any ongoing task force. All of which meant the investigation had been taken out of the hands of the Secret Service, leaving the people directly responsible for Blair's safety in the dark.

She was furious, but she needed more information before she knew precisely where to direct her anger. So she listened, her fists clenched under the table, her jaws clamped tightly enough to make her teeth ache. *Why didn't I know about this? Who in hell is in charge here?*

For a moment, the room was silent as each took stock of the others. Then the NSA man cleared his throat and said in a hoarse voice, "I'll let Doyle bring you up to speed on recent domestic developments. You'll find a summary of current information and analyses in the binder."

He passed prepared folders to each of them from a stack he had carried in with him. "From a national security standpoint, we're concerned about the president's upcoming summit meetings on the global warming agreement with the European Council members in three weeks. In addition, he'll be attending the World Trade Organization meeting in Quebec in just a few days. Any act of terrorism, including an attack on Egret, would obviously disrupt those plans."

"We don't have anything to indicate that Loverboy is a member of any group, national or international, with a political agenda," Doyle said, his voice hard-edged with a hint of Midwestern accent. His tone and expression suggested that he wasn't overly interested in Owens's national security issues.

"Nothing in the psychological profile suggests that he is philosophically or politically motivated," Lindsey Ryan, the behavioral scientist, interjected. "The message content—poetic verses, sexual ideation, the fixation on knowing where she is and what she's doing— these things indicate a distorted sense of reality. Despite this delusion, his ability to make repeated contact with her, and effectively elude capture for a prolonged period of time, indicates an intelligent and highly organized personality. All of his focus has been on her. He's obsessed with *her*. This isn't about the president."

"We have to assume that anything directed at Egret is related to the president," Owens said testily, his remarks clearly directed at Doyle.

Cam, working hard to contain her temper, listened as the two men engaged in verbal debate about whose agenda should take priority while ignoring the obvious importance of Ryan's assessment. It was clear to her that Blair was of much less concern to either man than establishing which of them had the greater stake in seeing the UNSUB captured.

"Exactly where do we stand on the degree of penetration as far as Egret is concerned?" Cam barely contrived to keep the wrath out of her voice. She couldn't get into a turf struggle now, not when she was so clearly out of the information loop. She needed to know just how close this psychopath had managed to get to Blair this time.

Doyle, looking impatient, raised his voice a notch and continued as if no one else had said anything. "Until the last ten days or so, all contacts from Loverboy have occurred via electronic transmission, specifically e-mail messages, delivered directly to the subject's personal accounts."

"What kind of intelligence do we have on the message points of origin?" Cam's voice was sharp as ground glass.

"Despite our attempts to trace the point—or points—of origin, we have been unable to verify a source. Changing Egret's accounts, rerouting through substations and aliases, and erecting electronic filters have all been ineffective. His messages to date have been"—he hesitated a moment as if considering how to phrase his comments, then continued—"mostly of a sexually suggestive nature."

"Is he escalating?" Cam's breath constricted in her chest. *This* was why she had been recalled. And if the task force had been ongoing for months, something had changed recently, and they weren't even close to having a handle on it. She tried not to think about the fact that Blair had almost slipped their surveillance yesterday.

Doyle shuffled a few papers, looking annoyed. "He was inactive for a period of time following the shooting earlier this year. Of course, every government agency including the Secret Service, FBI, and CIA was involved in the manhunt, and he didn't have much choice but to go under. He surfaced again about three months ago."

"Three months," Cam repeated, her eyes boring into Doyle's. "Three *months* and you're just advising her security detail *now*?"

"I knew," Stewart Carlisle said, unable to completely conceal his discomfort. He wasn't about to publicly explain that his decision—to have the task force run out of New York and by his people—had been overruled by the security director. He was still bitter, but he had orders to follow, too.

Cam turned to him, knowing better than to break rank in mixed company and question his judgment or his authority. But there was criticism in her eyes, and she knew Carlisle saw it.

"The Secret Service isn't equipped to handle this kind of scenario," Doyle said dismissively.

"We're on scene," Cam retorted, "and we're the ones who know the day-to-day situation best. A threat like this demands we increase our readiness level." Everything about the way they guarded Blair needed to change. *For God's sake, she's been underprotected for months!*

"We've had a presence," Doyle snapped. "We're more than capable of securing her."

"Not the way we can," Cam answered, still unable to believe that Stewart Carlisle had let this happen. "We need to take the lead in this investigation."

"You people knew about him in the beginning, and your security was so ineffective it almost got Egret killed." Doyle's color darkened as his lips curled slightly in derision. "I don't think you're up to it."

Cam's voice was cold, her words razor-edged. "By excluding the Secret Service from your intelligence, you put Egret at severe risk. Unacceptable risk. *Untenable* risk."

"Roberts," Carlisle warned from beside her.

She had effectively accused the FBI task force leader of endangering the life of the president's daughter, which at the very least constituted dereliction of duty and, according to strict interpretation, could be considered an indictable offense. Yet she couldn't back down, not when Blair's life was at stake.

She continued as if her supervisor hadn't said anything. "I want every piece of data, every transmission, every record, every projection and profile that you currently have. I want—"

"You'll get whatever I say—" Doyle hotly interrupted, leaning forward, the muscles in his formidable neck straining.

Cam stood quickly, placing her hands flat on the table, looking down at him. "Every single word, Doyle, or I'll *personally* file a report citing your negligence and hand-carry it to the Oval Office."

"You threaten me, Roberts"—Doyle came out of his chair faster than a man his size ought to be able to move—"and I'll find the dirt you think you've been able to hide and bury you in it."

Smiling faintly, Cam spoke in a voice that was quiet but very clear. "You don't know me very well if you think that will frighten me."

Neither of them heard the door open as they stared each other down, taking measure for the fight that was sure to come.

"From what I hear, you shouldn't even be *on* this detail," Doyle said derisively. "I'd like to know whose piss-poor excuse for a decision *that* was."

"I assume that would be mine," a deep male voice said calmly.

Cam straightened and turned toward the voice as the others hastened to stand for the president of the United States.

Chapter Five

Eleven hours later, Cam was back in New York City, having reviewed as much of the information regarding Loverboy's recent activities as she could access through channels. She knew there was more, but it would take her a while to get at it. Now that she understood why she had been recalled from Florida, her work could really begin. But first there was personal business she needed to put to rest, and she knocked resolutely on the penthouse door.

Admitted immediately, she stopped just inside the door and stared at Blair, who was clearly not expecting her and was obviously dressed to go out for the evening in a patterned silk blazer over a sheer ivory camisole and loose black trousers. Fleetingly, Cam wondered if she was meeting someone. She pushed that thought away because she was in no position to change it.

"What is it?" Blair asked, a quick surge of fear produced by the stony expression in Cam's eyes. "What's happened?"

"Why didn't you tell me?" Cam's tone was dangerous. She was struggling so hard to contain her anger she could barely get the words out.

"I'm not sure what you mean." Blair stalled, hoping it wasn't what she thought but knowing it must be; it couldn't be anything else. She had hoped, with Cam out of New York City, away from her detail, she could keep it from her. Keep her out of it. *Keep her safe.*

"You let me make love to you, you let me *that* close, and you couldn't tell me that he was back?" Cam seethed, her apprehension for Blair's safety and her fury at being excluded both by Blair and the FBI nearly making her insane. "How in God's name could you *do* that? I thought..." She'd almost said, *I thought I meant more to you than that. I thought we had something.*

Cam took a deep breath, closed her eyes for a second, and gathered her strength. This was not about her. Her relationship with Blair wasn't the issue anymore. She had to separate her personal feelings from what was happening now. The clear and present danger that Loverboy presented to Blair was what mattered. Not how she felt, not her disappointment, not her sense of betrayal. She concentrated on her duty, the one thing that always focused her, the one thing she could depend upon to drive the anger away.

Straightening with effort, she worked to hide her turmoil. She forced her fists to unclench, and when she spoke again her voice was cool—her command voice—calm and steady, uninflected, impersonal, infinitely professional.

"You should have reported it to Mac when the stalker contacted you three months ago, Ms. Powell, and you should have told me yesterday. In light of this new information, we have to assume a higher level of alertness. At your earliest convenience, I need to review the security protocols. If you could check your schedule now to confirm, please—I'd like to do this in the morning, as early as possible."

The silence deepened.

While Cam talked, Blair watched the flurry of emotions race across her face. She saw her go from anger and frustration to this implacable façade that she recognized as the barrier Cam erected between her emotions and everything else in order to do her job. In the rational part of her mind, Blair understood that this ability to compartmentalize her feelings was what made Cam so good at what she did, but it was not what Blair wanted to happen between *them.* She did not want Cam to distance herself in order to care for her. She wasn't sure exactly what she wanted, but she was very certain it wasn't that.

Her own frustration and fear boiled over, and she retorted caustically, "That's your solution to everything, isn't it, Cameron? Tighten the security, tighten the restraints around me. That's a simple answer and easy for *you.* However, it doesn't work for me."

"This isn't something that's negotiable."

"We'll see about that."

With effort, Cam explained quietly, "This man is serious. He's persistent, clever, and talented—and he's fixated on you. By all rights, you should be secluded somewhere until he can be apprehended."

At that thought, Blair's every survival instinct surfaced on a wave of irrational terror. She would *not* be made a captive. She had been imprisoned one way or another her entire life. Nothing mattered more to her than her freedom, nothing except one thing.

"I don't want you on this detail, Agent Roberts. I can't work with you. I *won't* work with you. If you won't resign, I'll do what I have to do to get you pulled off."

"I spoke with your father this afternoon," Cam said pointedly. "He seems to feel that I'm the best person for this job. So do I. This is one time your influence is not going to have any effect."

Blair stared at her, open-mouthed in astonishment. When she could find her voice, she asked incredulously, "You spoke with my *father?*"

Cam walked a few feet toward a nearby sofa and leaned against the back, trying to work some of the tension out of her body. She felt wound so tightly she was afraid she'd lose control, and at this point, Blair's very future could depend upon what happened between them. She needed Blair's cooperation, even if she couldn't make her understand why she had undertaken the job.

"It was unexpected. He showed up at the briefing about this... situation." Thinking back, it had been a strange encounter indeed.

The president had acted as if Doyle and Cam weren't about to fling themselves over the table at each other, merely motioning with one hand to the people gathered and saying, "Sit, please."

They did, everyone trying not to look uneasy. Clearly, no one had expected this visit. The NSA representative introduced the others and hastened to assure the president that everything possible was being done to protect his daughter. Andrew Powell said nothing, studying each face carefully as he listened.

After a minute or two, he said, "I'm sure that everything is being done appropriately. I'll expect my security director at the White House to be kept informed of any developments. I'm on a tight schedule, and I'd like to speak with Agent Roberts, if your meeting is concluded."

That was clearly a dismissal.

Lindsey Ryan stood immediately and began gathering her things, as did Stewart Carlisle. Doyle and Owens looked like they might object for a moment and then, with slightly disgruntled expressions, filed out of the room. When the door closed, Cam stood alone, facing the president of the United States for the first time in her life.

Their eyes met and Cam asked, "What may I do for you, Mr. President?"

A very faint smile flickered across his handsome face. She saw Blair in him as his features briefly softened, and in that instant, her anger turned to hard resolve. She would not allow Blair to become a pawn in some ambitious bureaucrat's political game, nor would she see her become the object of a psychotic's obsession.

"It seems that I need to rely on you again, Agent Roberts, to look after my daughter. I'm sure the task force is doing everything they can, but I know my daughter, and she is not going to make this easy for anyone."

"Sir," Cam began, intending to defend Blair. She knew, more than anyone else, just how much Blair suffered from the constant scrutiny of strangers.

He raised his hand as if he knew what she was going to say. He looked past her for a moment, as if seeing something she couldn't.

"She didn't choose this life, Agent Roberts. I chose it for her. It's been hard for her; I know that. She's strong and she's stubborn and I wouldn't change anything about her. I'm counting on you to see that both her freedom and her safety continue."

"Yes, sir, Mr. President," Cam said very quietly, her eyes never leaving his. "I'll do that, sir. You can depend on it."

He had nodded, thanked her, and left the room. Had she not had her own motives for needing to be involved, his unspoken command would have been enough. But she did have her reasons. And they were very personal.

Cam said softly, "I'm sorry, Blair. I'm staying."

I'm staying. The words screamed in Blair's head. Words she wanted to hear from this woman, but not this way. Not like this. Not *because* of this. She couldn't have this conversation any longer. She couldn't think about what it meant for either of them. *I'm staying.*

"Well, I'm not." She grabbed her bag from a nearby table and snapped, "I'm going out."

Cam made no move to stop her. She would not be her jailor. But when she spoke, her voice held a question. "Blair?"

Pausing at the door, Blair looked back, arrested by the defeat in Cam's tone. It was a weariness she had rarely heard from her, even after several days without sleep. Cam still leaned against the sofa. Blair had been almost too angry to see her clearly before, but now the shadows in Cam's face stood out in gaunt relief and her eyes gave away so much she was obviously trying to hide. They were dull with fatigue, suffused with something close to despair. She hadn't looked like that even when she'd been in the hospital recovering from gunshot wounds.

"What?" Blair asked, softer than she had meant, struggling with a nearly irresistible urge to cross the distance to her. It was so hard to hold on to her anger when she so wanted to hold her.

"Have you told them downstairs that you're going out?" Cam pushed herself upright.

"No," Blair answered curtly, irritated again as Cam resumed her official role.

"Is it a personal engagement?" Cam continued, keeping her voice carefully neutral. Now, the team would have to provide much closer coverage than they usually did, even for non-official functions. She had to ask in order to do her job, but she didn't need or want to know the details if Blair was seeing someone. "Will you need the car?"

She searched her memory for the day's itinerary, which she had reviewed the night before. Before her day in Washington. Before she knew that Blair wasn't really safe anywhere. "We didn't have you scheduled for anything tonight."

"It was a last-minute thing." Blair hated discussing her private plans with her security people. She always felt so exposed. This was worse. Reluctantly she added, "It's a party at Diane's."

"I see." Cam's expression didn't change, but she had no difficulty deciphering what Blair *wasn't* saying. It wasn't *official*, and if it was a date, it was none of her business. "Can you give me a few minutes to get someone for you? Stark and Grant are both off duty, and you'll want a woman."

"Fielding and Foster can wait in the car outside Diane's apartment." Blair opened the door and stepped into the hallway. "They always have before."

Following Blair out of the loft, Cam was already activating her radio. "Fielding, bring the car around, and find Ellen Grant or Stark for me. ASAP." She crossed to the elevator and said flatly, "I need someone inside."

"It's Diane's, for Christ's sake," Blair replied with irritation, punching the lobby button. "Do you think he's going to show up in drag?"

"I don't know what he's going to do!" Cam retorted in an uncharacteristically aggravated tone. "Until twelve hours ago, I didn't even know he was active."

Blair had no answer for that. She had ignored the first few messages she received by post, hoping they were just random crank mail, unrelated to what had happened before. Crank stuff did arrive from time to time, usually from disgruntled individuals who didn't like her father's politics. Sometimes from overenthusiastic supporters. Occasionally from people obsessed with her, asking for photos or dates or even articles of clothing. But never anything quite like these messages. Intimate, suggestive, and—most frightening—knowledgeable. Then when the e-mail started, she had confided in her friend at the Bureau, and that had been a mistake. Friendship has its limits, and her old school chum had decided that this was news she couldn't keep to herself.

"You didn't need to know. The FBI knew," Blair justified as the elevator opened onto the lobby. She was still angry with AJ for reporting it.

Cam didn't bother to point out that she needed to know for any number of reasons, not all of them professional. Because it was done. Blair had shut her out, and there was nothing to do now but regain control of the situation.

As Blair walked toward the front door, she was acutely aware that Cam had moved slightly ahead of her to go through first. Unexpectedly, she saw it all again in slow-motion replay—the bright sunlight, the screams of frantic men, the spreading blossom of rich red on Cam's chest as she dropped first to her knees, then collapsed to her back on the sidewalk. By then the other agents had pulled Blair inside, behind the glass doors, and Cam had been beyond her reach. She couldn't hold her.

"Blair?" Cam asked, concerned by Blair's sudden pallor.

Blair jerked at the sound of Cam's voice and hurried to cross the sidewalk, the flashback image of Cam's ashen face as she lay dying mercifully fading. Cam opened the car door, and Blair brushed her fingers lightly over Cam's sleeve, reassured by the solid presence of her. She didn't trust herself to speak but just slid into the rear of the black sedan parked at the curb.

❖

Diane Bleeker kissed Blair lightly on the cheek as she admitted her to a room already filled with people. The lights were conversationally dim; female servers in white shirts, black bow ties, and tailored black trousers moved carefully through the crowd with trays of hors d'oeuvres balanced in front of them. Soft music accompanied the murmur of voices.

"Your choice of escorts is improving," Diane remarked, a hint of surprise in her voice as she watched Cam move to one side of the spacious living room.

"I'm alone," Blair responded, slipping past her and heading for the bar that had been set up in one corner.

Diane threaded her way through the crowd in Blair's wake, reaching for a glass of white wine as Blair waited for the very attractive redheaded bartender in tight black leather pants to mix her a drink. "If you needed a date, I could have easily found you one. Marcy Coleman has been trying to get you to go out with her for weeks. You could do worse than a successful young surgeon, you know."

Blair took her drink, scarcely noticing the appraising glance that the bartender gave her along with the glass. She surveyed the other women in the room. As always at Diane's gatherings, there was a mix of aspiring artists—many of whom were Diane's clients—young professionals, and bar dykes from the Village who were there as escorts or just tagging along with someone they knew, hoping to get lucky. Diane always managed to provide something for everyone.

"I'm not interested in a *date*," Blair said acerbically, making an effort not to look in Cam's direction. She'd had years of practice at ignoring her security detail. Once she'd gotten used to their ubiquitous presence, they had simply become background noise.

When she was a preteen, it hadn't been as difficult, because her father had only been a governor then. Other than the fact that state troopers often drove her to school and parked nearby while she engaged in after-school activities, she'd been able to pretend she was like everyone else. Then when her father became vice president, the security around her had intensified and she had become very good at convincing herself that she wasn't being watched almost twenty-four hours a day.

But there was nothing she could do to ignore Cameron Roberts's presence. She could feel her as strongly as if they stood touching.

Diane smiled knowingly. "I was trying to be polite when I said date. I'm sure the very charming Dr. Coleman would be just as happy to spend the night with you, if that's what you had in mind."

Blair turned and met Diane's eyes, replying caustically, "If and when I decide I want someone to fuck, I'm quite certain I can manage the arrangements on my own."

If Diane was taken aback by Blair's sharp rejoinder, she didn't show it. She knew from long experience that the best way to get Blair to talk about anything substantial was to anger her. Blair had gotten much too proficient at disguising almost all her emotions, but when she was angry, her shields slipped. Diane was one of the few people who could actually goad her into revealing herself, which was probably the reason they were still friends.

"Well, if I had that criminally good-looking number watching *me* all night—especially with that smoldering expression in her eyes—I probably wouldn't be looking for anyone else either."

Blair didn't even have to look at Cam to know exactly the expression Diane meant. Cam had a way of looking at her that made her feel as if she were the only woman in the room—hell, the only other woman on the *planet*. She reminded herself that Cam was only doing her job, but no one—not even Paula Stark, for all her competence and despite the night they had shared together—ever looked at her in quite that way.

Blair's hand trembled as she raised the martini glass to her lips. "Don't, Diane. Not tonight."

Diane relented. Blair's voice was raw, and her eyes were wounded. Touching Blair's hand fleetingly, she said, "I don't know what you *think* is happening between you two, but she cares. She can't hide it any more than you can." She tossed her head in a practiced motion, her pale blond hair sweeping her shoulders. "You may not be in the mood for company tonight, but I am. It's time for me to prowl."

As she watched Diane slip sinuously through the crowd, Blair wondered how long it would take her to make her way around the room to Cam. And she wished to God she didn't care.

❖

When the athletic blond in the navy polo shirt, jeans, and Nikes walked in the door at a little before 0100 hours, more than a few heads turned in appreciation. She looked like an ex-soccer player, which, among other things, she was. It had taken Ellen Grant a little over an hour from the time John Fielding tracked her down at her mother-in-law's in Westchester to make it to the party at Diane Bleeker's Upper East Side apartment. She had considered changing her clothes and then decided not to, figuring she'd probably fit in with at least some part of the gathering.

Cam sighed with uncharacteristic relief at the sight of her backup. It wasn't so much her bone-deep tiredness that was taxing her, but the necessity of watching Blair dance with the same woman for the last half hour while trying to ignore the fact that the woman's hand rested very subtly on Blair's left breast.

"Sorry, Commander," Ellen Grant said when they managed to work their way over to one another. "I was at my husband's birthday party."

"No apologies required, Grant. I regret the need to call you away from your family." Cam gave a thin smile and passed her hand across her eyes, rubbing them briefly. "I'm afraid I got caught short tonight. You're bailing me out."

Grant glanced at her in concern, catching the strain in her voice and wondering if she was all right. Cameron Roberts was a legend to every agent in the field because of what she had done that day in front of Blair Powell's apartment, but to her own team, she was a flesh-and-blood hero. "Not a problem. I can take over now, Commander."

"Yes," Cam said. "Thank you."

Instead of leaving, Cam walked through the room and out onto a small iron-railed balcony with a view of Central Park. She rested both hands on the railing, aware of the ache in her left side along the ten-inch scar between her fourth and fifth ribs. It didn't usually bother her, or at least most of the time she could ignore it.

"Off duty now, Commander?" Blair asked quietly from beside her.

"Yes. Grant's taking over." They both knew that wasn't strictly true. She was never off duty, through choice as well as convention.

"You look like you could use some sleep."

Cam, still leaning forward, turned her head and glimpsed the quick flicker of moonlight playing over Blair's face. The sight caught at her heart. Surrendering for just an instant to the soft undercurrent of warmth in Blair's voice and the real concern in her gaze, Cam let herself relax.

"Airplane seats are always a little short for me to sleep in very well."

Blair stood next to her at the rail, close enough to touch her, but she was careful not to. She didn't trust herself enough to do that. She wasn't even sure why she had followed her outside, but the night was disappearing, and they were here, almost alone. Tomorrow, people would surround them again, and she had no idea when they would next have even a few moments of privacy. She couldn't bear to see her go, not yet.

"What's going to happen now?"

As Cam watched the headlights far below trace patterns of lights through the treetops, she considered the future. It never even occurred to her not to inform Blair of her plans, although it was distinctly non-regulation to do so. By long years of convention, the Secret Service never discussed procedure with a protectee.

But it was Blair's life that was affected, and she deserved to know.

"We'll need to go to high-alert status. I'll talk to Mac and Stark about that tomorrow. Inside, you'll have at least two agents with you at all times. Outside, four. Extra security at public functions, and we'll be disseminating far less information about your travel plans to the press."

"Everything will be closing down around me, won't it?" Blair sounded nearly as done in as Cam appeared.

"These are the things that will impact you most directly, yes," Cam allowed. There was much more that needed to be done, and she hoped she could accomplish them without making Blair even more unhappy. "I'm sorry."

Blair believed her. It had taken more than raw physical attraction to capture her heart. Cam, as no one before her, understood. Cam understood how she felt to be never alone, to be never free, to be never capable of spontaneous action. Cam understood even though she couldn't change it.

"I know." Blair did touch her then, a brief brush of her fingers over Cam's hand.

She caught her breath as Cam captured her fingers and caressed them gently. The light pressure of their palms sliding together was more achingly sweet than another woman's naked body pressing against her in the heat of lust. She stood there, buffeted by the chill night air, her head light with wanting her, and dared not move. Dared not break the fragile bond.

Finally, Cam sighed and released her. She was so very tired and she couldn't trust herself with Blair so near. She had just needed to touch her so much. And now she needed to go.

What she had to say next came hardest. It was difficult for her to even think it, but she had to. Everything between them had changed drastically almost overnight. They'd spent five frantic days trying to assuage nearly a yearlong thirst, and nothing had really been settled when they'd parted. Except they both had believed there'd be a next time.

She'd thought then that they'd have time to tackle the issues of Blair's notoriety and her own professional ethics, but the reappearance of Loverboy had changed all of that. Now whatever personal relationship they might have had was secondary. She knew Blair was hurt and angry, and she'd seen Blair in the arms of too many lovers not to know what she did when she was hurt.

She simply said what she had to say. "If you don't plan on going home tonight, please tell Grant. Let them protect you."

Staring straight ahead so that she would not see the good-bye in Cam's eyes, Blair replied quietly, "As you wish, Commander."

And then she was alone, the wind whipping at her tears.

Chapter Six

A t precisely 0700 the next morning, Cam walked through the command center toward the conference room. "Stark, Mac," she called as she passed each of them, "with me. The rest of you will be briefed later."

She closed the conference room door after they took their seats, and she remained standing, leaning forward slightly with her hands on the back of a chair. She was crisply attired in a steel blue suit, a tailored white linen shirt, and imported black loafers that matched the belt at her waist. Had the others been looking, they would have noticed that her knuckles were white where she gripped the leather. It was the only sign that she was distressed.

"This is what I know," she began, her tone and demeanor completely composed. "Approximately three months ago, Loverboy resumed contact with Egret via the U.S. mail. His messages consisted of short rambling notes professing his undying love for her, his desire to make love to her—put more crudely than that—and his intention to be alone with her so that he could convince her of his passion."

At her first few words, Stark and Mac sat up straight, clearly shocked.

"Commander! This is the first—" Mac sputtered, his face pale.

Cam held up her hand to silence him. "We'll get to that. Six weeks ago, he began electronic contact. This time, in addition to his verbal descriptions, he sent short video clips of explicit sexual activities he hoped they might...share."

"It's impossible." Stark couldn't contain her disbelief. "She would have told us. She's difficult, but she's not stupid. She would know that we had to be informed."

"The FBI knew. They formed a task force to monitor the situation." At that announcement, Mac swore. Cam continued, preferring to save the considerable explanations for later. "They've set up their own surveillance system with vehicles and agents tracking her whenever she's outside this building. They've attempted to establish alternate e-mail connections in the hopes of backtracking his messages to their source. So far, they've been unsuccessful."

Her fingers began to cramp and she forced herself to let go of the chair back. Her voice still quiet, she said, "I was called back because about ten days ago his messages changed. He's becoming more violent; he threatened her." She was surprised to feel her voice catch and hoped that Mac and Stark hadn't heard it. Quickly she continued, "The behavioral people at Quantico feel that he may be decompensating, either because he's been unsuccessful at gaining access to her or just because he's coming unglued. In any event, we must consider Egret at risk at any time."

"Oh my God," Mac breathed, "how could they have kept us out of the loop?"

Struggling now to contain her own anger, she answered, "They were investigating us." That wasn't strictly true. The FBI had been investigating everyone on the security team with the exception of Cam. She was exonerated by virtue of the fact that she had been an unintended victim of Loverboy's presumed attack on Blair.

"That's insane." Mac stood up, agitated. "We were all there with Egret—with you—when it happened. None of us could have been the shooter!"

"I agree with you." Cam shrugged. "But I don't have to remind you how paranoid our brethren in the FBI can be. They were floating the theory that if it was one of you, you might have had a hired hit man do the shooting. A stand-in to deflect suspicion."

"Oh, for Christ's sake," Stark muttered. "I don't believe I'm hearing this."

Cam almost smiled at that. Over the past year, Paula Stark had become the agent closest to Blair Powell. Cam could only imagine how furious she must be to have her professional integrity maligned and her efficiency undercut by people who were supposedly on the same side. She also believed that Stark cared for Blair, and she didn't think it had anything to do with the night they had spent in bed together. Cam didn't encourage any kind of personal attachment between her agents and those they guarded, but it privately comforted her. Blair deserved to be cared for.

"I'm sure members of the task force will be showing up soon to convince you that this is indeed all quite real," she went on. "Our official policy is one of cooperation."

Mac and Stark looked at her expectantly, waiting for her real orders.

"*We* are the Secret Service. *We* are the people assigned to guard her. *We* are the people with her twenty-four hours a day. This is our ball, our game, our rules," she said decisively. "Stark, you will choose a replacement to lead the day shift. Until further notice, you are Egret's primary guard. If at all possible, when she's outside this building, you will be with her. That means physically within sight of her. You'll be working split shifts to cover critical times and events, so review her itinerary carefully."

It was a tough assignment, and Cam watched Stark closely as she spoke.

"Yes, ma'am," Stark said immediately. "Understood."

"Mac, we need an agent, not just the video cameras, stationed in the lobby around the clock. The surveillance tapes need to be backed up every twelve, and I want them analyzed for repeat visitors, delivery people, public service crews—anyone who doesn't live or work here. Run the backgrounds again on everyone with access to floors above the lobby."

Mac and Stark were taking notes, but Cam had nothing written down. As she spoke, her gaze was distant, her mind clicking down the list of priorities as automatically as she dressed in the morning. She understood intuitively what few citizens of the United States did: that the illusion that the president and those close to him were untouchable was part of an image of invincibility essential to a world power. Unlike the leaders of many nations, the president of the United States was incredibly accessible. He could go jogging through the streets of Washington, DC; he could stand on an open podium and give a speech; and he could ride a bicycle through the dunes on Martha's Vineyard with only a few Secret Service agents nearby. He was at risk in ways that few people ever considered, unless, like her, it was their job to know.

In many ways, Blair's security was even more critical than his. The presidency was not a man, but an office. If the president were incapacitated, the line of succession was clear. But the president was susceptible to manipulation through his affections. The United States government did not negotiate with terrorists. Would that policy hold if the hostage were the president's daughter?

For an instant, Cam remembered waking with Blair in Diane's apartment, of holding her while she slept, naked and warm in her arms. All Blair's fury and fierceness had quieted in slumber, and Cam shivered inwardly at the image of her vulnerability. *Not Blair. Not on my watch. Not ever.*

She cleared her throat and picked up where she had left off with barely a moment's hesitation. "Her mail needs to be visually inspected before she picks it up. Any package, any delivery of *any* kind, requires verification of its point of origin before it goes to her, including ID checks for all delivery people. I'll arrange for a portable x-ray machine to be set up downstairs."

She took a breath and began to relax for the first time in days. It felt good to be in charge and comforting to know that the right people were providing Blair's safety.

"Mac, advise Finch I want to review all the data we accumulated on Loverboy's initial contacts last winter—including the building sweeps around the park. Those will need to be repeated. We'll go over the rest of the details with the team later today." Finally she asked the question she had avoided thinking about since she'd awakened at 0500 after a few hours of restless sleep. "I'll need a special briefing this morning with Ms. Powell. Is she on site?"

"No," Mac said carefully. "Grant checked in at 0600. She requested relief for continued surveillance at an off-site location."

She didn't come home. Cam had to work to ignore the swift surge of pain, but she said without inflection, "Right. See to it, then. I'd like a full report ASAP."

After Mac and Stark left the room, she finally sat, rested her face in her hands, and tried to dispel the image of Blair in the arms of another woman.

❖

Diane Bleeker eyed Blair speculatively across the small glass-topped table in her breakfast alcove. Watching her friend start on her second cup of coffee, she decided it might be safe to try conversation.

"Are you going to tell me why Roberts is your head spooky again?" she asked offhandedly, reaching for a croissant and hoping that she would live to eat it.

Blair looked up from the cup she had been mindlessly staring into, searching Diane's face for some hint of the motive behind the question. She wasn't up to verbal sparring at the moment. She definitely wasn't up to hearing Diane talk about how much she'd like to get Cameron Roberts into bed. It had never been enjoyable to hear, but now it actually hurt.

She didn't think Cam would be susceptible to Diane's brand of casual seduction, but she wasn't entirely certain. Diane was very beautiful, and Cam gave no hint of entertaining celibacy. All you had to do was look at her to sense her sexual energy. Blair recalled the rumor her contact in the FBI had recounted to her about Cam's secret lover in DC. For all she knew, Cam might still be involved with someone there. She didn't want to think about that, not when she couldn't get the feel of Cam's hands out of her mind. But Diane merely regarded her solemnly, patiently, without the slightest hint of confrontation. Friends, then, for the moment.

"Why?" Blair asked, trying not to snarl.

Not too bad. She didn't throw anything. "Because I got the distinct impression that while I was in Europe you made good use of my apartment, and I presumed you were with her."

Diane had seen the way the two of them had looked at one another for weeks before the shooting—as if they were struggling not to jump on each other and start tearing off clothes. And she'd seen Blair frantic with worry those first few days after Cam was wounded.

Even while the Secret Service agent was recovering and Blair had no contact with her, Diane had seen a change. Her notoriously restless friend hadn't been out hunting for a one-night stand in months. And then the use of her apartment—Blair must have wanted to be with someone very badly if she'd arranged to spend more than a night together somewhere. Since the president's daughter couldn't bring a woman to her own apartment right under the nose of the Secret Service, she had at least found some privacy here.

"It *was* her you brought up here, wasn't it?"

Blair just nodded, absently holding the coffee cup raised in front of her. Her mind balked at returning to those brief days and her wild hope of happiness. She wasn't sure she wanted to remember, not until she stopped aching every time she thought of Cam.

Diane continued as if she hadn't seen Blair's haunted expression. "Then we crossed in the air, and by the time I got back from Europe, you were off to China. I never *did* hear the juicy details. The next thing I know, we're sitting in a café, Roberts is across the room watching you on full spooky status again, and you're a mess."

"I'm fine," Blair responded, but her hands trembled slightly as she set the cup down.

In the past three days, she'd begun to wonder if she hadn't dreamed those five nights in June. Five nights, and then Cam had returned to Washington for her new posting as a regional director in the investigative division. They'd both expected it to be weeks before they saw one another again. Blair had the China trip with her father, and Cam would be in the field soon. She might have believed it a dream, she supposed, if her skin didn't still tingle with the memory of their last morning together.

When she awoke, she was alone. The shower was running in the adjoining bathroom. She turned on her side, toward the empty space beside her, imagining she could still feel the heat of her, still smell her— rich and dark and powerfully enticing. Her stomach tightened, and she lingered for a moment, eyes closed, remembering.

She drifted, pleasantly aroused, replaying the feel of Cam's fingertips along her thigh when warm lips brushed over her ear.

"Are you awake?"

"Mmm." She smiled, stretching under the light sheet that was still twisted from their passion the night before. "In some places."

"I was going to get breakfast." Cam leaned closer to kiss the sensitive spot at the base of her neck. "There's a service elevator in the building, isn't there? No need to announce my presence to whoever's on shift now."

Blair turned over on her back and was struck—as she always was when she saw her—by a surge of pure physical longing. Already her skin tingled. She grasped Cam's hair in one hand, tugging her down for a kiss, meaning only to say good morning. But she wasn't used to the feel of her lips yet, didn't think she'd ever get used to them. Firm and hot and wonderfully responsive. The first meeting of smooth warm flesh became a light bite and then a serious exploration as she sucked and licked and tasted, afraid she might starve if she couldn't have more.

"God," she gasped when she finally dropped back to the pillow, her fingers still wrapped in Cam's thick hair. "I'm hungry."

Cam was breathing hard, and her charcoal eyes burned as she looked down at Blair. She ran a finger between Blair's breasts and her fine mouth curled into a smile at one corner. "Why don't I think it's bagels you're talking about?"

"I can have bagels any day," Blair managed, the muscles in her stomach twitching as Cam stroked slowly lower.

She arched under Cam's touch, her hips lifting of their own accord. Heat burst between her legs like a bonfire that had smoldered for hours, then roared to life on a whisper of wind. She hadn't wanted anyone to touch her in so long, and now she couldn't stop wanting it. She couldn't think, was afraid to think. God, she was losing her mind.

"You have far too many clothes on," Blair whispered, reaching for the buttons on Cam's shirt, needing to distract her, because if Cam moved any lower and touched her just once, she would lose it.

Her nerve endings were already screaming for satisfaction, and it would be over far too quickly. That was something else she was afraid to think about. She had absolutely no control over her body with this woman. She'd made love to countless strangers, but the encounters had never touched her inside. She'd walked away barely aroused, but with Cam—one slow smile, one brief caress, and she was wet and ready.

"You're not helping," Blair half moaned as Cam's hands slid upward from her belly, cupping her breasts, her gifted fingers rubbing over taut nipples.

"Oh yes," Cam murmured, her voice heavy and smooth, "I am."

Blair lost patience and pulled the last button off Cam's shirt, then pushed it roughly down her arms. "Get your clothes off," she ordered, having trouble catching her breath. Her blood was boiling, and a terrible pressure pounded along her spine. She'd come without Cam touching her if she weren't careful.

"Cam, please," she pleaded before she could stop herself.

Something in her voice must have penetrated Cam's awareness, because suddenly she stood and threw off the shirt, her hands fumbling with the buttons on her jeans.

"Hold on to it," Cam urged, her breathing ragged, as she stepped out of her pants and reached over to fling the sheet off Blair's body in one motion. She moved over her, naked now, and slipped one long, lean thigh between Blair's legs, sighing as their flesh met. They were both so wet, and the moisture flowed along their skin, fusing them.

"You are so beautiful," Cam whispered, both hands framing Blair's face. Holding Blair's gaze, she began a steady rhythm with her hips, pressing into her, then away, then down again, harder, faster, each thrust working them both a little higher.

"You're making me crazy," Blair cried brokenly, biting her lip, struggling to ignore those first spasms deep inside. It was torture. She wanted to come instantly; she wanted it never to end. "What are you doing to me?"

"I'm going to make you come," Cam said, her voice hoarse, her eyes dimming with desire. She shivered, made a choking sound, and her lids flickered closed for an instant. "Ah, God. If...I...can last."

Blair, arms tight around her, back arched, trembled on the brink of dissolving and stared up into those dark, wild eyes, so close now—wanting to believe. "I lo—"

With her last shred of control, she stopped herself—too many years of guarding her secrets and hiding her fears stood in the way of the words. Running her hands along Cam's back, she found her hips, pulled her closer. "Take me away," she whispered into Cam's neck.

And Cam did. She brought one hand between them and grasped Blair's nipple, squeezing hard, timing it to the rhythm of her hips. Blair cried out as Cam jerked violently with the first rush of her own orgasm, and then they were shuddering in each other's arms, lost, and finally... found.

Drained by the memories, Blair stared at Diane as if she'd never seen her before.

"Wherever you just went," Diane commented dryly, "I'd give a lot to visit."

Blair laughed, but there was pain in her eyes. She shook her head ruefully. "So would I."

"So what happened?" Diane tried to remember the last time she had seen Blair so hurt, and couldn't.

With a sigh, Blair said, "She needed to go back to DC, and I had to leave the country. We talked on the phone, planned to meet as soon as we could."

She stood, walked to the small window that looked down upon the street. The nondescript black sedan bristling with antennae on the rear trunk that screamed *undercover car* was still parked opposite the entrance to Diane's building. She could make out a shadowy figure in the front seat. *Probably Stark by now.*

She wondered where Cam was, if she had slept.

"We knew it would be hard, but I thought..." Her voice trailed off as she recalled their last conversation before parting. *I thought we agreed she couldn't be on my detail. I thought we were going to work out a way to see each other. I thought she cared.*

"So what happened?" Diane asked from behind her, persisting gently.

Blair didn't turn, just kept looking off into the perfect spring morning, not seeing a thing. "The next time I saw her, she was at my door...and back on the job."

"Just like that?"

Diane was incredulous. It didn't seem like Roberts's style. The agent had always impressed Diane with her regard for Blair's feelings, even when she was pissing Blair off by insisting that she follow orders. She must have known how devastated Blair would be to be left out of a decision that affected her so personally. Blair's trust was so fragile, and Cameron Roberts simply didn't seem that cruel.

"Yes." Blair finally left the window, stalked to the counter, grimaced when she found the coffee pot empty. "Just exactly like that."

Diane wanted to ask more, but the moment had passed. Blair's fury had returned, and in a way, Diane preferred it to the pain. At least Blair had learned to survive with her rage. She wondered if Cameron Roberts had any idea how impossible Blair would be to control when she was not only angry, but also wounded.

CHAPTER SEVEN

S tark just radioed her position, Commander," Mac said when
Cam walked over to the communications station at Command
Central. "Egret is en route to the Aerie."

"Good," Cam responded, glancing at her watch. "It's almost 1100
hours. I'll inform her of the security changes at my scheduled 1300
briefing with her. Confirm that meeting time with her upon arrival,
please."

"Will do." He studied her as she stood perusing the monitors,
trying to read her mood. He hadn't missed the undercurrent of strain in
her voice, but he supposed it could just be due to the sudden escalation
of the situation with Loverboy. Considering the recent revelations
concerning the ongoing covert FBI task force, anyone else would
have been raging about the outside interference and the infringement
on their authority. But she looked just like she always did—calm and
controlled. *Too calm, maybe. The kind of utter stillness you feel just
before the bomb explodes.*

"Page me if you need me before then." She turned to leave,
needing to run off some tension. She had a splitting headache, which
she attributed to fitful, uneasy sleep. What she refused to consider was
that the pounding ache behind her eyes might be due to the fact that she
couldn't stop wondering if Blair had slept alone the night before.

"Uh-oh," Mac muttered as she turned to leave. "This looks like
trouble."

"What have we got?" She turned back suddenly to the monitors,
her heart suddenly racing.

Her eyes followed his to the central screen that gave a view of the building's double entrance doors and the doorman's desk just to one side in the lobby. Taylor, on day shift, could be seen checking the identification of two individuals, one of whom she recognized immediately.

"Here comes the cavalry." She muttered an oath under her breath, then rubbed her eyes and sighed. "Contact Stark and tell her I want her up here ASAP. Then bring our visitors back to the conference room. Get someone to take over out here for you."

"Yes, ma'am." Mac watched the man and woman cross the lobby toward the elevators and fought an almost irresistible urge to stand outside the door of the command center and bare his teeth. The first major battle of the turf war was about to begin.

"This is Special Agent Renée Savard," Patrick Doyle said officiously, indicating the woman with him. "She'll be assigned as personal guard to Egret until further notice."

Cam sensed Stark stiffen next to her. She commended her restraint but expected no less of her team. As she regarded Doyle, she was happy to see that he was beginning to perspire. Her voice was totally even in response.

"Agent Doyle, I already have a full complement of experienced agents. Agent Stark is currently functioning as Egret's primary guard. I don't need anyone else."

Mac kept his mouth shut, watching the volleys flow back and forth across the table between the two senior agents. It had been like this for the last thirty minutes, ever since SAC Doyle had arrived to inform the commander about the reorganization of Egret's security detail. It was clear that Doyle didn't have carte blanche from the security director in DC, or he'd just have walked in and taken command. But he was trying to bully his way to the top anyway. The commander had been cool, composed, and unyielding as stone. She hadn't given one inch, and Doyle was starting to crack. The guy clearly wasn't used to playing hardball.

"Look, Roberts," Doyle grated, his fists clenched on the stack of folders in front of him, "I can't run the task force effectively without an inside agent."

"As I understand it, you've been running it for months without one," Cam observed mildly. She waited a beat. "Although, as you say, not particularly effectively."

She was still incensed that he'd had the arrogance to keep the Secret Service on the outside when Blair was in imminent danger. On the other hand, she needed his intelligence as much as he needed her access. Her game, her rules, however.

"I'll be happy to have Agent Savard come on board as a liaison. She cannot, however, function as Egret's security. She's not trained for it, and I don't know her."

Doyle flushed. Next to him, the striking coffee-skinned woman lifted piercing blue eyes to Cam's, a flicker of anger hardening her gaze. Cam continued, unperturbed.

"In return, I expect daily briefings pertaining to any new information you might have."

"Are you suggesting that an FBI agent can't be trusted to secure the president's daughter?" Doyle demanded, half rising from his seat while handily ignoring the issue of shared intelligence.

Cam stood, gathering her papers. "I don't know *how* an FBI agent would react if Egret's life was at stake. I *do* know how every one of my people would respond." She glanced at Doyle and continued casually, "This isn't the time for on-the-job training."

"With respect, Commander," Renée Savard said, "I am fully prepared to assume responsibility for Egret's safety. I would like the opportunity to carry out my assignment."

Cam studied her, impressed by her composure when it was clear that she was insulted. Still, this wasn't about personal feelings. This was about the willingness of one person to die for another. Secret Service agents were carefully screened and extensively tested to determine their psychological willingness to sacrifice themselves for an individual or, in many cases, simply an ideology. For better or worse, this was what it took to do the job. The FBI and the Secret Service were not interchangeable, and she would not relax her requirements now, when the possibility of ultimate sacrifice was more than probable.

"Your request is duly noted, Agent. However, Agent Stark is primary on Egret's detail. If she can find a way for you to assist her, that will work. And that's the best I can do for you."

She turned around and walked out, leaving the two Secret Service agents and the two FBI agents measuring one another across the expanse of the conference table.

"I want a close-up look at your surveillance system and an overview of your tactical routines," Doyle demanded of Mac, trying to regain some semblance of dominance. If he couldn't get what he wanted from the hard-ass lead agent, he'd get it from someone else.

Mac stood politely, taking a page from his commander's book. "I can show you the relay station and the closed-circuit monitors. Right this way."

He ignored Doyle's hard stare and obvious displeasure. He wasn't going to offer any information on their video camera placement, building motion sensors, advance site preparation protocols, or anything else without the commander's clearance.

The men walked out, leaving Stark and Savard regarding one another in silence. Stark considered any number of options, including her preference, which was to stick Savard in the control room with Mac. She was still smarting that she'd been the object of an internal FBI review and had actually been considered a suspect in the shooting that almost killed her commander. She was also struggling with her own guilt over the fact that she had allowed Egret to unwittingly place herself in danger by eluding their surveillance. If to no one other than herself, she needed to make amends, and she wasn't going to miss her opportunity to do that. *I won't take any interference from the FBI.*

"I'm not trying to take your job," Savard said, surprising Stark with her bluntness. "I'm just trying to do mine."

Blushing profusely, Stark wished that she were better at masking her emotions. She envied the commander her ability to keep all of her feelings inside, something she had not yet learned to do.

She regarded her counterpart steadily, thinking that Savard didn't quite fit the standard FBI mold. Indeed, she wore the requisite navy blue jacket and slacks, with a tailored pale blue shirt and the hint of a bulge over her left hip where her weapon was holstered. *Cross draw,* Stark thought absently. And she appeared fit and confident, but Stark would've expected that as well.

Less expected was the challenge in her intense blue eyes that was surprisingly without malice. It was the kind of dare offered by a worthy opponent in a contest, not by a rival seeking to harm. Stark also couldn't help but notice that Savard was beautiful—beautiful in the way that cover models were beautiful—with elegant cheekbones and an exotic expression that suggested the Islands lingered somewhere in her background.

Stark tried not to think about that as she answered, "My job is to safeguard the president's daughter. I'm not sure what your job is supposed to be."

"My job is to apprehend Loverboy. Since Egret is what we have in common, I suggest we try to work together."

"I already have a partner," Stark said, but her resistance was wavering. It was hard not to respond to Renée Savard's compelling directness. "But there's room for a third," she finally relented, "as long as you don't interfere with me doing my job."

Renée Savard studied her opposite number. She envied Paula Stark. It was clear that her formidable commander respected her abilities and awarded her with the appropriate responsibility. She wished she could expect the same from Patrick Doyle, but she certainly didn't count on it. She had to admit, she also liked the way the dark-haired, feisty young agent tilted her chin in a faintly aggressive posture as she staked out her territory. Under other circumstances, she might have considered her cute.

"That seems fair to me." Savard stood and extended her hand across the table. "Looking forward to working with you, Agent Stark."

"Is Egret in the Aerie?" Cam asked Jeremy Finch, a bespectacled, mildly pudgy agent who sat watching a bank of six monitors that displayed strategic points throughout the apartment building. He was simultaneously running a real-time video of the previous twelve hours that had been captured by the cameras mounted at each corner of the external perimeter. Via the videotapes, he could review foot and vehicular traffic directly in front of the building for any time and from almost any direction he chose.

Most people would have found the multitude of flickering images overwhelming, but Finch seemed more at home in the electronic environment than in the real world. In addition to being a very solid agent, he was a computer wizard, and now that computer surveillance and analysis were a routine part of intelligence gathering, experts like him were essential.

From his personnel dossier, Cam knew that Finch had been a computer hacker in college, and that he'd distinguished himself by breaking one of the Department of Defense encryption codes. In point of fact, rather than considering such attempts felonies, the DOD and many major civilian corporations tacitly encouraged them. If a code could be cracked, it was considered defective, and discovering that fact provided an opportunity to improve security.

Jeremy Finch had managed it not once, but twice. Because of that, he had been targeted for government service. Apparently, he'd surprised a great many people by choosing the Secret Service over the much more glamorous Central Intelligence Agency.

Cam was happy that he had. Human intelligence was always critical, but in her area of operation they were heavily computer dependent, especially in the advance planning stages for Egret's public outings. Good intel was particularly critical for international venues like Paris, when security, motorcade routes, emergency medical evacuation plans, and personnel deployment all had to be juggled on a minute-to-minute basis.

Without taking his eyes off the screens, Jeremy answered, "No, ma'am. Egret went upstairs briefly and then directly into the park."

Cam glanced at the far upper-right monitor—the one that showed a panoramic view of Gramercy Park, the block-wide private park across the narrow street from Blair's apartment building. The heavily shaded, immaculately preserved square was surrounded by towering pre-WWI buildings and completely enclosed with a high wrought-iron fence. She couldn't actually make visual contact with Blair; the foliage was too dense to permit that. Nevertheless, she looked for her.

"That's where I'll be," she finally said.

"Roger that," he said, making a note on his handheld personal unit about something he had seen on the video that he wanted to review from a different angle.

Cam was very much aware that Patrick Doyle was still on site, but she had absolutely no intention of being his tour guide. She had work to do, and her most immediate duty was to inform Blair that she could expect several new faces in her security detail. Unfortunately, that was the least difficult of the topics they needed to discuss.

She let herself into the park by unlocking one of the gates that permitted access to those with clearance and a key. The park was nearly small enough to see across. At the midpoint, in front of a small fountain, she could make out John Fielding. He was standing, statuelike, to all appearances staring vacantly into space. She knew, however, that he held Egret within his sightline and was in all likelihood turning at regular intervals to keep the entire square under careful watch.

There was no way for a Secret Service agent to be unseen, and under some circumstances, invisibility wasn't even desirable. The visible presence of a bodyguard was often enough to deter people from casual approach. On the other hand, Blair, like most in her position, understandably did not want every moment of her personal life witnessed. Because of that, Secret Service agents were trained to walk a fine line between doing their job and actually impairing the lifestyles of those they guarded.

Cam nodded briefly in his direction, and he acknowledged her with an almost imperceptible motion of his head. She continued past him along a small gravel path flanked at discrete intervals by iron and wood benches until she came to one of the most secluded and idyllic corners of the park. A bevy of shrubs and flowers created a natural barrier offering privacy. Enough sunlight filtered through the overhead branches to highlight Blair in its pale shimmering glow.

Slowing as she approached, Cam told herself that she did not want to startle her. Actually, she wanted a few extra seconds just to observe her unawares. Blair was bent over a sketchpad, her legs drawn up under her on the bench. Her hair was loose, a tawny riot of curls reaching almost down to her shoulders. Cam knew the feel of those tresses, flowing silken over her hands as she kissed her.

Blair wore a sleeveless shirt that exposed her arms, muscled from hours in the gym and tanned from the sun. She was striking in any lighting, remarkable in any pose, but never as much as when she was lost in her work. That was perhaps the only time, except after making love, when Cam had ever seen her at peace.

"Ms. Powell," Cam said quietly.

Blair lifted her hair away from her face with one hand and looked up. The sunlight was behind Cam, casting her face in shadows.

"Good afternoon, Commander."

"Am I disturbing you?"

"No." Blair gestured to the bench beside her.

Cam sat down, barely suppressing a sigh as she leaned back, warmed by Blair's presence as much as the afternoon sun.

"You wanted to speak to me?" Blair knew she sounded stiff and formal but was unable to help it. It was so hard to be near her and pretend that there was nothing between them. It was even harder when she could see that Cam was tired. She was still angry with her—angry and hurt—but when she looked at her now, all she wanted was to pull her down against her shoulder and stroke her.

She pushed the image away with irritation. If Cam needed that, needed her at all, she would never have done this to them. Blair hadn't wished for this almost paralyzing ache that never seemed to lessen unless Cam was near. She had never wanted that, not with anyone. Ever since they'd slept together, ever since she had allowed herself to hope, being near this woman had become something very close to constant pain.

"More good news?" she asked sarcastically.

"The FBI made an official appearance this morning." Cam watched the light play through the leaves of the trees above them. Blair was inches away, but she felt as if their skin touched along the length of her body. She knew it was only visceral memory, but the sensation was so acute that her blood was racing. Would there ever come a time when she could be close like this and not respond? Did she even want these feelings to pass?

"I take it you're not pleased." Blair wondered at Cam's odd stillness.

"That, Ms. Powell, is considered classified information. According to any number of sections in the manual, personal observations on internal matters should not be shared, especially with civilians." Cam knew she sounded wintry. She could not think about the weeks that Blair had been a potential target and none of them had known without cold fury engulfing her. She offered a half smile to compensate, but this seemed lost on Blair.

"Well, we both know how dear the manual is to you," she rejoined sharply. "Why are you telling me, then?"

Cam didn't bother to protest. How could she? She'd chosen duty over Blair's wishes and had no defense. And ordinarily, she would never discuss matters of protocol with someone she guarded, but she and Blair had gone so far beyond the limits of acceptable professional behavior, it was ridiculous to stand on ceremony now. It was enough that she did not touch her. That was a hardship of her own making and she would learn to bear it. She would not place Blair at a disadvantage because she had overstepped her bounds.

"I thought you should know."

"Why?"

"At least one of them will be working with our detail in direct contact with you. I expect they'll add their own car as well."

"That's not too subtle, is it?" Blair asked pointedly. "If I go around with a parade following me, it's going to send a message that I give a damn what he says."

"It's going to send a message that you are well protected and not a ready target," Cam answered immediately.

Blair looked away, across the park, wishing she could be sitting there with nothing more on her mind than the sexy sound of Cam's deep voice, enjoying the flutter of desire that just being near her always provoked. She sighed.

"I guess it really doesn't matter. One more here or there won't change anything."

"They've been on surveillance for the last several months, and in truth, I don't mind taking advantage of their information-gathering capabilities. They've got access to much larger databases than we do, and at this point, I'll take everything I can get."

Blair sketched aimlessly as they talked, trying to absorb the words without letting them penetrate to her core. She couldn't live in terror every day. "Is this serious, do you think?"

It was a question she had avoided asking for months. Cam was the only one that she dared ask, because in spite of everything, Cam was the only one she trusted to see her frightened.

"I don't know." Cam watched Blair's hands move gracefully, with absolute certainty, over the surface of the paper, wishing she could touch her, just enough to comfort her. Her hands trembled she wanted to so much. The feeling was unbearably strong, and she pressed her palms flat against her thighs. "I have to assume that it is."

Blair nodded, not speaking. *There is nothing I can do about any of it—the crazy lunatic sending me messages, the FBI dogging my steps, or Cameron's determination to carry out the assignment my father ordered.* She was uncomfortable feeling that helpless, especially when she had struggled her entire life for some semblance of independence. For the moment, however, she couldn't see any other course of action.

"All right. I can live with it...if you can."

Cam laughed sharply. There was a tinge of irony in her voice as she responded, "We have something in common there, Ms. Powell. Neither of us has a choice."

The sketch was taking form on the pad. Cam looked down at the drawing, surprised to see her own face appearing. She studied the image, taken aback by the fierce, reserved expression, and wondered if that was all Blair saw of her. She knew the answer as Blair's talented hands sketched her eyes and captured the shadows in her soul.

"Blair," Cam said softly.

Blair's hand faltered on the paper at the gentle intimacy in Cam's tone. The way she did this, the subtle shifts she revealed, never failed to tear at Blair's heart. One moment, the agent was professional, aloof, and as impersonal as any of the scores of individuals who had ever guarded her. And then, she would say Blair's name with all the feeling she could ever hope to hear from another human being. It was everything she wanted, and everything she feared. She didn't raise her eyes, but continued drawing the sharp features and the wild gaze, unable to look at the woman, knowing if she did she would touch her.

"Yes?"

Cam took a deep breath, wishing she did not have to ask. "I'd like you to reconsider the race on Sunday. I'd like you not to go."

Blair stiffened, the pencil finally stilling. "I have to go. I'm the keynote speaker."

"Would you consider just arriving for the speech, but not racing?"

Blair put her sketchpad aside and turned on the bench until she was fully facing Cam. For the first time, she looked directly into her face, directly into her eyes.

"This event is more than political. This is personal."

Understanding all too well, Cam nodded. Sunday was the annual Race for the Cure, a huge fundraiser for the treatment of breast cancer. Blair's mother had died of the disease when Blair was nine years old. Cam understood what it was to lose a parent. "I'm asking you, recommending it *strongly* to you, that you do not run in the race."

"Why are you asking me this?" Blair knew that Cam could not order her not to race.

Cam hesitated before answering. It was her job not only to guard Blair physically but also to give her some semblance of normality, as ironic as that appeared on the surface of things. She didn't want to worry her unnecessarily. That's what *she* was getting paid to do—the worrying.

She didn't intend to tell her that the event was a security nightmare. That even coordinating with New York City police and the transit police, and putting agents physically with Blair along the race route, left Blair about as unsecured as she could be. Under any circumstances, the race would have been difficult. Now, with the threat that Loverboy posed, securing it was nearly impossible.

Perhaps I could go to the director of the Secret Service and request that he contact the president's security director—try an end run around Blair and get someone higher up to order her not to run. But Cam knew damn well that if anyone ordered Blair not to participate in anything, let alone something as important to her as this, they could expect her to do exactly the opposite. And probably lose all hope of any cooperation whatsoever.

She hedged her answer and tried for a hint of levity. "I'm not sure I can run fifteen miles."

"I need to do this," Blair stated calmly. "Besides, I've seen you run, Commander. You can handle the distance quite well. I'll be fine." She couldn't stop herself from adding, "And I'll enjoy your company."

Cam was silent a moment, considering the options. *This* was the reason that personal relationships were discouraged. She couldn't think clearly because she cared about what her decisions might do to Blair. She was afraid that she might care more about Blair's *feelings* than about her safety, and that kind of involvement undermined her position and her authority. Worst of all, it impaired her judgment. She cursed under her breath, then acquiesced. "I hope to hell that Stark can make it, too, because we both need to go with you."

"Thank you," Blair whispered, knowing that Cam had relented against her better judgment. She touched her hand briefly in appreciation. "It will be all right," she said, wishing somehow that were true.

CHAPTER EIGHT

C am knew that she should go. Blair had sought privacy and peace in a quiet corner of this tiny sanctuary, and Cam had brought danger and uncertainty into it. For the first time that she could recall, she resented her job.

"I'm sorry I had to bring that up," she said, surprising them both. "I should leave you to your work."

"You don't have to be sorry. And you don't need to leave."

Before Cam could even think to say anything, her earphone crackled to life. She turned her head slightly away, listening. Her mood turned grim, but she kept her voice completely uninflected as she spoke briefly into the tiny microphone attached to her wrist.

"Send him in, then." Turning again to Blair, she explained, "It seems we have company."

Blair looked past Cam across the tiny park as a large man hurried toward them. "This would be the FBI, I presume," she noted, a look of faint repugnance on her face.

In spite of the situation, Cam laughed. "Very observant, Ms. Powell. Perhaps you should consider a future career in intelligence."

"Believe me, Commander, by this time I can recognize every branch of our esteemed intelligence agencies by the cut of an agent's suit and the arrogance in their walk." Blair smiled faintly, but there was no laughter in her eyes. "At least the Secret Service has always been polite."

"Ms. Powell." The burly man pointedly ignored Cam. "I'm Special Agent in Charge Patrick Doyle, Federal Bureau of Investigation. I wanted to meet you in person since I'll be spearheading your security detail until such time as we have apprehended the UNSUB."

Blair saw Cam go rigid beside her and said very coolly, "Mr. Doyle, my security is a matter for Commander Roberts. If you have something to relay to me in that regard, I suggest you do it through her. One daily briefing is all I can tolerate."

She gathered her sketchpad and drawing pencils and stood abruptly, forcing Doyle back a step. She glanced at Cam, whose expression was most likely unreadable to Doyle, but she saw the hint of laughter in her eyes. She smiled gently at her and turned to go. "I'll leave you two to sort out your territory."

Patrick Doyle turned on his heel and watched the president's daughter walk away. A muscle stood out in his jaw as he ground his teeth. When he faced Cam again, his fury was tinged with contempt and condescension. "She doesn't know what's good for her. I suppose you think you do?"

Cam stood, and when she did, she was nearly eye to eye with him. "I don't pretend to know what's good for Ms. Powell, but I can assure you of one thing. I know precisely what's good for her security. I can also advise you that if you have any suggestions or recommendations regarding that matter, you bring them to me. That's the chain of command, and I suggest you follow it."

He moved forward a step, trying unsuccessfully to force her back. Their chests were almost touching.

"Listen here, Roberts," he growled, his face livid. "You get in my way on this thing, and there just might be a little leak to the media about what you like to do in your off hours, and who you like to do it with."

"We've been down this road before, Doyle," Cam responded, her eyes never leaving his. "You're wasting your time."

"The directors in DC might not think so if your activities happen to involve the president's daughter."

"Doyle, you really are a fool if you think you can take on Blair Powell." She smiled at him, a thin smile, cold and hard as granite. "She'll have you for lunch."

Ignoring his bluster, she stepped lightly around him and walked out of the park the way she had come.

She glanced across the street, thinking that Blair was probably already secure back in her apartment. It crossed her mind to go after her, and then she stopped abruptly when she recognized the reason. She missed her already.

❖

Nine stories up, Blair leaned against the window frame, staring down at Cameron Roberts. Her security chief was standing just outside the gates of the park, her hands in her pockets, one shoulder braced against the stone pillar that marked the entrance to the square. Patrick Doyle stormed through the gate and passed her without a word.

She looks so tired. Blair could only imagine how difficult it must be for Cam to deal with the FBI presence. She'd been around politics all her life, and she knew that interagency power struggles were vicious, and self-interest paramount. Often, in their eagerness to advance their own positions, agents lost sight of their objective. She had no doubt that Patrick Doyle cared a great deal less for her personal safety than for his own desire to be the one to apprehend Loverboy. She wasn't foolish enough to think that she really mattered to him, and she didn't care.

She knew—more importantly, she *felt*—that to Cameron, she did matter. She'd felt that caring the first time Cam walked into the loft and made it clear that she would do her job, but that she'd try to make it tolerable for Blair. Most importantly, she'd seen it manifest in horrific detail the day Cam had stepped in front of her and almost died from the bullet meant for her. She didn't want Cam standing in front of her for any reason, but certainly not for a reason that could cost Cam her life.

God, I don't want to see that again. Why couldn't you just have told him no?

She'd wondered the same thing a hundred times, but she knew the answer. Cam hadn't accepted this assignment just because the president of the United States had requested her. She'd taken the assignment because that was what she did. That was who she was. Some part of Blair could respect that. Some part of her could even understand it. But knowing it and understanding it did not change what she felt. She resented that she needed protection from anyone, but at least she had made some form of peace with that. She didn't want or need it from Cameron Roberts.

What she did want from her was the one thing she had given up hoping for, or had simply stopped looking for, in another human being. Cam touched her in some deep place that others never imagined existed, and that's what she so desperately needed. Cam didn't try to tell her to accept her circumstances or be grateful for her privilege, as so many others before her had. She was equally oblivious to Blair's status, a welcome respite from the solicitous attentions of so many. Most importantly, Cam understood her anger and forgave her fury.

Blair watched her walk around the corner toward her own apartment building, and after a moment, she turned back to her empty loft. Seeing Cam, being as close to her as they had been just moments before, had left her restless and edgy with the low throb of desire. It always seemed to happen when they were anywhere near each other. She didn't want to feel it, and she didn't want to think about it.

Her gaze fell on a large oil canvas, and she studied it critically from across the room. She didn't consider the details at first, but rather the gestalt, the sense of it. She felt it, rather than saw it. Slowly, after a minute or two, she focused her attention on the elements of the painting—the colors, contrast, and movement of the eye over the images. By the time she'd advanced from the window to stand in front of her work, contemplating what she needed to do with it, her mind was clear, and briefly, her heart was free.

Cam was happy she had decided not to go after Blair. It was much safer to run—safer than seeing Blair again so soon. It had been the same since the first time she'd met with her, this rebellion of her body in the face of good sense. She was aware of it now, in the simmering tension that ran along the tendons and the muscles and the nerves in her legs, twisting through her like a starving beast. She knew what it was; she'd felt it for months before she had finally relented.

Being with Blair hadn't blunted the urgency, touching her hadn't lessened the wanting, making love with her had not muted the desire. She could feel Blair's skin hot under her hands and the hard beat of her under her lips. She could taste her still.

There were other ways to deal with the body's demands—safe, simple, unencumbered ways. Pleasant, mutually satisfying, emotionally secure ways. She was reminded of Claire's note, left for her to find after their last night together.

If ever you need...anything, call me. C.

Cam tossed her jacket on the bed, shrugged out of her shoulder harness, and began unbuttoning her shirt. *Yeah, right,* she muttered, stripping down to her briefs and pulling shorts and T-shirt from a drawer. *Simple.*

She wasn't certain any longer that Claire's admittedly talented ministrations could assuage the hunger. Still, physical desire—that was something she could deal with, one way or the other. But it was more than just the wanting, and that was the problem. It was the aching in her heart that tormented her.

Blair didn't just arouse her, she also awakened her. Every emotion so carefully stilled came roaring back to life when she thought of her. Blair's ferocious will stirred her senses even as Blair's tenderness, so invisible to others, comforted her. Blair made her nearly mad with frustration yet soothed her with the barest of touches. *She devastates me with a smile. God, I miss her.*

She exited her building and hit the pavement running, desperate to stop thinking. She just needed a few weeks to assess the seriousness of the threat to Blair. Once she had access to all the available intelligence, she could turn over more of the day-to-day security to Mac. Maybe then, she and Blair could talk; maybe then, they could...

What? We could what? Carry on an affair under Doyle's nose? Risk Blair's privacy and the president's public image with a backroom love affair that the media would make into tabloid headlines? Perfect. Great idea, Roberts.

She pounded steadily along the East River, although the scenery barely registered. All she could think about was the look in Blair's eyes when she'd told her that she was commanding the security detail again. *I hurt her.*

Knowing she'd hurt her, seeing it in her face, was harder than anything she'd ever had to bear. Even harder than when Janet had died, because then, and for months after, she'd just been numb.

Mercifully numb. Frozen with the senselessness, the stupidity, the guilt. She should have known about the raid that morning. It was her job to know those things; it was her responsibility to know those things.

But she had not been part of the plan. Despite the fact that she and her team had been investigating the same splinter faction of cocaine dealers as the other agencies, the DEA had orchestrated the entire scenario that morning. The ATF and the Secret Service had only been informed of the impending maneuver at the last minute. By some all too common breakdown in the local-federal law enforcement communication lines, no one had realized until too late that the DC Metropolitan police had an undercover narcotics agent inside the warehouse where the exchange of very authentic counterfeit money for a huge cache of drugs was to take place.

Janet had already been on site when the assault began. The sting operation had gone bad almost from the beginning. A lookout no one anticipated had seen the armored cars approaching and radioed the Colombians in the building where the buy was going down. The men inside had been heavily armed and prepared to defend themselves. Shots had been fired as soon as the battering rams cracked the wide double doors. Janet had been directly in the line of fire.

Cam had gone inside right behind the first wave of tactical officers. The air had been heavy with the smell of cordite and thick with the sounds of screaming—orders, curses, cries of agony. Janet had taken one of the first bullets and was down before Cam shouldered her way past the splintered remains of the reinforced doors. By the time she reached her, Janet was almost gone. She'd held her, called her name, begged her to hold on. She would never be certain how to interpret the look in Janet's eyes those last few seconds as the spark slowly faded. She couldn't help thinking that it had been an accusation.

If it was, I deserved it.

She ran into Central Park, sweat pouring from her face, oblivious to the cramps beginning in her thighs or the faint ache behind her eyes.

I should have known. I should have protected her.

CHAPTER NINE

At 0700 Sunday morning, Cam waited in the lobby of Blair's apartment building along with Stark and Savard. She had sent Mac on ahead to coordinate the details in Prospect Park and to advise the commanders of the municipal security teams that she wanted to meet with them personally before the start of the race.

The New York City Transit Bureau would station squadrons of officers in the subway system, the New York Police Department would provide security along the race route, and the mayor's detail would be on the speaker's platform where he, Blair, and others would address the public at the completion of the race. It was standard operating procedure for the Secret Service to coordinate all the security forces whenever a high-level protectee was making a public appearance.

Cam was sifting through the details in her mind when the elevator door opened and Blair entered the lobby. She was dressed for the run almost identically to Cam—a light nylon windbreaker over a T-shirt, running shorts, and shoes. She had caught her hair back at the base of her neck as she usually did for public outings, substituting a length of dark ribbon for the customary gold clasp. Her light make-up was superfluous on a face made for the camera. Even her attitude was different—she walked quickly, purposefully, with barely a glance at her surroundings.

She, too, had a job to accomplish, one she had been performing in her mother's absence for over fifteen years. She was the reigning queen of her father's dynasty and often accompanied him to state affairs or represented him when the social circumstances required it. Today, she was appearing as the president's daughter, and although the role was not always comfortable for her, it was one she knew well.

When she saw Cam, she hesitated briefly. They smiled at each other, forgetting for a moment that there was anyone else in the room. It was one of those automatic responses that neither of them could prevent, that brief surge of pleasurable recognition that was beyond volition or better judgment.

In an instant, their smiles disappeared, and they greeted one another formally.

"Good morning, Ms. Powell," Cam said as she turned and walked beside her, Stark and Savard falling in on either side.

"Commander." Blair nodded quickly and continued toward the front door without breaking stride again. Per routine, Stark held the door open, and Cam went through just slightly ahead and to the right of Blair. Cam hesitated fleetingly at the sidewalk as she looked up and down the street and then across the park, just as she had the day the shot was fired. It was so subtle that no one except another agent would have noticed. No one else except Blair.

She was always acutely aware of the way Cam positioned herself between her and any potential threat, even when they just walked down the sidewalk together. In this particular location, she would never lose that involuntary instant of stomach-churning fear.

Cam sensed Blair stiffen beside her and murmured in a voice too low for anyone else to hear, "It's just procedure. Try to ignore it."

"I'd like to be able to," Blair said just as quietly as they crossed the sidewalk toward the black limousine. "It would be so much simpler if I could. But I can't."

Stark and Savard proceeded to the Suburban idling just in front to lead the caravan, while Cam held the door to the second car, allowing Blair to slide in, then followed after her. An FBI vehicle fell in behind, and as the convoy pulled away, Blair announced in a businesslike tone, "I'll be meeting some people when we get there."

Cam regarded her carefully, slightly surprised that the information was volunteered, while at the same time mildly annoyed that she hadn't been informed sooner. Blair wasn't required to tell her security detail everything, of course, but it was always helpful to have as much advance data as possible. She was grateful, however, for this small improvement in communication.

"Will they be joining you for the run?"

Blair nodded, watching out the tinted windows of the limousine as the city slid by. "Yes. I've invited Diane and another friend."

No details. And I won't ask. Cam wondered, though, if she would be spending another day watching the admittedly attractive Dr. Coleman pursue Blair. *You put yourself in this position, and you knew what it would mean,* she reminded herself. But she hadn't even come close to imagining how difficult it would be, and she hadn't expected it to be so complicated for the two of them to talk. The lack of privacy didn't help, but it was more than that. She had to admit that part of it was pride, and some of it was pain, and a great deal of it was a lifetime of defenses, on both sides, standing between them now.

"Noted. Savard, Stark, and I will be with you along the route."

"We'll have a party," Blair murmured, turning from the window to study Cam's face, a face she never seemed to tire of observing. Just seeing her made something pulse inside, swift and sharp and hot—part desire, part longing, and, so unexpectedly, part tenderness. It defied explanation, but in spite of everything, she welcomed the sensation.

"Special Agent Savard is quite the beauty," Blair added dryly.

Cam raised an eyebrow but decided a comment was probably not required. Renée Savard was indeed an attractive woman, now that she considered it. She hadn't thought about it earlier; in fact, she hadn't paid much attention to her other than to consider what to do with her.

Savard was an agent under her command by circumstance, but under her command nonetheless, and that was the only way she thought of her. When she noted Savard's appearance at all, it was merely to reflect that despite her photogenic beauty, almost anyone paled when compared to Blair. Blair's beauty was fired by her passion and her temper and her absolute unwillingness to yield. She was beautiful in a way so primal that being near her made Cam's skin burn.

"What?" Blair asked quietly.

"I'm sorry?" Cam blinked, uncharacteristically startled.

"You were smiling," Blair said, a slight edge to her voice. "Thinking of Savard, were you?"

"No. Actually," Cam said before she could stop herself, "I was thinking of you."

Across the narrow expanse of the limousine where they sat facing one another on opposite seats, their legs nearly touching, Blair's blue eyes darkened to indigo. "You should try doing that more often," she said, her tone throaty with invitation.

Cam met her gaze, captivated by the heat in those eyes. For a moment forgetting everything else, she said, her voice husky, "No, Ms. Powell, I shouldn't. It's too distracting."

"Well, Commander," Blair said very slowly, very quietly, staring at the pulse that beat rapidly in Cam's neck, "I like you when you're distracted. In fact, I like you that way very much...or have you forgotten?"

No. I haven't forgotten.

"You're distracting me," Cam complained playfully as she tried to read the newspaper.

"I like you when you're distracted," Blair responded, running her hand over the soft cotton fabric of Cam's sweatpants. "In fact, I like distracting you."

They were in Diane's apartment, lying together on the couch in the late afternoon sun. They had finally managed to shower and dress, which for the first eighteen hours they'd been together they hadn't been able to accomplish. Every time they made it into the shower, one or the other would start something, and they'd end up back in bed. Starvation finally drove them to get up, and Cam made a trip to a nearby deli for sandwiches, newspapers, and something to drink.

"What do you imagine they think I'm doing up here?" Blair mused, her fingers tracing the seam along the inside of Cam's thigh.

Cam sighed, most of her attention focused on the light pressure of Blair's fingers moving rhythmically up and down the same fine line, over and over again, creeping higher up the inside of her leg each time. She settled back against the cushions, her muscles twitching faintly at Blair's touch.

"They're not supposed to think anything about it at all." Her voice caught as Blair stroked closer to the heat between her legs.

"Maybe they're not supposed to, but they are human, aren't they?"

Blair lifted the edge of Cam's shirt and circled her hand over Cam's stomach, absently drawing one finger up and down the center of her body. "I've come so many times in the last twenty-four hours, I didn't think anything could excite me," she said in wonder. "But, God, you do." She pressed her palm swiftly to the triangle between Cam's thighs, making her jump, then just as quickly moved it back to her stomach. "So...you were saying about discretion?"

Cam's voice was low, heavy with the urgency of mounting desire as she answered. "Their jobs depend upon it. But it's more than that..." Aware of the fact that her breath was coming a little faster and that her sentences were a bit choppy, she knew she was wet again and hardening with the rush of blood and need. She took a desperate breath. "Believe it or not, we understand that what we do is an infringement. The very least we can do is not speculate upon what we observe."

She looked down, watching Blair's fingers move under her T-shirt and wondering at the ease with which Blair was able to ignite every nerve ending with a caress. She had absolutely nothing to say about it. It was as if her body succumbed to Blair's touch, bending to her will as a tree yielded to the wind. "Blair," she warned huskily, wondering if Blair had any idea what she was doing to her.

"You have the most amazing body," Blair observed casually, massaging her palm over Cam's rib cage, brushing fleetingly over her chest, smiling as Cam's nipples stiffened rapidly. Cam groaned and reached for her, and just as quickly, Blair leaned away. "I think you should just read the newspaper and ignore me," she said with a perfectly serious expression.

"You're kidding." Cam's eyes widened slightly, her hands rubbing lightly up and down Blair's arms. Her skin felt hot. "I don't think I could concentrate."

"Try," Blair suggested with a hint of command in her voice. "In fact, why don't you read the headlines out loud? A synopsis of today's current events would be good. Make yourself useful."

"For your information," Cam said, ominously now, "I've been trained to resist torture."

Blair burst out laughing and loosened the ties on Cam's sweatpants, slipping to the floor to kneel between Cam's legs. "Oh really? Well then, Commander, let's put that training to the test. Go ahead, read."

"Uh, let's see." The New York Times *pages fluttered in her right hand as her fingers trembled. "Uh...dot-com stocks rose finally—" She gasped when Blair pulled at the skin of her lower abdomen with her teeth. "God..."*

"I'm listening," Blair murmured, eyes nearly closed. She licked the red spot she had just bitten and pulled the cotton fabric down Cam's

hips. She pressed her palms to the inside of Cam's legs, bringing her thumbs very close to the visibly swollen clitoris. Cam's hips arched and she groaned again.

"Not until I hear the sports scores," Blair whispered, leaning forward and kissing the soft skin at the top of Cam's thigh. "How about them Yankees?"

"Blair, come on," Cam gasped, tossing the paper aside. "I can't... read. I can't talk...I can barely breathe."

When Blair's thumb brushed lightly over the tip of her clitoris, Cam pushed back against the couch, neck arched, her hands fisted by her sides. Another teasing stroke followed, and she uttered a strangled sound. She found Blair's face with one hand, moved her fingers into her hair, and pulled her closer.

"I'm ready...do that again...to divulge...ah, yes, right there...state secrets." Her voice cracked with need. "Suck me."

Blair held off another second, but apparently not without effort. She was shaking. "God," she whispered. "I want to taste you."

When Blair's lips finally encircled her, Cam jerked, her fingers convulsing in Blair's hair. She clamped her jaw down on a moan and tried to think of anything except the waves of pleasure coursing down her legs, up her spine, through her guts. She wanted it never to end. Reflexively, she pushed against Blair's mouth, dimly aware that she might bruise her, trying not to press too hard. But she couldn't stop, couldn't get enough air, couldn't hold it back.

"Blair—" she cried, lifting off the couch as her legs stiffened, pounded by the fury of the orgasm whipping through her. Before she regained her bearings, Blair was in her arms, straddling her thigh, rocking hard on her leg, face pressed to her neck.

"You make me so hot," Blair moaned, clutching Cam as she climbed frantically to her peak. "You make me...oh..." Her words were lost in a choked cry, and all Cam could do was hold on to her, embracing her securely while she took her pleasure.

The limousine pulled to a stop on the edge of the green in Prospect Park. Cam shuddered faintly and struggled to keep her voice steady. "I'm not interested in being distracted."

"That's your problem, Commander," Blair said lightly, reading the dark eyes liquid with unspoken emotion, and sensing the arousal Cam couldn't successfully hide. "Not mine."

As she slid across the seat toward the door, she ran her hand down the length of Cam's thigh. She smiled to herself as Cam gasped sharply. "I told you once before that your body never lies."

Prospect Park, the starting point for the race, was slightly more than half the size of Manhattan's eight-hundred-acre Central Park, but it nevertheless housed a wildlife center, a music pagoda, a lake, and many other opportunities for city dwellers to escape the urban stresses for a few hours.

The area of Brooklyn around the park was a study in contrasts. The west boundary was Park Slope, a conclave of historic brownstones that housed the wealthy and privileged. The eastern extent of the sprawling park abutted Crown Heights and Bedford-Stuyvesant, areas that in recent years had become dangerous territory for tourists and inhabitants alike. This early on a Sunday morning, there were usually a few early-morning enthusiasts enjoying the opportunity to run or rollerblade in relative solitude.

Such was not the case today.

Long Meadow, an open, rolling ninety-acre section nearly a mile in length, was already bustling with people. The Race for the Cure drew more supporters than almost any similar event because the disease itself affected so many. It was a media event as much as anything else, especially with Blair as the keynote speaker, and photographers and news vans were already present in abundant numbers.

Cam stood next to her by the side of the car, scanning the hundreds of participants gathering for the start of the run. "It's going to be very crowded along the entire route, especially when we get into Central Park. I'd appreciate it if you'd not lose us."

"You're very good at your job, Commander." Blair met Cam's eyes, and for the first time in a long time, she couldn't read the expression in them. Even though they had been physically separated since Cam's return, she'd at least had the comfort of seeing what was behind the professional façade when she looked into her dark eyes. This new barrier stung. "I'm sure you'll manage somehow."

Then the president's daughter abruptly turned and walked off toward the area where the race organizers had set up information booths, leaving Cam alone to stare after her. Stark and Savard approached from the second vehicle, and Cam signaled the two women to accompany Blair while she radioed Mac for his position.

"Do you have the commanders of the other teams there?" she asked without preamble, watching Blair disappear into the crowd of men and women clustered around the long registration tables. It bothered her that Blair was out of her visual range and that she couldn't see who was around her. *Terrific.*

"I'll be right there," she snapped into her mike. Her lapse in concentration on the ride over had left her unsettled. So did the simmering remnants of desire. She ignored the physical annoyance with effort and checked Blair's position again.

Across the wide field, she could see her talking to a number of people, Diane Bleeker among them. Cam resisted the urge to scan the other faces nearby for the very handsome Dr. Coleman. She assured herself that Stark and Savard were well positioned and headed over to join Mac and the other security chiefs.

It was hot, sunny, and, surprisingly for late July, without the heavy humidity that often blanketed the city in summer. After greeting the appropriate people and allowing the media types their few minutes of photo-ops, Blair found a quiet spot in the shade to stretch and prepare for the run. As she leaned over, legs braced, stretching her hamstrings, Diane's familiar voice remarked from beside her, "I see you've brought along a new addition. A very nice one, too."

Blair shifted to look up at Diane. She didn't have to ask whom she meant. She had seen her friend's appreciative and frankly appraising expression when Savard came into view a few minutes before. "That would be the FBI's contribution to my team."

Diane reclined on the grass next to her and leaned forward, touching her toes effortlessly. "What's going on?" she asked, moving smoothly into a yoga pose.

"Nothing." Blair reached for one ankle and crossed it over the opposite knee, rotating her torso.

"Listen, my friend—just how dumb do you think I am?" Diane asked, breathing deeply in the prescribed ujjay manner. "First Roberts makes a surprise appearance, and now you've got the FBI following you around. That means something."

"I know you're not dumb, which is why I wouldn't lie." Blair turned over and pushed off ten fast fingertip push-ups in perfect form. Returning to the sitting position, she said, "It's just routine."

Somehow talking about it made it much too real. She didn't want this in her life. Except for her first tentative discussions with her friend AJ at the Bureau, she hadn't told any of her acquaintances. She had intentionally avoided briefings with the FBI. The only thing she wanted to know from them was that they had caught him.

"Believe it or not..." Diane folded both legs into a full lotus position and slipped one arm behind her back, twisting slowly in the opposite direction. "I can keep a secret if I need to. Besides, my feelings will be hurt if I'm the last to find out and I miss all the fun."

Blair snorted in disgust. "Believe me, if you think this is a treat, you can take my place any day."

She rose quickly and began to alternately lift each leg to her chest in rapid succession. She looked across the gathering crowd and easily picked out Cam where she stood talking with several officious-looking individuals. There was nothing flashy or showy about the agent, but she stood out from the others. The air around her seemed charged. It was amazing...and frightening.

Diane studied Blair's face as she followed her gaze. "She's gotten to you, hasn't she?"

"Oh, yeah," Blair said without thinking. She looked away, shrugging. "She's back because my father wanted her here. I've been getting a little more fan mail than usual, and you know how seriously these people take those things. It's nothing, really."

Diane nodded, knowing there was more but willing to wait for the details. Eventually, she'd get the rest out of her. She rose and stood beside Blair, waving to a familiar figure making her way through the crowd toward them. "Marcy's been asking about you."

"Is that so?" Blair looked at her friend, an eyebrow raised in question.

"Yes." Diane grabbed them each a water bottle from a nearby table. "She wants to know how available you might be."

"Then she should ask me herself," Blair said impatiently. "For God's sake, we're all adults."

"I think she wants to avoid being shot down. Your signals were a little mixed last weekend at my place," Diane pointed out dryly.

Seeing Marcy's friendly smile as the doctor drew near, Blair was a little embarrassed to realize she hadn't given any thought to the events at Diane's gathering. She'd been too rattled the last week by Cam's abrupt reappearance and the emotional chaos that followed to give anything, or *anyone else*, much thought. It hadn't occurred to her that Marcy Coleman might have other ideas, but, recalling what had happened, she supposed it should have.

It had all started after Cam left the party.

Blair watched Cam move through the crowd, murmur something briefly to Ellen Grant, and then walk out the door. She did not look back to where Blair still stood in the shadows on the balcony.

After a moment of foolishly hoping that her security chief might suddenly reappear, Blair rejoined the group in Diane's living room. Lights were turned down low, and couples were dancing. A daring few in secluded corners were carrying on more intimate exchanges.

Dr. Marcy Coleman, a willowy blond in her mid-thirties, approached, a smile on her face and a question in her eyes. "I didn't see you for a while. I thought you might have left."

"No," Blair said, her mind still on the image of Cam standing outside, alone in the dark, the night wind ruffling her dark hair. Once she had been challenged by Cam's solitude; now she was wounded by it. The change was not a welcome one, and she brushed the reflection from her mind.

"Another dance?" Marcy asked, lightly taking Blair's hand in hers.

"Sure," Blair answered absently. At least it would distract her from the way her body still vibrated from the brief touch of Cam's fingers. Or so she thought.

She stepped into Marcy's arms, rested her cheek lightly against the other woman's shoulder, and closed her eyes. The music was something slow and sultry—perfect music to get lost in. She wanted to be lost for a while. Not to think, not to struggle, not to mourn. To want nothing was to never be disappointed.

Marcy's body was sleek and sensuous, and she moved against Blair with practiced intimacy. It had been like this countless times before, with other bodies, other faces. Brief diversions, momentary escape. The act of pleasuring was satisfying in itself, but Blair was careful always to remain in control. Safe, simple, emotionally unencumbered. No promises—just pleasant, mutually satisfying biological proceedings.

As Marcy pulled her a little closer, rotating her hips slowly, insistently, against Blair's, there was a subtle shift of pressure that she almost didn't notice at first. And then something unexpected happened. Without realizing it, without consciously willing it, she was becoming aroused.

A year ago, even six months ago, she would never have noticed the first spark of fire. And even if she had, she would have been able to ignore it. The excitement would have settled into the back of her mind like a pleasant afterthought, untended and unanswered. Now her nerve endings were raw and acutely sensitive. And she was afraid she knew why.

Since Cam, something had changed. Something she had been able to contain for many years had been unleashed. The practiced disconnection she had so carefully constructed between her emotions and her physical self had dissolved with the first touch of Cam's hands.

She knew her breathing had gotten erratic, and she felt Marcy's heart beating rapidly, echoing her own. When Marcy cupped her breast as she had done briefly earlier that evening, her nipple stiffened against Marcy's palm. She bit her lip to keep back a moan and tried to concentrate on something other than the liquid heat surging between her legs.

Marcy lowered her head, her lips brushing the outer edge of Blair's ear. "You are a great dancer," she said, her voice throaty and slightly breathless. As she spoke, she rubbed her fingers very lightly over Blair's nipple.

Blair gasped as a ripple of excitement flickered through her, running down her spine and coiling in her stomach. The sensation was so unusual it took her completely by surprise, and before she was fully aware of it, she had parted her legs and pressed harder against Marcy's thigh. The pressure against her swelling clitoris was exquisite, and for a moment, she couldn't think of anything at all.

"I'd like very much to be alone with you right now," Marcy continued, deftly directing them closer to the hallway that led back to the guest room in Diane's apartment. "I want to touch you so much it's driving me crazy."

Blair flashed on the last time she had been in that room, and almost instantly, Cam's face, intense and consuming, filled her mind. For a moment, it was Cam's hand on her breast, and Cam's leg between her thighs, and a spasm shuddered through her as her arousal escalated. She stumbled slightly, trembling.

"I don't usually do this sort of thing in other people's houses," Marcy said urgently, closing her arms around Blair. "But if I don't do something soon, I'm in danger of exploding."

By now they were in the hallway, alone, and Marcy had maneuvered Blair up against the wall. She had both hands under Blair's sweater, on her breasts, squeezing them as she worked Blair's nipples between her fingers.

Struggling to stay upright, Blair pressed her palms flat against the wall, her head tipped back, her eyes closed, verging on orgasm. She wasn't thinking of the woman who touched her now, but of the woman who had done so much more than just touch her body.

"Blair," Marcy whispered.

Not Cam.

"Marcy," Blair groaned, forcing her eyes open, backing away from the edge through sheer willpower. "We...should...stop."

Marcy's lips were on Blair's neck, biting her lightly as she pressed harder against her, one hand pushing under the waistband of Blair's pants. "Oh God, I don't want to." She moved her hand to the triangle between Blair's thighs and squeezed rhythmically. "God, I know how close you are. I can feel it."

With effort, Blair pulled away as much as she could, struggling to contain the surging pressure building between her legs, knowing that in a second, she would lose the fight. Dimly, she wondered why it mattered, and she did not want to know the answer.

"Stop now, please."

"I'm sorry." Marcy brought her hands to Blair's waist, holding her but not pushing her any further. She shuddered, gasping, her forehead resting lightly on Blair's shoulder. "I don't know what happened."

"Neither do I," Blair laughed shakily, "but you don't need to apologize."

"I usually have better control than that." Marcy leaned back, her eyes still molten with desire. She smiled a little tremulously. "But I don't think anyone has ever done that to me before."

"You mean teased you quite so unmercifully?" Blair laughed, with more strength this time. "Maybe I should apologize."

"Oh no, don't even think of it." Marcy ran one finger along the edge of Blair's jaw. "What I meant was, no one has ever made me so hot so fast. No one ever made me lose my mind like that."

"I didn't mean to do that." Blair stepped sideways enough to put space between them. "It took me by surprise, too."

Marcy brushed her shoulder-length blond hair back with a still-trembling hand. "I think we should go back into the other room. I seem to be dangerous out here."

"A very good idea, Dr. Coleman." Blair took her hand in a friendly but not intimate gesture, and laughed. "Come on."

"I'd like that to happen again," Marcy said just before they rejoined the others. "Somewhere, some time, when we won't have to stop."

Blair did not look back, and she did not answer.

"I didn't intend to send her any kind of message at all." Blair started to walk. "Nothing happened."

"That's not the way she tells it," Diane said offhandedly. "To hear her, you are the answer to a woman's dreams. She appears to be in danger of spontaneous combustion just from being in the same room with you."

"I can't help that," Blair said in irritation. "I can't control what other people fantasize."

"I absolutely agree, Blair," Diane responded, her tone uncharacteristically serious as she followed Blair through the crowd toward the start line. "I like her, though. I like you, too."

"You have a point here?" Blair challenged her with a look.

"I thought I did. God knows, I'm the last one to give advice. Just be careful with her. Especially if you know there's no chance."

Blair looked back and, just beyond Marcy, saw Cam. The contrast was striking—one blond, the other dark; sunlight and midnight. Her heart hammering, she said, "I'm not sure of anything anymore."

Chapter Ten

Stark glanced over at Savard and grimaced. She hoped her lithe companion, running effortlessly beside her, could not see her struggling to catch her breath. *Running. I hate running. Stupid form of exercise. Terrible for your feet. Murder on your knees. Give me a bike, or better yet...rollerblades.*

Savard cast her a sideways look and grinned, a surprisingly charming grin. "Isn't this great?"

"Oh yeah, fabulous! Love it." Stark hoped she sounded appropriately excited. No way was she going to let the FBI agent think she couldn't keep up. She'd run on bare feet first. Just to prove it, she picked up her pace a little bit.

"Could be worse duty," Savard commented, not even breathing hard. *Or worse company.*

She was enjoying her posting with the Secret Service more than she had imagined she would. She missed the prevailing sense of urgency that permeated everything the FBI seemed to do, even if it was just a routine wire tap, but she couldn't deny that Roberts and her team ran a tight, well-organized operation.

And she also had to admit that Paula Stark was an interesting combination of straight-arrow dedication and startling naiveté. She couldn't help but wonder if her refreshingly unsophisticated counterpart really had no clue as to how attractive she was or the fact that other people might think so. Savard reminded herself to stop watching Stark's butt and keep her eyes on the main target, who, come to think of it, had a very nice butt herself.

At that moment, Stark was doing the same thing, but without quite the same appreciation. The commander and Egret were a few feet ahead of her, and neither of them looked as if they had even broken a sweat. In between ignoring the pain in her calves and attempting to look consumed with zeal for this madness, her primary responsibility for the day was crowd surveillance. *Another nearly impossible chore, but a far more achievable goal than pretending enthusiasm for the next only-God-knew how many miles.*

The entire security team had been provided with photos of individuals expected to be in Blair's immediate vicinity during the run— primarily the race organizers, representatives of cancer organizations, and various political dignitaries. When Stark occasionally spotted someone she didn't recognize, she radioed a verbal description to Mac in the communications van that was following behind the mass of runners. More often than not, he made an immediate identification. If there was any question or concern, she could beam him an image from her handheld personal unit.

He and several other agents conscripted from the local office for this particular event had been on site since daybreak, quietly photographing individuals as they arrived in the park. They ran all unknowns through computer links to the DMV, Armed Forces directory, and the state police files. She didn't know for sure, but she assumed that the FBI were doing the same thing from their own van as well. It would have been more efficient to combine their search capabilities, but the FBI hadn't offered access to their databases. *So much for interagency cooperation. Huh—what else is new.*

Not all of this was routine. The fact that Egret was now considered a high-risk subject dictated the extra precautions. Stark shifted the weight of her pistol in the quick-release fanny pack she wore and said a small prayer of thanks as they crossed over the Brooklyn Bridge into Manhattan. She looked ahead, never so grateful in her life as now to see the Bowery.

Cam kept pace to Blair's right and just a half step behind her, a vantage point from which she could see anyone approaching from the right, left, or rear. What she was watching now, however, was Marcy Coleman leaning close to say something to Blair, her hand resting casually on the small of Blair's back. It might have been a friendly gesture, but Cam didn't think so. Not from the way the blond doctor had been looking at Blair for the last few miles.

Cam had seen Blair with other women before. Hell, she'd seen her have sex with other women. It had been different then. She hadn't particularly enjoyed watching her have casual sex with strangers, the biggest reason being that she had always thought Blair exceptional, and she couldn't help but think that she deserved something more than anonymous couplings. But it hadn't been her business then, and she had been able to put it out of her mind enough to work around it.

It still wasn't her business, but the problem now was that she carried the imprint of Blair's skin branded into her nerve endings. She had surrendered to her and taken her, and she knew the wonder of holding her when she was completely without her usual defenses. Now it was intolerable to see another woman touch her.

She looked away, scanning the nearby faces, forcing herself to review yet again the details of the rest of the day. As she took refuge in her responsibilities, she settled back into a comfortable rhythm, mentally and physically. They were approaching Fifth Avenue, and before too long, they would enter the south end of Central Park. Once there, security would be at its most difficult, and Blair would be at greatest risk.

Just like every day, the park was filled with people—runners, bladers, people pushing strollers, and tourists of all size and description. Students picnicked on the grass, and lovers trysted amongst the outcroppings of rocks. The race ended in Sheep Meadow, a huge open field where a stage had been erected, equipped with sound and video for the closing activities. Blair, the mayor, members of the American Cancer Society, and a few celebrities would be speaking.

The area was impossible to isolate and contain. Blair would be exposed on the podium the entire time, particularly so when she gave the keynote address. The anticipated crowd would number in the thousands. The New York State Police would be providing the NYPD with additional troops for crowd control. That would leave the mayor's security detail to concentrate on the area directly around the speaker's stands. Cam had met the mayor's security chief before, and she was good. That was a plus. She intended to make full use of all of the additional manpower. Her mental planning was interrupted as Blair dropped back to run next to her.

"Are you enjoying yourself, Commander?" Blair was actually surprised to find that *she* was. She loved the exercise, but the event itself took a toll on her emotionally. It reminded her, even after all these years, of the horrible year when she was nine and everything in her life seemed to change overnight. She focused on Cam's face and let the memory slip away. "Beats sitting in front of the video monitors, wouldn't you say?"

"It's a beautiful day," Cam agreed, smiling when she looked at her because she couldn't help it. There was a faint sheen of sweat on Blair's face, and her T-shirt was damp between her shoulder blades. She looked healthy, strong, and altogether beautiful. "Can't complain about a chance to spend a few hours like this outside."

"Uh-huh," Blair acknowledged with a slow smile, thinking that Cameron Roberts had to be the most naturally graceful, physically striking woman she had ever seen. And at the moment, there were shadows in her deep gray eyes. "Then why do I get the impression you'd rather be elsewhere?"

"I'd rather *you* be elsewhere."

"So I gather." Blair shook her head, frowning slightly, but her eyes were dancing. "You are nothing, Commander Roberts, if not doggedly persistent."

Cam's eyes became even more serious. "I assume you want me to tell you the truth, Ms. Powell. Especially when it affects you."

"I do, Commander." Blair's chin came up and her voice was chilly. "I just wish you'd tell me *before* you decide on something. Especially when it affects me."

Cam looked ahead, checking their position. Nothing out of the ordinary. Then, for a moment, she looked nowhere but at Blair. "I know. I'm sorry."

"Yes"—Blair could take no comfort from that admission—"you said that before."

"I'll have to review a few things with you once we arrive at the stage." Cam needed to keep them both focused on what was important for the moment. Later, later somehow, they would talk.

"I'll try to spare a minute or two," Blair answered dryly. Then she picked up her speed and rejoined Diane and Marcy Coleman.

❖

The area around the viewing stands was controlled chaos, just as Cam had expected. Sound and video technicians were crawling over and under the surface of the stage, running last-minute cables and adjusting microphones. The mayor was taking every occasion for photo-ops, and more reporters were jockeying for a comment than Cam would have liked. The media were easily identifiable by their badges, but it was a simple matter to counterfeit a press pass.

"Let's go up the back way to the stage," Cam suggested as she and Blair approached the area. "There are too many people in front."

"I should make an appearance here first," Blair said matter-of-factly, noting the local and national television crews. At Cam's frown, she added gently, "I am identified with this event. The American people know my life story and the story of my mother's death. I need to be seen. It's expected."

"You'll be seen by millions of television viewers in about twenty minutes," Cam pointed out as she took Blair's arm and started to move around to the side of the high temporary stage. "That will have to do."

"Cam," Blair said quietly.

Cam stopped in her tracks at the sound of her name spoken as only Blair could say it.

"He doesn't want to hurt me. If he did, he wouldn't be sending me the messages he's been sending."

At mention of the UNSUB, Cam felt a sudden sense of foreboding and immediately looked over the faces in the direct vicinity, imprinting each on her mind. She saw Stark and Savard already posted at opposite corners of the stage and Mac in conversation with the mayor's security chief. She was as satisfied as possible that all was as it should be.

When she looked back at Blair, there were no barriers in her eyes this time. No professional distance, no orders or rules or protocol between them. "I don't know what he's going to do. I don't know when he's going to do it. I don't know nearly enough." She struggled not to touch her, and for the barest of instants, she brushed her fingertips over Blair's hand. "Blair, I just want you safe."

"Yes, I know," Blair responded, no anger or resentment in her voice. She could not argue with the honest caring in Cam's face. This wasn't how she wanted it—and it was not what she wanted from her—but it was real nonetheless. "And you've done what needs to be done to ensure that. Now, I need to go and do this."

Cam nodded, knowing she would never be comfortable with it, but accepting that Blair would not let this threat interfere with her life or her responsibilities. "Let's go see the mayor, then, Ms. Powell. You'll make the photographers a lot happier than he does."

"Why, thank you, Commander." Her smile was for Cam, not the mayor or the photographers.

❖

When Blair stepped to the podium, Cam was positioned to the right rear, just a few feet behind her. Stark and Savard were at ground level directly in front of her, and several FBI agents on loan from the New York office were interspersed in the crowd near the stage.

Mac, coordinating the various teams from the communications van, was linked by radio to Jeremy Finch, the driver of Blair's car; to Ellen Grant, in the second backup vehicle; and to the mayor's security chief, as well as the NYPD crowd-control captain. So far, for that sort of affair, it was proceeding without a hitch. The audiovisual equipment actually functioned; the speakers were keeping to their preplanned schedule; and the hundreds of people scattered about in Sheep Meadow were surprisingly orderly.

Blair had exchanged her running gear for warm-up pants and a dry T-shirt in one of the tents, as had Cam and the others, and she looked casually stylish as she faced the mass of onlookers. When she began to speak, the sound of camera shutters clicking fluttered through the crowd like something alive. Every eye and lens was focused on her.

While part of Cam's attention was completely preoccupied with the crowd activity in the area within visual range of Blair, another part listened to her speak. She had a beautiful speaking voice—deep, warm, and strong. Cam knew the story, of course. Everyone did. A man could not run for the presidency of the United States and have something as critical as his wife's valiant battle with breast cancer not be a prominent issue during the campaign. This personal tragedy was part of Andrew Powell's image, part of his public face, no matter how private the pain.

And because her father's life was open to intense scrutiny by virtue of his position, Blair's loss became public knowledge, too. The president's daughter had secrets she guarded, but this was not one of them. To fight this war, she had willingly exposed her deepest anguish.

She spoke eloquently, urging lawmakers to allocate funds for treatment and diagnosis, exhorting women to practice vigilance and to be their own best advocates, and, above all, encouraging every person touched by the disease to never lose hope.

Cam thought she was magnificent.

When she turned away from the podium. Cam stepped immediately to her side, careful not to touch her but walking close beside her toward the rear of the stage and the shelter of some overhead canvas tarps.

"Are you all right?" she asked gently, because she had heard the tears beneath the noble words. Although she had rarely seen Blair shaken, she could sense her fragility now. There were some things that always hurt, no matter how many years had passed. "Can I get you anything? Some water? You were standing in the blazing sun up there for half an hour."

Blair glanced at her, aware of what Cam *wasn't* saying and grateful to her for not remarking on the fact that she was shaking. "So were you," she pointed out.

"Yes," Cam murmured, passing her a bottle of water, "but I had sunglasses on."

That made Blair laugh. "Well, that explains it. I'm all right, but I'd like to get out of here now."

"Of course." Cam spoke quickly into her microphone. "Egret is flying."

Blair smiled wearily. "Egret is actually dragging, but carry on, Commander."

"Destination?" Cam asked. They moved down the steps and across the field toward the waiting cars parked along the far edge of the grass. The meadow itself was large enough that the vehicles were actually quite a distance away on one of the main roads running north to south through the park. Cam wasn't happy about the expanse of open ground they had to cross, but it was the terrain she'd been given to deal with. Stark and Savard fell in behind, and Mac, upon hearing Cam's announcement, radioed the drivers to prepare for departure.

"I'd like to inform the drivers where you need to go." She said it as casually as she could, and hoped she sounded only professionally interested. She was acutely aware of the fact that Blair had spoken privately to both Diane and Marcy Coleman just before she had joined the other speakers on the stage. Cam assumed that she was making plans for the rest of the day. She had tried hard not to consider the particulars of those plans.

"Home," Blair responded.

Diane had invited both her and Marcy over to her apartment for dinner and drinks, but she had decided to pass. It had been a long day and a longer week. She didn't have the energy for conversation or the desire to deal with Marcy's obvious interest. She might have to deal with it soon, but not when she knew her emotional armor would already be breached. She'd need a little time to rally her defenses again.

As they walked, Cam relayed the information and tried to keep the relief from showing in her voice. "That was quite a speech. They were right to have you give it."

"Thank you." Blair smiled, pleased despite her weariness.

Cam merely nodded, anxious to get Blair into the safety of the waiting car. They were thirty feet from the vehicles, Stark and Savard keeping pace to either side, when they heard someone call out.

"Blair!"

Blair looked back over her shoulder, then stopped as Marcy Coleman hurried toward her. *This could be awkward,* she thought, very conscious of Cam beside her. She didn't want to have a personal conversation with Marcy in front of her. It shouldn't have mattered, and she was well used to ignoring her security guards, just as they were well schooled in appearing totally deaf and blind under such circumstances.

In fact, she had no doubt that Cam would behave as if nothing were happening, but Blair would know she could hear. She wasn't sure what Marcy would say, or precisely how she herself would respond. She *was* certain that she didn't want to deal with a request for a date, no matter how delicately worded, in front of Cameron Roberts.

"Sorry," Marcy said, suddenly flustered as she looked at the cadre of Secret Service agents loosely ringing Blair. For the first time, it was abundantly clear to her just whom she had been trying to seduce. *Jesus.*

She held out a white envelope, smiling uncertainly when Blair regarded her with a slightly confused expression on her face. "Sorry— Diane told me you weren't coming by later, so I thought I should give you this now."

Cam listened with half an ear to the vehicles starting their engines behind them while thinking that the attractive doctor was making a very serious attempt to capture Blair's attention. She tried to tell herself that her annoyance was merely due to the hiccoughing coming from the motor of one of their cars. She'd have to speak to Mac about the maintenance schedule. She couldn't have Egret's vehicle breaking down.

Assuming it was a personal note from Marcy, Blair took the envelope and was about to tuck it into her fanny pack when Marcy added, "He said you'd want to look at it right away. That you'd know who sent it."

Blair faltered, staring from Marcy to the envelope. "He?"

"Wait," Cam ordered sharply, reaching for it when the significance of the engine's stuttering finally registered. Roughly, she grabbed Blair and pushed her to the ground, shouting, "Everybody down!" just as the air exploded with heat and thunder.

Momentarily stunned by the noise, Blair was shaken and disoriented by the force of landing hard with Cam on top of her. As the weight pinning her down eased, she heard Cam's voice, raw and urgent.

"Extricate! Extricate! GoGoGo!"

Then she was suddenly being dragged away by Stark and Savard, too confused and shocked by the sight of the burning car to resist until she saw Cam running. But Cam was running *away* from the direction of the evacuation, away from safety—and directly toward the inferno that had been Blair's vehicle.

"No!" Blair cried, struggling to escape the hands that restrained her. The second vehicle careened to a halt beside them, and the doors flew open. As Stark pushed her into the back of the car, Blair had only a fleeting glimpse of Cam stepping deliberately into the blaze, one arm extended, reaching for what remained of the door on the flaming wreck.

Then she could see nothing, and all she could hear was the wail of sirens and her own silent screams.

Chapter Eleven

The next thing Blair was clearly aware of was the wild rocking of the car as it careened around curves on the narrow twisting road through the park. She could barely breathe because Stark was practically lying on top of her in an attempt to shield her in the eventuality that projectiles were directed at the windows. Shifting on the seat, Blair pushed Stark none too gently away, then sat up and stared at the two women with her.

"What's happening?" she asked urgently.

No one answered her. Stark and Savard, their faces grim, both with a hand to their small earpieces, alternately listened to and then answered their respective colleagues. Stark was rapidly switching frequencies on her transmitter, issuing rapid-fire, one-word responses. Blair assumed it was some kind of code concerning their evacuation route or destination, because she couldn't make any sense of it.

"Where is Cam?" Blair demanded, her voice louder, stronger now that she had caught her breath. "Agent Stark...*Paula*...are you talking to her? Is she all right?"

Something about her tone caught Savard's attention. She had been listening with only part of her mind, and when she registered the edge of fear in Blair's voice, she misinterpreted it. "Ms. Powell...are you injured?"

"Am *I* injured?" Blair stared at her, barely able to contain her escalating panic and anger. This was an all too familiar nightmare—a déjà vu so horrifyingly real she wanted to grab Savard and shake her. Everyone was focused on protecting *her*, as if her life were so much more important than everyone else's. It was insane.

She struggled for control amidst the disorientation of being whisked away to some unknown destination while the threat of danger enveloped her like an oppressive, invisible cloak. Even worse than the infuriating helplessness of having no control over her own safety was the terror of knowing that Cam might be hurt—might be seriously injured—and she was not there. Again.

Knowing these women were only doing their jobs, Blair took a deep breath, and asked once more, "Is there any word from Cameron? Is she all right?"

"I don't have any information as to specifics," Stark said, her voice tight with stress but still polite. She hesitated and, against regulations, added, "Emergency medical services are on the scene. I have no word on the extent or nature of casualties."

Stomach clenching, fighting to quell the choking fear, Blair held Stark's gaze. "Can you tell me if she's hurt? Can you just tell me that?"

Stark shook her head, and, unexpectedly assaulted by a sudden wave of nausea, barely managed to say, "Ms. Powell, I can't. I don't know." Then the pain struck, and she gasped at the sudden onset of a near-blinding pounding in her head. "Oh, jeez..."

For the first time since they had piled into the car, Savard actually looked at Stark, who was seated beside her. Then her heart skipped a beat—which, at the rate it was already racing, was no small feat. Still, she managed to state calmly, "*You* appear to be injured, Agent."

Through the haze of her own anxiety, Blair, too, finally focused on Stark and saw that she was mopping up a steady stream of blood that ran down her face. Her handkerchief was saturated. A three-inch gash in her forehead was bleeding copiously.

"She's right," Blair said. "You need a doctor. Tell whoever's driving this thing to go to a hospital."

"I'm fine," Stark said, although in truth she was having a little trouble clearing her vision and her stomach was heaving. *Just the bumpy ride.*

At this point, protocol dictated no diversion from the prescribed evacuation route for any reason except a serious injury to Egret. In addition, she was the ranking agent present, and she had much more pressing matters to attend to than a little crack on the head. She wondered where the commander was, but she pushed that worry from her mind.

Concentrating on procedure, she confirmed their position with Grant and radioed it to Mac. "We are en route, on schedule, to checkpoint alpha. Please advise."

"Continue to that location, blackout procedures in effect until further notice," Mac's voice directed. "Terminating transmission now."

Until such time as the scope of the assault could be determined, Stark knew it was standard operating procedure to assume that their radio transmissions were being monitored. That also meant that she, Ellen Grant, and Renée Savard, an unknown entity in this situation, had full responsibility for Egret's safety until the commander, or Mac if the commander was unavailable, contacted them on a preset frequency and sent a coded, predetermined all-clear message.

"Your clothes are torn," Savard remarked to Blair, indicating a long tear in the thin fabric of her pant leg. The material was spotted with blood. "Is it serious?"

"No."

"Are you otherwise uninjured?"

Blair nodded an affirmative. Her thigh burned with what felt like a scrape from her contact with the gravel on the path when Cam had thrown her down. She wasn't concerned about her aches and bruises, however. All she could think about was Cam racing toward the burning car.

Nearly sixty minutes later, they stopped. Blair had only a brief glimpse of a moderate-sized colonial structure artfully hidden from the neighboring houses by fences and hedgerows before the car went around the corner and stopped beneath a vine-covered breezeway. She guessed they were in one of the affluent bedroom communities just north of the city limits where the homes had a small amount of land and an impressive amount of privacy, all of which came with an enormous price tag.

"It'll just be a few more minutes," Stark advised as she opened the door, slipping her revolver from the quick-release compartment in the fanny pack. "If you'd wait in the car, please, Ms. Powell."

"Let *me* check the perimeter," Savard said quickly, moving to slide out behind her.

"I've got it," Stark replied stubbornly. When she discovered Renée Savard by her side, she relented grumpily. "Fine. You take the back, I'll go around front." Leaning down toward the driver's partially open window, she added, "Keep the motor running, Ellen."

It seemed like more than a few minutes, but eventually, Blair found herself in the living room of a surprisingly tasteful house that most likely sat unoccupied for months or years at a time, waiting for someone like her to need shelter. She had no idea how many such places there were scattered over the country and probably in other countries as well. She knew that anywhere her father traveled, anywhere she traveled, or, for that matter, anywhere *any* of the immediate members of the president's or vice president's families might be, contingencies were made to secure them in safe houses not only in the case of a threat to their personal safety but also in the event of a national emergency.

She'd always thought that such precautions were unnecessary holdovers from the paranoid days of the Cold War, when everyone feared that a nuclear attack was imminent. But taking in the comfortable accommodations, she grudgingly admitted to herself that in this instance, maybe the paranoia had been a good idea.

"There is a bedroom down the hallway to your left with an adjoining bath," Paula Stark informed her as she glanced at a floor plan on her handheld unit. "There should be clothes to fit you there as well."

"Look," Blair began, about to object to being sent off when what she wanted was information, but then thought better of it. She *was* cold, but it was a chill she wasn't certain any amount of clothing could warm. And she also realized that her protectors most likely knew no more than she at this point.

"Thank you, Agent Stark," Blair said quietly. "You should see to that wound at some point. You're dripping again."

"Yes, ma'am, I'll do that at the first opportunity."

Blair thought she saw a faint smile play across Savard's face at the serious reply, and it occurred to her fleetingly that there was something tender in that smile. "Good," she responded, and went in search of something to exchange for her torn and dirty clothes.

When she returned from the bedroom in a pair of gray sweatpants and a long-sleeved, dark blue T-shirt, she found Ellen Grant in the kitchen, making coffee of all things. It seemed like such a mundane, commonplace thing to do that Blair was afraid she would burst out laughing at the absurdity of it. Even worse, she was afraid that if she began to laugh, she would begin to cry. And then she wasn't sure she would stop.

The aroma of brewing coffee was surprisingly comforting, and she had a feeling she was going to need it. She doubted that she would be sleeping for some time to come. Watching the agent set cups down on the counter, she asked when she could trust herself not to come apart, "Is there anything I can do?"

Grant cast her a startled glance and then a faint smile. "I don't think so. There's some food in the freezer—pizza and the like. I'm afraid that will have to do for the time being. Coffee should be ready in just a second."

It was almost surreal, Blair thought, to be standing in some strange house, talking to a woman she had seen almost daily for the last year, and to realize that they had never had a conversation before. The Secret Service agents did their jobs so well, remaining always in the background, that most of the time Blair did not think of their personal lives. She studied the wedding ring on Ellen Grant's hand.

"Does he mind your job?" she asked. Under other circumstances she never would have asked. Somehow these extraordinary conditions created a familiarity that might otherwise have never existed.

As if what Blair had asked were the most natural of questions, Grant replied, "If he does, he's never said. He's a cop."

"Does it bother you, what *he* does?"

Grant smiled, a distant smile, and her eyes were focused somewhere far away. "Yeah, sometimes."

"What does he say?"

"I've never mentioned it. It's what he does."

They're all alike. Relentlessly responsible. No matter what it costs. Blair sighed and helped herself to coffee. "Someone should get Stark to a hospital."

"One of us will take care of that as soon as she's free to leave. In the meantime, I'll look at her. We've all had EMS training."

"I know," Blair said dryly. "The team is completely self-sufficient."

"To some extent, yes." Grant ignored the edge of sarcasm in Blair's voice. "You'll be perfectly safe here with us."

"I don't doubt it," Blair said, meaning it. She wasn't in the least concerned for her own safety. It wasn't her safety that had ever been her concern. "When it's possible, I'd like to talk to my father. He'll be worried."

At the mention of the president, Grant nearly came to attention. "Of course. I'll relay the information to Stark. She's acting chief until the commander returns."

"Do you know where Cam is?" When the agent didn't answer, a quick stab of fear knifed through her chest. "What is it? Do you have any information?"

Grant looked uncomfortable. "Agent Stark is in command temporarily, Ms. Powell, and I'm sure she'll brief you soon."

Recognizing a stone wall when she ran into one, Blair resisted the urge to push for more. She could hear Stark and Savard's murmured voices in the adjoining room, and assumed they were still apprising whomever it was they needed to apprise of the situation. It was approaching two hours since they had departed Central Park—two hours that felt like an eternity; two hours that felt like a nightmare from which she could not awake. She went to join them.

She wasn't planning on waiting much longer for information.

"How's your headache?" Savard asked calmly.

Stark leaned against the breakfast bar in the dining alcove, a radio transmitter in one hand and a telephone receiver in the other. She glanced across the room to where Savard sat at a small desk, her PDA in her left hand.

"What headache?" Stark grunted, trying to carry on three conversations at once.

"The one you're pretending you don't have," Savard noted absently without looking up, punching information into her handheld.

"Feels like my eyeballs are going to fall out," Stark responded flatly.

"Thought so," Savard said, making a note in her daily log. "You're going to need a CT scan."

"Yeah, sure. Next month maybe." Stark listened to Mac relay the status of the investigation in Central Park while juggling equipment and trying to jot notes. She'd gotten the all-clear call just a minute before. At least this location was felt to be secure, and they could stay put for a while. She was glad because she thought she might vomit if she had to ride in the car again. She closed her radio transmission, simultaneously hung up the receiver, and crossed her arms over her chest, trying to stave off another wave of nausea. "Where's Doyle?"

Savard looked up in surprise, noting immediately that Stark's color was lousy. "Don't know. Haven't heard from him. I'm assuming he's going to want me to stay with the team, so all I'm trying to do is organize my field notes from today. Once we get the first stats on the crime scene evidence, we'll have something to work with. We'll need to review the preliminary psych profile on this guy ASAP, too. I don't think anyone expected a bomb."

"That's an understatement, Agent Savard," Stark grumbled, her expression grim. And beneath the anger in her tone sounded a hollow note of pain. "At least I hope no one did. Because if anybody had any idea of this and didn't tell us about it, there'll be hell to pay. We lost an agent today."

A sharp gasp from the doorway caused them both to turn quickly in that direction. Blair Powell stood there, white as a sheet, and for a second, Stark thought she might faint.

"Are you all right, Ms. Powell?" Stark asked in genuine concern.

"Who?" Blair steadied herself with one hand on the back of a dining-room chair and waited until she was quite sure her voice was steady. "You said you lost an agent." She heard herself speak in a surprisingly calm voice that couldn't possibly be her own, because she was quite certain she was screaming. "Who?"

Stark looked uncomfortable and a little uncertain. "I'm sorry, that information—"

"Jeremy Finch," Renée Savard interjected immediately. She ignored the quick look of surprise and uncharacteristic anger from Stark, her gaze returning to Blair. "He was driving the lead car."

"My car," Blair said softly. She recognized the quick rush of relief that accompanied the sound of his name, but she couldn't bring herself to feel guilty. This time it wasn't Cam. *It wasn't Cam.*

"I'm sorry."

"There's no reason for you to be sorry," Stark said, gently now, too. "You are not responsible for what this maniac does. It has nothing to do with you."

Blair shook her head, appreciating Stark's kindness, but unable to accept it. "It *does* have something to do with me. Agent Finch was assigned to me. His job was to protect me."

"It still doesn't mean that what happened to him was your fault," Stark persisted.

"That's a very fine distinction you're making, Agent Stark." Blair smiled, a sad smile.

"It's the fine distinctions that make all the difference," Savard responded in a firm but compassionate tone.

"I wish I could accept that," Blair said, almost to herself. She regarded them both and asked one last time, "Have you talked to Commander Roberts?"

"Not yet, ma'am," Stark answered, and Blair believed her.

"I'll be in the other room. Could you please let me know when you have more information?" She was more emotionally exhausted than physically tired. There was nothing she could do, and she couldn't bear the conversation another moment. She assumed that her father had been informed that she was safe and that his security director, the director of the Secret Service, the FBI, and all the other alphabet agencies entrusted with her protection would be doing whatever it was they did. She was the one player in all of this who apparently had no role to play. She knew that she wasn't a prisoner, but in many ways she felt like one.

I don't know where I am or how long I'll be here. I'm not allowed to call out. I can't get any word on Cam. She could be...No. She's fine. She has to be.

"Please advise me when I can call my father." Her tone was harsher than she intended.

"Yes, ma'am," Stark said crisply.

When Blair left them, Stark looked at Savard in annoyance. "It's not exactly procedure to discuss classified information with her."

Savard regarded Stark thoughtfully, and chose her words with care. She didn't know the compact, dark-haired agent all that well, and she knew the others on the Secret Service team even less. "Can I speak to you off the record here?"

"I'm not going to report anything you say to me, Savard." Stark glanced over her shoulder and saw that Grant was posted by the front entrance and Blair was curled up on the couch staring blankly into space. They were alone. "I'm not the spy here."

Renée let that jibe go, appreciating that not only was Stark injured, but she had also lost a colleague. "I just meant that I have no desire to offend you by talking about your commander."

As she expected, Stark's shoulders stiffened, and she looked ready to go to battle despite the fact that she also seemed in imminent danger of falling down at any second. It amazed Savard that every one of the Secret Service agents in Egret's detail was totally dedicated to their reserved, formidable commander. She admired and respected the sentiment.

"What about the commander?" Stark asked.

"Blair Powell is in love with her."

Stark's mouth dropped open. It was some seconds before she managed to close it.

She still hadn't found her voice when Savard continued, "And I think the feeling is mutual."

Staring at the floor, Stark was silent, trying to think, but her thoughts were racing in circles. She thought about the five days that Blair had spent in Diane Bleeker's apartment not quite two months before. While Blair had been inside, she had spent a large part of that time sitting in a car outside that apartment building. And she and everyone else knew that there was no way that Blair Powell was up there alone that entire time. They hadn't spoken of it, even amongst themselves, but privately, she had wondered.

She was sitting there with a cold cup of coffee in her hand, staring up at the darkened windows in the oddly foreboding building, working hard not to wonder what was happening upstairs. Struggling, too, not to replay the night she had ended up in Blair Powell's bed as a result of a very ill-advised wave of pure, mindless lust. She had been so damn scared that night, and so damn naïve, and so damn crazy for her...and Blair had been kind, if not tender.

Blushing in the dark and hoping that Fielding couldn't see it, she recalled that tenderness had not been high on her list of requirements at that point, not when she had been frantic to get Blair's hands on her burning skin. She had never done anything like that before, and she hoped to God she never would again. She hadn't expected it, hadn't even considered it, but then she rarely thought about things like that. No—she thought about passing her firearms recertification, or her next shift assignment, or what she would have done if she had been the one to look up and see the sun glint off a rifle barrel pointed at the president's daughter.

Sipping the acid dregs in the mushy paper cup, she remembered what it felt like to be touched the way Blair Powell had touched her. Even though she managed to put the memory from her mind most of the time, every now and then she would look at the president's daughter and remember her kiss. Then her blood would race, and she'd long to feel that way again.

Stark realized that her mind was wandering down very inappropriate avenues and, ignoring her pounding headache and the faint disconcerting stirrings elsewhere, she considered the facts. The commander had been in town during those five days; Stark had seen her briefly in a bar with Blair Powell. The timing certainly fit. It was more than that, though. It was a hundred little things that she had noticed since then but never quite consciously seen. It was the way they looked at each other, and the way they walked together—not touching but connected just the same. Neither of them had been obvious, but when she considered everything as a whole, she thought that Savard might be right.

"How can you say that after only a week of being around them?" It bothered Stark that the FBI agent had seen something she hadn't.

Savard smiled. "I know what women look like when they're in love."

Stark blushed and immediately cursed herself mentally for the reaction. The answer was not quite what she'd expected, and she hated the fact that her heart raced in a highly undisciplined manner. *We are in the middle of a crisis situation, and I have responsibility for Egret's security until such time as Mac or the commander arrive on scene, and here I am discussing something very improper with an FBI agent who might very well be reporting every word back to her dickhead of a superior.*

To make matters even worse, she was having decidedly unprofessional thoughts about that agent.

"Well," she began, then stuttered to a stop when she realized that Savard was softly laughing. "What?" she asked belligerently.

"I apologize if I've upset you," Savard said, the lilt in her voice playful.

"I'm not upset." Stark was definitely defensive now. She squared her shoulders and reached for the telephone. "I'm just busy, that's all."

Savard simply smiled again and returned to her report. She had been right about Stark the first day they'd met. She *was* cute.

CHAPTER TWELVE

Hours had passed in silence, it seemed, with Stark or Savard or Grant standing guard duty at the front door. Finally, Paula Stark stepped into the living room, where Blair still sat, trying fitfully to read a paperback novel she had found on a small bookcase in the den.

"Ms. Powell, if you would pick up the phone on the table next to you, please."

For a moment, Blair hesitated, staring at the instrument with a mixture of apprehension and wonder. Such a simple thing—contact with the outside world. Exhilarating, and somehow frightening, because she wasn't certain she was ready for the news. Then she had to reach for it. "Yes?"

For a moment, all she heard was strange static and then a faintly metallic version of the only voice she wanted to hear. "I'm sorry. I couldn't get away before, and I just now found a scrambled line. I can only talk a minute. Are you all right?"

"I'm fine." Suddenly, Blair didn't care where she was or how long she would have to be there. This was the one thing she needed. "Are *you* hurt?"

"No."

The answer came too quickly, and even with the electronic interference, Blair heard that tone in Cam's voice that she always got when she was being official and avoiding a question. If she hadn't been so relieved to hear from her, she would have been pissed. There would be time for that later.

"Cam? What's happening? Where—"

"I'm sorry. I can't talk now, but I'll be there as soon as I can."

"Be careful."

Then there was only silence on the line. Nevertheless, for the first time since the explosion had rocked her world, Blair was able to draw a full breath without feeling a hard ball of pain in her chest. Cam was safe...she was *safe*...and she had found the time, in the midst of what must be pandemonium, to call.

Replacing the receiver, she glanced toward the front door where Stark stood, gazing out the window. It was already close to ten p.m. "What are Mac and Cam doing back there?"

"I haven't been informed of that." Stark turned from the window, satisfied that the two new FBI agents who had arrived an hour earlier were well positioned outside. She welcomed the additional surveillance assistance, because she, Savard, and Grant were tired and stressed. Despite rotating shifts, they couldn't adequately cover both the grounds and the interior. And even with the Fibbies, they were still undermanned, but that would get better once the commander and the rest of the team arrived.

Blair watched her, waiting for more than a stock answer.

Stark's response had been an automatic nonresponse, because the Secret Service did not comment on procedure, even to the protectees. But when she looked into Blair's face, she caught an unguarded glimpse of her worry. And then she remembered what Savard had said about the commander and the first daughter. *She needs the truth.*

"I imagine they're meeting with the crime scene techs and the ATF bomb unit. You can often profile a bomber from the specifics of the bomb itself. The first walk-through is always the most important. The commander wouldn't leave that to anyone else."

"The walk-through?" Blair had an uneasy feeling she knew what that meant.

For her part, Stark hesitated. It wasn't exactly a pretty picture, and she was already uncomfortable with the conversation.

"The epicenter of the explosion was the lead vehicle," Renée Savard said, walking in from the kitchen with yet more coffee. "Depending upon the nature of the accelerant, the amount, and the exact placement of the device on the car, the blast radius could be anywhere from ten feet to a hundred yards. Anything and everything remaining in that area is potential evidence."

"Aren't there specialists to take care of that kind of thing?" Blair asked, her throat dry. *Everything* included human bodies, too, she supposed.

Stark nodded. "Of course. All the agencies—the ATF, the Bureau, and most likely the NYPD and the State Police, too, will be there. It's probably a real jurisdictional snafu right now."

"That's putting it mildly." Savard snorted. She was quite sure that was why she hadn't heard from her own commander. Doyle was undoubtedly trying to direct the activities by claiming that federal interests had priority.

"So Cam isn't really needed there, is she?" Blair persisted. She couldn't imagine the horror of sifting through the debris of an explosion that had claimed the life of someone she knew. *God, why can't Cam just let someone else do this part?*

Stark stared at her, incredulous. "There's no way she's going to walk away until there's nothing else to find. Not when *you* were the target."

There was such certainty and unmistakable pride in the young agent's tone, Blair began to see why it was so hard for Cam to relinquish her position on the team. She was so clearly the leader. "It could be a long time before they're done, then, couldn't it?"

Stark regarded her seriously for a moment, then smiled. "If she said she'll be here, Ms. Powell, then you can count on it."

Blair wasn't sleeping, just lying quietly in the dark. The soft tap on the door brought her bolting upright, her heart pounding and her pulse racing. She glanced at the red digits on the bedside clock. Three twenty-two a.m.

"Yes?"

"Ms. Powell, it's—"

"Come in," she said urgently, fumbling on the bed for the terrycloth robe someone had considerately thought to stock in the bathroom.

She was standing by the bed, tightening the belt, when the door opened slowly, briefly admitting a shaft of light from the hallway, and then closed again. She hadn't turned on the bedside lamp, but the glow from the security lights cleverly hidden in the nearby trees outside her window was enough to illuminate Cam's unmistakable form. "Cam? Are you all right?"

"Just tired," Cam responded, her voice raspy.

They were six feet apart, both of them leaning forward slightly, and the silence hung heavily between them.

"Are you?" Cam whispered at length. "Stark said you were okay, but—"

"Fine. I'm fine."

Cam took one unsteady step forward, hesitated, and then another. When she spoke, her tone held none of its usual reserve. Tentatively she asked, "Would you mind very much if I...touched you...just to be sure?"

Something that had lain cold and frightened in Blair's heart warmed. She trembled faintly with the kind of anticipation she barely remembered, from a time before she had learned to expect disappointment from a lover's promise.

"No, I wouldn't mind that at all."

Blair took one step to meet her, and then Cam's arms closed very gently around her. Blair scarcely dared breathe, afraid that she might suddenly awaken to find it all a dream. Awaken and discover herself alone in the dark yet again, waiting for a woman to come and touch her. Waiting for a lover's touch to set her free. She held very still and willed the moment not to end.

Cam sighed, contenting herself with absorbing the warmth of Blair's body. As she held her, Blair's energy penetrated the numbness that had settled in her mind and body somewhere during the endless night. She still hurt...everywhere. But being close to Blair—feeling her heart beat, listening to her quiet breathing, leaning on her strength, being with her—was soothing the edges of her pain.

Eventually, Blair ran her hands slowly up and down Cam's back, cautiously, assuring herself that this woman was real. When she lifted her arms to encircle Cam's shoulders, pressing closer to her, Cam gasped sharply.

"You *are* hurt!"

"It's nothing," Cam rested her cheek against Blair's hair and closed her eyes. *God, it's so good just to be near her.* She hadn't realized how truly tired she was. There'd been so much to do.

Once she'd finally been assured that Blair was unharmed and secured at the safe house, she'd had to deal with the scene. They'd had to cordon off the park in the immediate vicinity of Sheep Meadow, an impossible task in itself, and then there was the evidence collection, and the interviews. She'd had to call Jeremy Finch's sister in Omaha, having nothing to offer but her presence on the line as the woman cried. And then report on a secure line to DC and brief the deputy security advisor and her own director, confirming that there was no imminent threat to Blair. Then came the decisions about where to move her, and when, and how deeply to sequester her.

Goddamned Doyle argued with me every step of the way.

Every minute of the previous twelve hours had been overlaid with wondering if Blair was hurt, even though Stark had reported no injury, and worrying that Blair might still be in danger, or that she was simply just frightened, and alone. Twelve hours apart from her had felt like a year. She tightened her hold on Blair and gasped again at the sudden surge of pain down her arm. She was having trouble closing the fingers of her right hand.

"Tell me," Blair whispered.

"Just a few burns," Cam mumbled, nearly asleep on her feet. It really didn't hurt so very much just at that moment. She lifted her uninjured hand to stroke Blair's face. "You're sure you're all right?"

"I am now." In that moment, she realized how badly Cam was shaking. And as much as she didn't want to let her go, Blair knew it was essential. "Cam, you need to lie down."

"Let me just stand here a minute," Cam replied, her voice eerily flat and her words forced and slow. "I'll be fine if I just don't move for a minute. Doesn't really hurt if I don't move. Just a little tired is all."

"I know," Blair said. She began to move them both toward the bed, one careful step at a time. It worried her that Cam followed without protest. That wasn't like her. This wasn't just fatigue. "Cam?"

"Hmm?" Cam asked dimly, trying to remember what she needed to do next. "Stark...Stark's report. Need that."

"Did they give you anything for the pain?"

Cam felt her legs hit something unyielding and she sat down. Bed.

How did I get to the bed?

"No. I told them no. I have to talk...to...Mac."

"Are you in pain now?" Blair asked, guiding her back against the pillows, one arm behind her shoulders.

"Not so much, really," Cam muttered. Now there was the strangest tingling in her right hand. Then she was aware of Blair lifting her legs onto the mattress, removing her shoes.

"I shouldn't be in here," Cam remarked suddenly, as if just realizing where she was.

"You're safe for the moment," Blair said gently, staring at the white gauze bandage, spotted in places with dark blotches, wrapped around Cam's hand and arm. She hadn't seen that before. She swallowed around the lump in her throat and stroked Cam's cheek lightly. "I don't think you're in any condition to break any rules tonight."

"This is definitely...against...regulations," Cam remarked drowsily, reaching for Blair's hand but only managing to brush her fingers over Blair's palm.

"Yes," Blair whispered, leaning down to kiss her very softly on the mouth. "I know that, Commander."

Then Blair pulled the covers over the sleeping woman and quietly left the room.

CHAPTER THIRTEEN

B lair pulled the bedroom door closed behind her and came face-to-face with John Fielding, who was standing in the hallway three feet from the room. She raised her eyebrows in question.

"Do you need something?"

"Mac would like to speak to the commander."

"Not now. She's asleep."

If he was surprised by her response, he gave no sign of it. He merely nodded and walked to the far end of the hall. Then he situated himself in a position where he could see out the window as well as back along the hallway, past the closed door of Blair's room, and into the rest of the house.

In the living room, Blair immediately noted an unfamiliar man standing next to the front door in the place Stark had occupied. Savard was on the couch, leaning back, her eyes half-closed. She looked worn, but her smile was still electric.

"Couldn't sleep?" she asked, surprised to see Blair. It hadn't escaped her notice that when Cameron Roberts walked through the door the first person she'd asked for was Blair Powell. After issuing a few curt orders, Roberts had disappeared down the hallway to Blair's room. Savard didn't know exactly what she thought might happen next, but it wasn't this. She hadn't expected to see Blair up in the middle of the night, a fierce expression in her eyes, looking like she wanted to go ten rounds with someone. "Anything I can get you?"

Ignoring the question, Blair said, "You should go to bed, Agent Savard. Even the FBI can't require that you work twenty-four-hour shifts."

"I was thinking about doing that," Savard admitted with a faint smile. "I just thought I'd wait until Grant came back from the hospital. She took Stark to be checked out about half an hour ago. I wanted to... hear how she was."

"How did she seem?" Blair heard the edge of worry in Savard's voice.

"Cranky. Fussing about leaving her post." Savard chuckled. "She wouldn't have gone if the commander hadn't ordered her to either be examined or be relieved." She smiled, a smile soft with feeling. "Stark's a regular Boy Scout."

Blair recognized the undercurrent of affection in her voice. *Interesting.* "Where's Mac?"

"The dining room." Savard indicated the room opposite. "It's apparently our new command center. I think he's waiting for the commander in there."

"Then he'll have to wait," Blair said flatly. "She's exhausted. If anyone goes anywhere near that bedroom, they'll answer to me."

Interesting, Savard thought as she moved to get up. "Right, then. I'll go tell him."

Blair stopped her with a raised hand. "Never mind. I'll tell him myself."

The proprietary tone in her voice was unmistakable, and for an instant, the two women's eyes met in silent understanding.

Mac looked up from the notebook computer he was using as Blair Powell entered the room. He was relieved to see that other than a weariness she couldn't quite disguise, she looked uninjured. Considering the devastation of the blast, he couldn't even think about what might have happened if she'd been fifteen feet closer to the vehicle when it exploded.

"For God's sake, Mac, sit down," Blair said quickly when he started to stand. The man looked surprisingly fresh at first glance, but there were hollows beneath his eyes she'd never seen before, and his clothes were smudged with soot.

"How are you, Ms. Powell?" he asked politely.

"I have no idea how to answer that question." She laughed grimly. "Other than the fact that I feel like I've been dropped into the middle of some awful B-movie, I'm basically fine."

"It's been a hell of a day. And tomorrow will be hectic, too." He smiled sympathetically and moved some file folders off the chair next to him. "You're welcome to sit down. The commander will want to fill you in herself, I'm sure."

"In the morning, Mac."

He stared, surprised and clearly confused. "I'm sorry?"

"Have you *looked* at her?" Blair was unable to keep the irritation from her voice. *What is wrong with these people?* "She's falling down on her feet, and she's hurt. She's asleep right now, and no one is going to wake her up."

This time, Mac's incredulous expression was followed very quickly by an unmistakable look of respect. "Of course. There's nothing that won't keep a few hours."

"She couldn't tell me very much." Blair sighed, finally sitting down on the straight-backed dining-room chair across from Mac. "Just how badly is she hurt?"

"Uh..." Mac looked away, uncomfortable talking about something that he knew Cam wouldn't want discussed. Herself. He'd rather Blair had asked him to reveal top secrets.

For a few seconds, Blair thought he wouldn't answer. "Mac?"

Then he met her gaze and responded quietly, "As far as I can gather, she's got fairly severe burns on her right arm, shoulder, and neck. A state trooper who was near the blast site grabbed her and dragged her away from the car before she could sustain more serious injuries."

He wasn't about to tell her how damn scared he'd been watching helplessly from the surveillance vehicle. First, he'd seen Jeremy's car rock on its axles, then burst into flames. Then people were being thrown to the ground for fifty feet around from the percussive waves. When he had looked to the spot where he had last seen Blair's group, all that was visible was a cloud of smoke. For a moment, he'd been paralyzed with the fear that they were all dead. Fortunately, Grant was cool in a crisis, and she was already racing in the backup car toward Egret's last known location.

Almost the instant the air cleared slightly, he'd seen the commander running straight into the raging inferno as if she didn't even notice the flames. Then Stark's voice had clamored in his ear that Egret was secure, and while he was frantically trying to clear the lines of communication and direct the evacuation, he'd seen a burly state trooper dive into the blaze and tackle Cameron Roberts. While Grant sped from the scene, the trooper dragged the commander away from the fire-engulfed car, beating at her smoldering jacket with his hat. Mac had an eerie sensation that if that officer hadn't grabbed her, she might not have moved. He took a steadying breath, banishing that disquieting image.

"It took me the better part of two hours to get her to let the EMTs near her. But they checked her out and bandaged her in the field."

"What did they say at the hospital?"

He stared at her blankly.

"You *did* take her to the hospital?"

"Uh...we were pretty busy out there, Ms. Powell. I—"

"I can't believe it." Her voice had dropped dangerously low, and her heart pounded with a combination of fury and fear. The horror in the park, the hours of waiting, the memory of Cam's last brush with death still so fresh—all of it strained her control past the breaking point. "Has it occurred to any of you that she's flesh and blood? Just how much do you think she can take?"

She rose quickly and walked to the window, her back to him. She would not let him see the tears.

"I...I didn't think...I—"

"I'm sorry," Blair interrupted, turning back, relieved that her voice was steady and that the shadows hid the moisture on her cheeks. "It's not your fault. I'm sure a presidential order wouldn't have gotten her to leave."

Mac laughed as the tension dissipated. "Agreed."

"Was anyone other than Agent Finch seriously injured? I had a friend with me. Dr. Coleman?"

"I don't have the figures yet." He was solemn now. "There were a number of bystanders with bumps, bruises, and assorted fractures, but as far as I know, Jeremy was the only casualty."

Blair heard the slight waver in his voice. She realized with sudden clarity that Mac had lost a friend as well as a colleague yesterday.

"I'm so sorry."

Mac nodded mutely. There really wasn't anything to say, especially to Blair Powell. He supposed he shouldn't even be briefing her, but in the months that he had served as the head of her security team, he had gotten to know her better then he might have otherwise. He didn't presume to think that they were friends, but he understood her isolation a little bit better now. It wasn't right to keep her in the dark, especially when the events so clearly involved her.

"You should get some rest, Ms. Powell," he said. "It's relatively quiet now, but I doubt that it will be in the morning when the FBI shows up in force."

Blair realized that indeed she was exhausted. She had been running on pure adrenaline for hours, waiting to know. And now that Cam had arrived, alive and more or less intact, she could allow her fatigue to surface.

What she really wanted to do was go back to her room and stretch out on the bed next to Cam. *Perhaps that isn't the best idea, considering the house is filled with Secret Service agents, not to mention the FBI. If I go in there now, they're not likely to be able to ignore the fact that I'm sleeping with Cameron Roberts.*

She almost smiled at the sheer absurdity of the situation.

"I'd say that's good advice, Mac, and you should probably take it as well."

"I think I will," he said with a smile. As Blair rose, he added, "This is a very large house, and other than this room, the living room, and the kitchen, all the other rooms are bedrooms."

She studied him thoughtfully, but she couldn't read anything in his clear blue eyes. "Thank you, Mac. I think I'll go find an empty one."

He watched her leave the room, thinking once more how glad he was that he did not carry the ultimate responsibility for safeguarding her life.

Shortly after seven the next morning, Blair walked into the small galley-style kitchen. She found Cam in the process of pouring a cup of coffee, juggling the pot somewhat awkwardly with her left hand. The security chief was wearing blue jeans that were an inch too long, a loose-fitting pale blue button-down-collar shirt that looked suspiciously like police issue, and running shoes. The shoes, at least, were hers. Remarkably, when she glanced at Blair and smiled, her eyes looked clear and rested.

"How in the hell do you do that?" Blair grumbled, stumbling in the direction of the coffee cup Cam held out to her.

"Do what?" The corner of Cam's mouth lifted again in an irritatingly knowing grin.

"Look so damn good after no sleep."

Cam thought Blair looked just fine in her gray sweatpants and navy blue T-shirt, although both were a little too large for her. She was happy to see that Blair's primary mood appeared to be grumpy, rather than frightened. She knew from experience that the fear must be there somewhere, and that eventually it would surface, but for now, they could let it rest.

"I don't need very much sleep."

Ignoring her, Blair leaned against the counter and gratefully sipped the steaming brew. After the first few scalding swallows, she asked, "What happened to your own clothes?"

Cam hesitated for a second, then said nonchalantly, "I had to throw them out. I borrowed these from the trunk of an NYPD patrol car. The officer assured me they were clean."

Blair didn't smile. Cam seemed fine now, but Blair remembered her exhaustion and pain of just a few hours before. She stared at the bandage wrapped around the palm of Cam's right hand and disappearing under the unbuttoned sleeve of her blue shirt. "How bad is that?"

Cam shrugged and started to speak, but Blair interrupted impatiently. "And don't say 'it's nothing' one more time, or I swear to God I'll forget that you're sore and take you down right here." As she spoke, she lifted a hand and turned back the unbuttoned collar of Cam's shirt, drawing a sharp breath when she saw the angry swatch of blistered skin that extended along the lower side of her neck onto her shoulder. "Jesus, Cam."

Using her left hand, Cam set her coffee down and then met Blair's eyes. "It's been looked at," she assured her. "It's just superficial—nothing too serious. It should be a lot better in a few days."

"The doctors said that?"

"Ah...well." Cam hesitated again. "Not exactly...no."

"Never mind. I already know that you didn't go to the hospital."

"Checking up on me?" Cam asked, one eyebrow raised, but a smile in her eyes.

"What were you thinking?" Blair demanded, unswayed by Cam's attempt to distract her from the subject of her injuries. She was rapidly accumulating memories of Cam in danger, or hurt, or literally dying, and the images didn't get any easier to take with reviewing. Her fear only fueled her anger. "Damn it, don't you *care* if you get hurt? Don't you think *I* care?"

Cam looked away. It had happened so quickly, and then, after, there had been so much to do—so many things to check and organize and confirm. She had put it from her mind.

"I wasn't thinking," she said softly.

Surprised, Blair just stared at her. "You're *always* thinking. What happened this time?"

"I..." Cam faltered, suddenly uncomfortable. Doyle was likely to show up at any minute, and she needed to brief the team and discuss strategy before that. "We should talk about this some other time."

"There will never be *some other time*," Blair said flatly. "Or a better time. Not for us, Cam. Tell me what happened out there."

"It was the engine stuttering that reminded me," Cam murmured.

An uneasy feeling fluttered through Blair's chest. Cam looked pale. Blair stepped a little closer, resting her fingers lightly on the top of Cam's hand where it lay along the edge of the counter.

"Go ahead. It's okay."

Cam drew her mind from the past and focused on Blair's face, smiling gratefully. Blair's touch steadied her, anchored her in the present.

"I was late for school, and my father said I could ride with him on his way to the embassy. He went out ahead of me to tell the driver about the change in plans while I got my books. When I came down the steps, I could hear the car engine coughing like it was going to stall."

She hesitated, running a hand quickly over her face. She was sweating, the cold sweat of fear and dark memories. A faint nausea made it hard to speak.

Blair forced herself to breathe, but it was difficult around the choking dread as she began to understand what Cam was saying. They had never talked about it. They had had so little time to talk at all. Not about what mattered, she realized. "You were right there?"

Cam nodded. "About twenty feet away, I guess, when the bomb exploded. It knocked me down." She was clutching the counter and made a conscious effort to relax her grip, to keep her voice even. "When I got up, the flames were so high, and it was so hot...and I...I couldn't get close." She looked at Blair, her eyes shadowed with old misery. "I was too scared."

"Cam," Blair whispered, lifting her hand to caress her cheek. "Even if you could have...you know..."

"I know," Cam said. "But I should have *tried*."

"You were a child then," Blair argued gently. "And yesterday you weren't, and you still couldn't have saved either of them."

Cam closed her eyes briefly, seeing her father disappear as his car roared into flame. She wasn't sure who she had been trying to rescue yesterday, but she'd failed. Again. "I know."

Hearing the guilt still heavy in Cam's voice, Blair shook her head in frustration and sympathy. Knowing and believing were two very different things. She was torn between wanting to shake her and wanting desperately to hold her. "Do you have any idea how crazy you make me when you do things like you did yesterday?"

"Some," Cam admitted, turning her palm so that their fingers met briefly. "I don't mean to."

"You aren't indestructible, you know."

Cam laughed shortly. "Believe me, I *do* know that."

"That's some progress, I suppose." Blair sighed.

"I don't want you to worry about m—"

"Please! Don't push your luck, Roberts," Blair snapped. She withdrew her hand and pointed to Cam's arm. "What about changing the bandages?"

"I'll have Stark or Savard give me a hand," Cam said with a shrug. "I was just about to go shower. I still smell like smoke."

"The hell you will." Blair narrowed her eyes. "I might *just* trust Stark, but I have no intention of letting Renée Savard put her hands on you for any reason, under any circumstances."

"I can assure you, Ms. Powell, you have no need to worry." Cam's voice was dark and intimate. *Don't you know that?*

Unconsciously as they'd talked, they had moved slowly closer, until Blair's hand rested on Cam's hip, and Cam's fingers brushed tenderly up and down Blair's arm. There was space between them, but those few inches shimmered with heat.

"Thank you for coming to my room last night." Blair's lips were inches from Cam's. "I don't think I could have stood waiting much longer."

"I'm sorry it took me so long." Cam found her eyes unable to leave Blair's. She shuddered faintly as Blair moved near enough for their thighs to touch.

"You're driving me out of my mind, Cam. First you show up and announce you're back on my detail...now this."

"I didn't mean to hurt you, Blair." Her voice was suddenly heavy and thick. "I never meant that. I don't know any other way to do this."

"You really piss me off, Commander," Blair murmured, moving her hand upward to rest her palm against Cam's chest. "And I'm not saying I like any of this, and I don't intend to change my mind any time soon. But still..." She slipped her hand under the collar and caressed the uninjured side of Cam's neck "You make me crazy."

This time it didn't sound like an accusation. Cam answered the call in Blair's deep blue eyes and lowered her head to kiss her. She stopped at the sound of footsteps behind them.

"Good morning, Commander, Ms. Powell," Renée Savard said smoothly as she walked through the door and headed directly toward the coffee machine. She'd always thought that the best way to handle an awkward moment was to move through it. And since her presence would have been obvious in another second, retreat was not possible.

Cam straightened and stepped back from Blair. "Agent Savard," she said easily.

The instantaneous change in Cam's demeanor was amazing, and Blair watched more in fascination than anger. A second before, she had felt the heat and the urgency rippling through Cam's taut body. Cam had been aroused, about to kiss her. Now, she seemed totally cool, not a hint of disturbance or discomfort on her face.

Renée Savard undoubtedly suspected what had been about to happen between them, but suspecting and observing were two different things. Though Blair did not think it would matter to Savard what went on between her and Cam, she had to admit that if it had been Patrick Doyle who had come walking through that doorway, the situation would have been difficult.

She'd been forced to make that an uneasy acknowledgment many times in her life, growing up in the public eye. She'd had no choice but to be cautious, and sometimes she had been forced to hide. She hated it; she had never accepted it; but there had always been more than her personal integrity at stake. There had been her father's career to consider, and her sacrifice of silence had seemed acceptable in the short term. She had compromised because she hadn't had a good reason to fight. Watching Cam slip effortlessly into her professional persona, she thought that perhaps she might finally have found that reason.

Chapter Fourteen

W e'll be briefing at 0900, Agent Savard," Cam said as Savard started out of the kitchen with a cup of coffee. Her voice was steady, but her autonomic nervous system was still responding to Blair's hands on her. She felt her own hands trembling and buried them in the pockets of her jeans.

"Yes, ma'am," Savard replied from the doorway. The commander met her gaze directly, her gray eyes completely unreadable. It wasn't that hard to read Blair Powell's expression, however. She was still looking at Cameron Roberts like she wanted to swallow her whole. Savard figured if she hadn't walked in at such an indelicate moment, Blair might have been better able to hide her feelings. It seemed she usually did.

"Anything you need from me in advance, Commander?" Savard asked, withdrawing onto safer ground. She imagined privacy was rare for these women, and it wasn't her job to infringe on what little of it they shared.

"I don't suppose you have a report from the FBI field team on when I'll have their videotapes from the park, do you?"

For a moment, Savard looked away, embarrassed. She didn't want to admit that she was out of the loop, and had been ever since she'd told Doyle that she'd be happy to work on the inside with Egret's security detail but that she wouldn't pass him information outside of channels. He'd been angry, but he couldn't order her to do it. It was a messy situation, but she was still FBI, and she would keep the Bureau's dirty laundry private.

She shook her head. "I've had no updates since arriving here, Commander."

Cam had expected nothing different. She knew Doyle would keep his intelligence reports from her as long as he could. "That's all, then."

Savard left without another word, and Cam turned to Blair, a rueful smile on her face. Blair's eyes were still deep with desire, and it took all of Cam's willpower not to touch her again.

"I had better get to work. We should have some food supplies within the hour, and your clothes will be coming later today. I sent Grant back to the city this morning. I thought she would know what you needed."

"What about Stark? Is she all right?" Blair asked, her throat oddly tight with the lingering ache of arousal. *Much more of this torture and I'm going to lose my mind.*

"She was cleared for duty, but I suspect she's downplaying her symptoms," Cam said, distracted by Blair's fingers caressing the side of her coffee mug. *She has such sensitive fingers. She always manages to find just the right spot, and then she strokes it so...* She swallowed and pulled her eyes away. "Since we won't be traveling for a few days, she may be okay."

Blair tore her gaze from Cam's mouth, which she had just been imagining on her skin. Struggling to sound businesslike, she asked, "You expect this to be an extended stay, then?"

"I don't really know yet."

The space was too small, and Blair was too close—she couldn't concentrate. Cam moved to lean against the opposite counter, but the three feet of distance failed to solve her problem. She was having trouble thinking about anything at the moment except the way Blair touched her when she was hungry.

"How long do you *think*?" Blair ran a hand through her hair in frustration. *I'll really go crazy if I have to stay cooped up in here with you. It was agony last year, and I hadn't slept with you then.*

"Ah, well—at the very least, another day. I hope to have preliminary reports from the ATF bomb center in a few hours. I expect that the FBI profiler and the ATF commander will be here sometime later today for a briefing. All the videotapes from our cameras and the FBI teams, if they cooperate, will be arriving here along with our computer equipment this afternoon."

"Why can't I go home?" Blair asked, thinking that there she would at least be able to touch her, just *touch* her, without someone walking in on them.

"Your apartment building has to be checked again, just to be certain we don't have any breach in security there." Cam wanted to hold her—just long enough to comfort. "I know it's hard."

Blair tried to absorb the magnitude of the investigation, realizing that this was not something that was going to disappear overnight. A complex machine had already been set in motion, and there would be no stopping it. It all centered on her, and all she could hope was that there would be enough privacy for her to breathe, and to steal a few moments with Cam.

"Tonight, then?" she asked hopefully.

Cam shook her head. "We don't know enough yet. We assume that the car bomb was some kind of message from Loverboy, but it could just as easily be a terrorist attempt on your life...or a warning to the government from some extremist group that wants recognition. It could be the first of a series of bombings that don't involve you personally at all."

She paused for a deep breath, wishing she had better news to deliver. By rights, she shouldn't tell her anything at all, but there was too much between them for that.

"You're safe here, and until we gather intelligence from the CIA and the antiterrorist divisions of the NSA and FBI, plus get an analysis of the bomb and a few hundred other bits of information, you can't go home. It's never easy getting intel from other security branches. I'm sorry—but for the next few days, I'm using this as our command center. I'd like you to remain here for at least that long."

Cam waited, knowing that what she was saying was probably more threatening to Blair than the physical attack on her life. This kind of focus would mean an even greater assault on her privacy and a more pervasive objectification of her life. There would be very little time, and almost no place, for her to live normally in the midst of such scrutiny.

"Do I have a choice?" Blair felt her anger rising quickly. She could barely imagine being surrounded by strangers twenty-four hours a day. Not just in the background anymore, but literally in the same room with her.

"We could have a helicopter take you back to the White House, where the White House guard would be responsible for your security."

Cam held her breath, knowing that, in theory, Blair should be perfectly safe inside the White House. Except that she knew damn well that Blair wouldn't *stay* inside the White House, and there was no one there that she trusted to guard her. And she'd go crazy if she thought that Blair was likely to slip away from her security detail and inadvertently place herself in danger. And she didn't think she could stand being separated from her now.

"Why can't you come back with me to DC?" Blair asked, risking disappointment but needing so desperately just to *be* with her.

"I have to stay here, Blair." Cam hated to say the words that she knew would hurt her. "At least until I'm sure that I'm getting all the information I need. It's going to make a difference in the future. Sooner or later, you'll be visible again." She didn't state the obvious, that Blair would be vulnerable again then, too.

"Well," Blair commented dully, struggling to hide the ache of rejection, "better the enemy you know. I'll stay."

"Thank you," Cam said softly. "A few days, and I'll try to get you home again."

Anger and disappointment warred with desire. "I hope so, because I'm not sure how long I can stand this."

"Blair," Cam whispered, her voice husky with the need to soothe her, "I'd give anything in my power to make this different for you." She couldn't bear seeing the pain in her eyes. She couldn't bear being the cause of it one more time. "But I can't."

"God, Cameron. You don't get it at all, do you?" Blair took one step closer, clenching her fists to keep her hands off her. "I don't *want* you to fix it. I want you to touch me." She trembled, uncertain whether she wanted to scream or cry. *I want you so much!*

Cam didn't have the strength to look into Blair's eyes and lie to her. She couldn't say no to her, because she couldn't tell her she didn't want her. Not again. She wavered slightly on her feet, rapidly losing the battle with sense and reason. "Come with me," she finally said hoarsely as she turned abruptly and walked away.

Blair hesitated for half a second, staring after her, then she hastened to follow. She caught up to her at the beginning of the hallway that led to the rear of the house where most of the bedrooms were situated.

"Fielding is down there," Blair said in an urgent whisper.

"I know that," Cam said curtly. "I posted him there last night."

They reached Blair's bedroom door and Cam opened it, stepping to one side so Blair could enter before following her through and closing the door. When Blair turned, confusion in her eyes and a question on her lips, Cam reached out with her left hand, gathered the fabric of Blair's oversized T-shirt in her fist, and pulled Blair roughly to her. Lowering her head, she captured Blair's mouth and swallowed her gasp of surprise with a kiss. She kept her hand twisted in the material, forcing Blair against her as she slowly walked them across the bedroom toward the open bathroom door.

Blair had no choice but to hold on. She raised one arm and wrapped it around Cam's uninjured shoulder, threading her fingers through the hair at Cam's neck. John Fielding, and the fact that the house was filled with federal agents and other assorted individuals, was completely forgotten. At that moment, she couldn't have cared less. All she was aware of was the heat pouring from Cameron Roberts's body and the demanding press of her mouth.

The kiss was anything but gentle, but even in her haste, Cam was careful not to hurt her. They were five feet from the adjoining room when Cam relinquished Blair's mouth and moved her lips to Blair's neck, biting her hard enough to draw a startled cry.

"God, Cam," Blair exclaimed, struggling to keep her voice muted. "If you leave a mark, everyone out there will know."

"Shut up." Cam quickly released the shirt and in the same motion, drove her hand beneath it until she found Blair's breast.

When Cam's fingers closed firmly on the taut nipple, Blair's legs began to quiver so unexpectedly that she stumbled. She pressed her face to Cam's shoulder, eyes squeezed tightly closed, struggling desperately to contain a moan. They were still staggering toward the bathroom, and she reached between them, trying to work the buttons open on Cam's jeans. Her hands shook so much she couldn't manage.

"I'm going crazy," she gasped against Cam's neck. "I'm so hot I can't stand it."

Cam pushed her up against the wall beside the open bathroom door and dragged down the loose cotton sweatpants that were the last tangible barrier between them.

As she bared Blair's thighs, she looked into her eyes and said, "I know."

Then, still staring into Blair's eyes, she slipped her hand between Blair's legs, gliding smoothly through the wet heat, entering her in one fluid motion. She held her breath, watching Blair's pupils dilate and her lids flutter nearly closed.

"More," Blair managed to gasp, before she caught her lower lip between her teeth and arched her hips with the sudden pleasure. As Cam pressed deeper, Blair's head thudded against the wall and her entire body shook.

Cam straddled Blair's thigh, pressing herself, swollen and hard, against Blair's leg. She withdrew her fingers, added another, and entered her again, deeper this time. Their lips were a fraction of an inch apart, their gazes locked.

"I'm coming," Blair whispered brokenly. She spasmed repeatedly around Cam's fingers, clutching desperately at Cam's hips, trying to stay upright.

"I know," Cam murmured, leaning her forehead against Blair's, stroking almost completely out and then moving into her again, pushing deeper still with each thrust. "I know."

Blair clung to her, shuddering as wave upon wave of sensation flooded her body. She buried her face against Cam's shoulder again, trying to contain her cries, whimpering softly as the last contractions fluttered through her belly.

"Don't let go," she gasped finally.

Cam was still inside her, and they were pressed tightly together, using the wall as support. Her breath heaved through her chest as she hovered on the brink of orgasm. "You...neither."

With a tremulous laugh, Blair finally succeeded in getting her fingers to work. She gently grasped Cam's wrist, forcing her to ease out, then pulled open Cam's fly and pushed her hand inside Cam's jeans. Immediately, Cam jerked into her palm.

"Oh God," Blair whispered. "You're so wet."

"Uh-huh," Cam grunted, pressing harder against Blair's fingers. She couldn't think, couldn't see; all she knew was the ferocious pressure pounding between her legs and the desperate need to release it.

Blair felt Cam shiver and knew she was on the edge. Another time, she might have teased her, but it had been too long for both of them, and she wanted her to come. She wanted to feel her lose control and she wanted to hold her. And she wanted to have her, completely, for just a few moments. She worked her hand deeper inside Cam's jeans until she could cup all of her in her palm. Then, bringing her thumb slowly and deliberately along the length of Cam's clitoris, she massaged her rhythmically.

Cam braced herself with one hand on Blair's hip, her body bowed, her head down, gasping. Her thighs trembled as the blood seemed to halt in her veins and every muscle clenched. The next knowing stroke of Blair's fingers sparked the explosion, and her breath burst out on a low tortured groan. Dimly, she heard Blair moan softly, almost in exultation, but all she could do was struggle to stand as her bones melted before the onslaught of sensation.

"Oh, yeah," she finally murmured, sagging against Blair. Her head was still pounding.

Blair laughed faintly as the last ripples of Cam's orgasm pulsed against her fingers. She ran her free hand up and down Cam's back, soothing her. She didn't think anything had ever satisfied her as much as having Cameron in her arms, trembling and so unguarded.

"I wish I'd known sooner that all I had to do was ask," she remarked breathlessly, unbuttoning Cam's borrowed shirt so she could run her palms over her chest.

"You don't need to ask." Cam sighed and straightened up, leaning back to look into Blair's face. Their legs were still pressed together and just the sensation of Blair's skin against her own was exciting her again. She grinned, but was very serious. "I can't even be near you without wanting you."

"Really?" Blair asked, aware of Cam's hips rocking persistently against her own, and realizing, too, they weren't done yet. She stripped the shirt off Cam's shoulders, easing it gently down her injured arm. "Is that a problem for you, Commander?"

"Not at the moment," Cam muttered distractedly as she hooked her fingers under the edge of Blair's T-shirt, lifted it upward, and pulled it off over her head. She tossed it somewhere behind them and brought both hands down to Blair's breasts, her eyes fixed on the tight pink nipples under her thumbs. "No problem at all."

"Cam," Blair said urgently. "You're bleeding."

"What?" For the first time, Cam was aware of a burning discomfort along her right palm. The gauze wrapped around her hand was bright red with blood. "It's nothing," she said, dismissing it, as she lowered her lips toward Blair's breasts.

Blair caught Cam's chin with her fingers, halting her motion. "We need to look at it."

"Later," Cam warned, her eyes dangerously dark, her expression impatient with need.

"No." Blair pivoted slightly and slipped out from between Cam and the wall. Grasping Cam's good hand in hers, she dragged her through the doorway into the bathroom. "I want to look at this, now."

"Blair, God damn it."

They faced each other in the small space, Blair completely nude, Cam naked from the waist up with her jeans open. The air around them shimmered with urgency as they stared at one another, flushed and breathing heavily.

Then Cam advanced on Blair, her expression determined. "I'm not waiting."

"Yes, you are." Blair sidestepped quickly and yanked the knobs on the shower to full on. She turned back just as Cam reached her. She hooked her thumbs over the waistband of Cam's jeans and pushed down. "Get out of these."

Relenting, Cam stepped free of her jeans as Blair backed into the shower. Cam followed, her eyes riveted on Blair's. She reached for her, and Blair gently captured her injured hand between her own.

"Let me unwrap this," Blair said tenderly as they stood together in the streaming water.

Momentarily defeated, Cam held out her right arm so that Blair could remove the bandages. She set her teeth as the water hit the cracked and crusted patches. Along the length of her arm, on her shoulder, and the side of her neck, the skin was blistered and raw. In places, blood still oozed slowly.

"How does it feel?" Blair asked, hoping that her voice was steady. The burns looked terrible, and for one horrifying moment she imagined what might have happened if someone hadn't been nearby to drag Cam away from Jeremy Finch's car.

"It doesn't hurt." Cam turned slightly so that Blair could not see the injury. With her other hand she caressed the side of Blair's face. "It'll be okay."

"Why don't I believe you?" Blair murmured, wrapping one arm around Cam's waist.

"Because," Cam whispered softly, her lips moving against Blair's ear, "you don't trust the Secret Service, Ms. Powell."

Blair tipped her head back, offering Cam her neck. "That's because you keep secrets, Commander."

As Cam worked her way along Blair's jaw and down the column of her throat, Blair found Cam's uninjured hand and brought it to her breast. She gasped faintly at the swift sharp pressure of Cam's fingers on her nipple and she quickened, her clitoris twitching rapidly at the renewed stimulation. "Oh, that's trouble."

Slowly, Cam knelt.

When she leaned forward to taste her, Blair braced herself with one hand against Cam's shoulder. "Be careful..."

Dimly, Cam heard a moan as she moved her mouth over her, finding Blair still swollen and firm. Drawing her between her lips, Cam knew it would not be long. She tried to make it last, sucking gently, careful not to work her too quickly or too hard, but it didn't matter. It was already too late. Blair was too sensitive and too close, and almost immediately, she began to come.

With the first pulse of release, Cam pressed harder, pushing Blair rapidly to another peak. She would have kept going if Blair hadn't fisted a hand in her hair and pulled her away. The water streamed into Cam's face and she had to shake her head to clear her eyes. Blair's face was soft through the curtain of moisture.

"Stop," Blair gasped hoarsely. "I can't."

"You can."

Blair laughed, drawing Cam up next to her. She leaned into her and wrapped her arms around Cam's waist.

"You're right. I probably could, if I had a little more time and I didn't think that John Fielding was going to burst in here at any second to find out why I'm screaming."

"No one will come in," Cam said firmly. "They'll assume we're having a private briefing. It's perfectly normal under the circumstances."

Blair kissed the pulse at the base of Cam's neck. She wanted her again. She wanted to lie down with her and touch every part of her and taste her again and again. "There's nothing normal about any of these circumstances, Cameron. If letting you go now means that I'll be able to have you again, I'd rather stop."

Cam closed her eyes and held her tightly. "Will you believe me if I tell you there *will* be another time?"

"I'll try, because I don't have a choice," Blair whispered. "I have to believe it."

CHAPTER FIFTEEN

Y our hair is wet," Blair commented as she watched Cam gathering her scattered clothing. She leaned against the bathroom door, wearing the terrycloth robe that she had donned the previous evening when Cam had appeared at her door. "If you leave my room and go to a briefing like that, you might as well wear a sign that says *I slept with the first daughter*."

Cam grinned as she buttoned the borrowed shirt. "It'll dry while I put on my own clothes. I've got a suitcase in the other room that Mac brought." She pulled on the jeans and smiled faintly. "Somehow I fell asleep last night before I got around to unpacking."

"That's because you were out on your feet," Blair remarked with a combination of irritation and concern. "Will you get someone to take care of those burns?"

"I'll ask Stark. The EMTs left something for me to put on them." She crossed to Blair and put her hands lightly on her waist. "I'll take care of it, I promise."

"You'd better," Blair said, her voice husky. As much as she hated to, she added, "You should go."

"Yeah." Cam sighed, reluctant to leave. "I'm going to be tied up all day with the briefings. Stark will see to anything that you need."

Blair smiled wryly. "As long as she doesn't make me play pinochle with her. That's where I draw the line."

"Understood." Cam pressed her lips lightly to Blair's forehead. She didn't dare do more, because she was afraid if she felt the softness of Blair's lips, she might not be able to stop with one kiss. She couldn't seem to control herself the way she was used to—couldn't seem to stop wanting this woman.

Finally, she stepped away and crossed to the door, pausing with her hand on the doorknob. "By the way, Dr. Coleman is fine. I think she might have ended up on the bottom of the pile when we all hit the ground. She was shaken up a bit by the blast, but she's all right."

Blair studied her for a moment, looking for some sign that there was a hidden message in Cam's words. She should have known there wouldn't be. Cameron Roberts did not play games. "Thank you. I was worried."

"I thought you might be." Cam nodded and opened the door.

"Cam?" Blair said quickly, and the agent turned back. "You do know there's no one, don't you?"

"I'd hoped," Cam replied softly, and then she was gone.

Two hours later, Blair stood in the doorway of the makeshift command center and surveyed the people grouped around the long dining room table in the center of the room. Cam, attired now in a dark gray suit and silver silk shirt, sat at one end of the table while Patrick Doyle occupied the seat opposite her at the far end. Mac was to Cam's left, and Stark, a bandage on her forehead and a very impressive bruise on the side of her face, was beside him. Across from them were a man and woman Blair did not recognize. Savard looked mildly uncomfortable situated between Stark and Doyle.

Patrick Doyle frowned and asked tersely, "Can I do something for you, Ms. Powell?"

Blair studied him for a moment, then walked around the table and pulled out a chair next to Cam. "I'd like to get some idea of what's happening."

Obviously annoyed, Doyle cleared his throat and rearranged some of the papers in front of him. When he looked up at her, his gaze was wintry. "I think at this point anything I could tell you would be premature. I'll advise you of any facts you need to know at a later date."

It was obvious to Blair that Patrick Doyle did not want her there, but it wasn't his opinion she cared about. Silently, she turned to Cam. No one could keep her out of the briefing, although it wasn't routine for her to sit in on one. "Commander?"

"We're just getting started." Cam didn't even look in Doyle's direction, instead introducing the redhead next to Blair. "Ms. Powell, this is Special Agent Lindsey Ryan, a profiler from the behavioral science division at Quantico. I've asked her here to give us an idea of what to expect from Loverboy in the future."

"I think we should discuss the crime scene evidence and find out what we have from the bomb," Doyle immediately countered. "What we need is hard data, not theory."

Cam did stare the length of the table at him then, but responded evenly. "*Everything* is important. My primary objective at this juncture, however, is to anticipate the potential threat to Ms. Powell—"

"She shouldn't be here," Doyle snapped. "Protocol—"

"And to that end," Cam continued as if he hadn't spoken, "I'd like to have as much information about the perpetrator as we can get." Indicating the handsome dark-skinned man next to Ryan, she continued, "Captain Lane is our liaison from the ATF bomb division, and he'll fill us in shortly regarding the information you're interested in, Agent Doyle."

Doyle's color rose, and although it appeared that he wanted to object further, it would be difficult and politically inadvisable to argue that Blair's safety was not of primary concern. It was also clear that he was irate at having been subtly outmaneuvered. He merely closed his jaws tightly and gave a curt nod.

"If you would go ahead, please, Agent Ryan," Cam said.

Lindsey Ryan sat forward slightly. "After the incident yesterday, I reviewed all the information available on the UNSUB beginning with the first contact early this year. My specific intention was to track his behavior, looking for any kind of cyclical or repetitive pattern. I was hoping to identify some kind of trigger that could help us predict what he would do next. This is a rough timeline." She passed out several pages to each person at the table.

"What we see," she continued, her voice practiced and steady, "is a fairly erratic temporal pattern marked by predictable sequential events. Namely, he attempts seduction, and when that is unsuccessful and his overtures are rejected, he follows with aggressive retribution."

"Does this explain why someone who is presumably obsessed with Ms. Powell would also want to harm her?" Mac asked, frown lines deepening between his brows.

Ryan nodded. "Initially, he left a written message delivered to Ms. Powell's door, suggesting that *he* was the most worthy recipient of her attentions. He also indicated underlying anger by suggesting that she was misguided in placing her affections with people who were *unworthy*. In essence, he was offering himself as a suitor."

She waited for the subtle agitation around the table to settle. "Clearly, when this approach failed, his anger escalated, and he made his first attempt on Ms. Powell's life. This is not inconsistent with his obsessive attraction, in that very often a rejected suitor resorts to aggression. It's the old case of *If I can't have you, no one else can either*."

"What about the fact that he's changed his methods? First a sniper attack and now a bomb?" Cam did not look at Blair, but she was acutely aware of their arms resting only inches apart on the tabletop. It had to be difficult for Blair to hear herself being discussed so impersonally by relative strangers. Cam wished she could spare her that. She knew, however, that that was neither feasible nor desirable. Blair had a right to know about the threat that involved her, and keeping her in the dark would only result in losing her cooperation. And if Blair didn't cooperate with them, she would be in even greater danger. "Doesn't that run contrary to the opinion that a repeater usually uses the same form of attack—once a gun always a gun?"

"Unfortunately, in this case, I don't think so," Ryan said with certainty. "He doesn't seem to be attached to any particular form of violent expression, as some psychopaths appear to be. I think it's more likely that he chose a more dramatic method of expressing his displeasure because his tolerance for failure is decreasing. Nothing else he's tried has worked, so he's going to be sure that she takes him seriously now."

A hard fist of anxiety clenched in Cam's chest. "So, are you saying we can expect an escalation in the violence?"

"Probably in both timing and form. This latest action is a statement. He's reminding us that he has power, that he's in control, and that he should not be ignored. Frankly, I'm surprised he hasn't made some attempt at personal contact before this."

"He has," Blair said quietly.

Cam stared at her, a muscle in her jaw clenching. It took all her effort not to raise her voice. "Has he approached you in some way?"

"Not exactly." Blair hesitated, then met Cam's penetrating gaze. "He sent a message saying he wanted me to meet him."

Doyle rose halfway from his seat, barking out, "When did this happen? Why weren't we made aware of it?" He glared at Cam. "Roberts, if this is some kind of attempt by the Secret Service to cut us out of the loop, I'll—"

"I didn't tell anyone," Blair interrupted him, and he sank back into his seat, apparently speechless.

"Why not?" Cam questioned softly.

"I didn't realize at the time that it was significant." Blair's eyes shadowed with worry. "He'd been sending messages regularly, mostly e-mails and the...videos. You know that...I reported that. I thought it was just more of the same."

Cam's stomach turned as she recalled the explicit sexual images that Blair had received, and the graphic messages describing in excruciating detail what this nameless, faceless man fantasized about her.

"What was it this time?"

"It was just another message. At least that's what I thought." Blair's voice trembled slightly. "I just logged on, and it came up on the screen. He said...he said he'd been waiting for me, and he couldn't wait any longer for me to make up my mind. He said he would have to do it for me."

Stark looked at Doyle accusingly. "What happened to the FBI's mighty Carnivore program? I though you guys were supposed to be able to selectively monitor her servers, waylay all messages. How did this e-mail get through and we didn't know?"

"You're out of line, Agent," Doyle growled.

"She has a point. An important one," Cam stated. "Why didn't any of us know this?"

"We'll find out from the computer analysts later," Savard interjected, looking the length of the table at Blair. "When was this?"

"A little over a week ago." Blair glanced at Cam, her voice pitched low. "The day you came back."

Blair didn't need to say anything more. Cam realized that part of the reason Blair hadn't informed anyone about the message was because she hadn't been thinking about the threat to her life. Her attention had been focused on Cam's sudden reassignment to the security detail.

Savard continued, "It could have been a virus implanted previously and activated by something as simple as a piece of code buried in an innocuous e-mail advertisement. Even though Ms. Powell's system has been swept, it doesn't mean he hasn't infiltrated something else more recently."

"Did he kill Jeremy Finch because I ignored him?" Blair looked at Lindsey Ryan, her face pale. "Is it my fault?"

"No," Cam said quickly, vehemently. "None of this is your fault."

"Commander Roberts is right," Ryan interjected. "You're not responsible for Agent Finch's death. The only one responsible for that is the individual who placed and triggered the bomb. There is no way you could've satisfied his demands, because he is not even aware of what actually drives him. Regardless of what you do or do not do, he will never be content."

Doyle took that moment to add contemptuously, "*You* are certainly not to blame. However, no one would have been able to plant a bomb if security measures had been adequate."

His criticism was clearly directed at Cam, but it was Mac who responded.

"You sorry son of a bitch!" He was on the move, rising from his chair, when Cam's voice cut him short.

"Mac." Her tone carried a clear command.

Mac remained half standing, his hands braced on the table, his expression murderous as he glared at Doyle.

"Let's take a break," Cam said calmly, pushing back her chair. She stood but didn't move until everyone except her and Doyle had left the room.

"If you have something to say to me, Agent Doyle, say it now," she said, facing him squarely.

"*You* lost a man, Roberts, not me." His expression was smug. "I have no idea why you're still in command, but I wouldn't get too comfortable if I were you."

Cam waited until he had walked out before she sank slowly into her seat. She would have argued if he hadn't been right.

"Cam?" Blair stood at the door of the dining room. "You don't believe that, do you?"

Cam had been staring blankly down at the table. At the sound of Blair's voice, she straightened quickly and forced a smile. "Eavesdropping on federal business, Ms. Powell?"

"You know better. And don't try to distract me with that charming smile." Cam's automatic attempt to hide her feelings didn't mask the pain in her eyes.

"I heard what Doyle just said. He's wrong to blame you."

"No, he isn't." Cam sighed wearily, slumping slightly now that no one except Blair was there to witness her fatigue. "A man died under my command. That's my responsibility."

Blair's first instinct was to argue, because she couldn't bear to hear the anguish in Cam's voice, but she knew it wouldn't make a difference. She understood Cam's feelings of accountability, even though rationally, no one could be expected to anticipate every eventuality. Not only was Cam trained to assume the blame, but also Blair knew that she was just made that way. This was one of the reasons she admired her, and, she admitted reluctantly to herself, it was also one of the reasons she loved her. Unfortunately, it was also one of the things keeping them apart.

"I talked to my father last night before you got here." Blair crossed the room and pulled out a chair, sitting at Cam's left. She extended her hand on the tabletop until her fingers just touched the back of Cam's wrist. It wasn't enough, but it was all she could have at the moment. "He told me that he had every confidence in you, and that I should listen to you."

Cam couldn't help but grin. "Why do I think you ignored that last part?"

"Well," Blair laughed softly, "I don't always do *everything* he tells me." She stroked her fingers lightly over the top of Cam's hand. "But I do agree with him that you are doing everything that can be done. And I'm so sorry for what happened to Agent Finch."

"So am I," Cam whispered, remembering the terrible silence on the end of the line when she informed Jeremy's family that he had been killed. Their stoic response and gracious thanks to her for calling them personally made it all the harder to bear. But that wasn't the worst of it. "You could've been in that car, Blair. Another thirty seconds, and it would have been you."

"I wasn't." Blair responded urgently to the naked torment in her eyes, her fingers closing on Cam's arm. "Don't torture yourself."

"I don't know what I would have done," Cam murmured, trying hard not to think about the possibility.

"Don't do this. I'm all right, and as long as you're safe, I'll be fine."

Cam smiled. Blair's presence, as always, banished the nightmare images from her mind. "We seem to be in the same situation then, Ms. Powell. Because as long as you're safe, I'm all right, too."

"Finally, we agree on something, Commander."

For a moment, they simply rested with one another, their hands very lightly touching, but their connection much deeper than physical.

Reluctantly, Cam said, "I need to finish up the briefing. Do you want to stay?"

"Will you fill me in later?" Blair asked.

"Yes."

"In that case, I think I've had enough of people and procedures for a while. Is there any rule against me going outside?"

"Not as long as you don't mind company," Cam said. "And I'd prefer if you stayed on the grounds, at least for this afternoon."

"You know, I don't even know where we are."

"I'm sorry, I never thought to tell you." Cam looked momentarily chagrined. "Croton-on-Hudson," she said, naming a small, scenic community on the Hudson River.

Blair pushed her chair back and rose reluctantly. "I'll see you later, then, Commander."

Cam stood, too, and watched Blair disappear into the other room, then squared her shoulders and followed. Mac was waiting just outside the door. "Let's get this done, Mac," she directed. "Bring everyone back in."

"Doyle is trying to make trouble for you," he seethed.

"Let him try," Cam said resolutely. "Let's not forget our priorities. We need to stay focused on Egret's safety, and I think he's got information we need. Let's use him."

Mac looked in the direction that Blair had gone, then asked in a low voice, "Are you going to tell her about the photograph?"

"Yes."

"Service protocol dictates that we never advise the protectee about threats." He grimaced. "Of course, it's a little late now."

"I know what the protocols are, Mac." She answered him because she liked and respected him. She didn't ask him if he approved, because she didn't require his approval. She also had a feeling that he wouldn't agree, but then the decision wasn't up to him. "She needs to know."

❖

It was close to sundown when Cam finally finished the briefing and went to find Blair. She found her sitting on the side of a small dock on the edge of the river that ran along the rear of the property. Ellen Grant watched from under a small clump of trees twenty yards away, while Harry Rodriguez, another Secret Service agent Cam had brought in from the New York City field office, scanned the river and opposite shore with binoculars. She and Blair were as alone as they were likely to be for the foreseeable future.

Cam eased down beside her. "Hello."

"Long meeting, Commander." Blair smiled softly.

"Yes."

"Anything new?"

"Not much yet." Cam sighed in frustration. "A lot of conflicting theories about the bomb, but not much hard data. It appears to have been a high-order explosive, probably RDX, the current material of choice. Captain Lane says that the limited range of the blast indicates a small charge that could have been detonated with something as innocuous looking as a radio pager." She tugged at a small splinter on the dock and then flipped it into the water.

"We have no idea how or when it was placed, but the vehicle was serviced three days ago. Doyle has a team at the shop now—interviewing employees, tracking parts that might have been used... anything."

"But surely someone was watching the car while it was worked on?"

"Yes," Cam confirmed, "but Lane said it wouldn't take more than a second to slip something under the carriage with a magnet or even a quickbond of some kind. It could even have happened yesterday while the car was following us along the race route. Jeremy would have had to go slowly and make multiple stops because of the crowds."

Blair shivered, but could find no words to express her horror.

"There's something else." Cam handed her the small white rectangle she had been carrying in her pocket for hours.

"I don't understand." Blair stared at the photograph. It was an image of herself standing on the platform in Sheep Meadow, with Cam visible just behind her, clearly taken the previous day during her speech. Her eyes were riveted on the circled *X* inked in red over her chest. "If he targeted me while I was on the stage, why didn't he...shoot?"

"Turn it over," Cam said gently.

Blair did and read in chillingly familiar block print on the back: IT COULD HAVE BEEN YOU. She caught her breath, and her hand trembled.

"This is what was in the envelope that Marcy was trying to give me, isn't it?"

"Yes."

"What is he saying?"

"Agent Ryan believes that you were never the intended target yesterday. Loverboy didn't mean to kill *you* at all. He simply wanted to send you the message that he *could* have if he'd wanted to."

Blair stared at Cam, a horrible realization dawning upon her. "And the rifle shot outside my building? Was *I* the target then...or was it you all the time?"

"That's unclear." Cam looked uncomfortable, but she wouldn't lie to her. "It's impossible to reconstruct the scene exactly, because we don't have adequate video documentation. I didn't realize there even *was* a reconstruction until this afternoon. The FBI had confiscated all of the tapes from your building that showed the day of the shooting, and none of us had ever seen them." Another splinter sailed into the river.

Blair waited, watching Cam's face.

"You can't tell from the camera angle the precise sequence of events when the shot was fired. Even with digital remastering and time sequencing, it's unclear whether the trajectory line was toward you or me, because we were so close together, and there aren't good sightlines on the video." She paused a heartbeat. "I just can't say for sure."

"I don't believe this. Are you telling me you spent all afternoon watching a videotape of yourself being shot?"

"Well, not *all* afternoon," Cam said, hoping to defuse the anger she heard brewing in Blair's voice. It hadn't been that difficult after she had seen it the first time and recognized how quickly everyone had responded and how well protected Blair had actually been. Reviewing the tape had relieved a great deal of her anxiety about Blair's vulnerability.

Blair stood quickly, wrapping her arms around herself. Although the night air was still hot and humid, she was chilled. She tried but could not comprehend what it would take to sit there and watch something like that.

"Blair," Cam stood and went to her side, "it's all right."

"No, it isn't," Blair snapped, unable to contain the buffeting storm of emotions. "It most certainly is *not* all right. It's bad enough knowing that you might have been killed trying to protect me. It's worse thinking that you might have been killed just to get my attention."

She turned so suddenly in Cam's direction that their bodies touched briefly. Cam took a half step back, uncharacteristically startled, as Blair's fiery gaze locked onto hers.

"Now do you understand why I don't want you on my detail?" she demanded. "Can't you understand that I don't want to lose you?"

"Blair..." Cam was desperate to reassure her. "We'll get him. I promise. We have thousands of feet of video from the park, and hundreds of still shots. We have Marcy Coleman's description of the person who handed her the envelope. Lindsey Ryan's profile is running through every database in the country right now. The ATF bomb squad is constructing a profile from the bomb remnants. Every hour that passes, we have a better idea of how to find him."

"And until that happens, you're in danger," Blair argued, her chest tight with panic. "You or Stark or Mac or Savard or someone whose name I don't even know might die."

Cam took her hand, uncaring that Grant would see them. "Every single one of us is well trained, and we're all aware of the danger. Nothing is going to happen."

"You can't know that."

"You're right, I can't," Cam said, her voice rising with a combination of frustration and sympathy. "But I don't intend to walk away. I know how to do this job, and I have more reason than anyone else to do it right." She clasped Blair's other hand and stared intently into troubled blue eyes. "I have to do this. Damn it, Blair, I love you."

"If you did, Cameron, you'd leave me alone," Blair protested, pulling her hands free. Then she turned and climbed hurriedly up the slope past Grant and disappeared into the house, leaving Cam staring after her.

Chapter Sixteen

When Cam walked back into the house just after eight in the evening, Patrick Doyle was piling folders into a large battered briefcase, obviously preparing to leave. He glanced up as she entered the living room, and said, "My team says that Egret's building is secure. I told her she could go home any time she's ready."

"Where is she?"

"Packing, I suppose."

"What part of the fact that you don't have any say in her security don't you understand, Doyle?" Cam was indignant, for the first time not bothering to hide her irritation. She'd had a hell of an afternoon, and her recent exchange with Blair had left her nerves raw. "You don't have a say in where she goes or when she goes or how she gets there. You don't have anything at all to do with her movement or her protection."

"Just trying to help you out," Doyle replied, feigning surprise. "Since you're down a man, I thought I'd give you a hand with her."

"I don't *need* your help with her, Doyle." She moved a step closer to him, a dangerous glint in her dark eyes. "All I need is for you to keep me apprised of any intelligence regarding Loverboy. That's *it*. That's *all*. Is that too complicated for you to comprehend?"

Mac walked into the room just in time to hear Cam's last remark, and the edge in her voice surprised him. He had never seen her give even the slightest hint of losing control. Anyone who didn't know her probably wouldn't notice anything amiss even now; however, he saw her hands clenched tightly by her sides, and there was something just a little dangerous in her eyes.

Savard must have thought the same thing. She was watching both Doyle and the commander carefully as she stepped cautiously nearer.

"Hey, we all want to catch this guy." Doyle closed the clasp on his briefcase and reached for his suit jacket, which he had left lying over the back of a nearby chair. He paused and grinned at Cam, a taunting grin completely without humor. "But, you know, it's hard to catch fish if they don't bite, and they almost never bite if there's nothing on the hook."

Cam moved so swiftly that Mac and Savard were completely taken off guard. She had her hands on Doyle's shirtfront before he had a chance to stop her. In the next instant, she had shoved him up against the wall, her fists twisted in the fabric of his shirt, pulling the collar tight across his throat. His usual ruddy complexion rapidly turned crimson. When she spoke, her tone was low and lethal, but everyone in the room could hear her.

"Blair Powell is *not* bait. She is not part of this, and she never will be. Don't suggest it. Don't even *think* it. You don't go near her without clearance from me." Each phrase was punctuated by a slight shove. "You don't talk to her. You don't brief her. You don't so much as look at her."

Doyle's face was purple and he was gasping for air, but he outweighed Cam by seventy pounds, and he was a trained agent. He chopped down on her right forearm with both of his fists, and even if she hadn't been injured, he probably would have broken her grip. As it was, her face went white as pain exploded through her arm, and she let go of him, reflexively taking a step backward.

He lunged for her, but Savard caught his arm, restraining him. Mac stepped in front of Cam, effectively separating the two.

"You're out of control, Roberts," Doyle wheezed. "And we both know why, don't we? Maybe if you weren't trying to fu—"

"Shut up, Doyle," Cam growled while trying to edge around Mac to get at the FBI agent again. She was having trouble staying on her feet, though, and a wave of nausea followed fast behind the burning pain that streaked up her arm. She marshaled every ounce of strength she had left and said very clearly, "Remember what I said. Stay away from her."

"Commander," Mac said calmly, "you appear to be bleeding. You should sit down."

"Come on, sir," Savard persuaded, wedging herself in front of Doyle and widening the distance between the two senior agents. "Everybody's on edge. Let's all cool off."

Doyle looked at her as if just now realizing she was in the room. "Just remember whose side you're on, Agent Savard," he warned as he finally picked up his briefcase and headed toward the door. He glared at Cam, rubbing his neck where the collar of his shirt had left a raw spot. "Your reputation won't protect you forever, Roberts. Heroes are quickly forgotten."

Cam didn't answer. She was having trouble getting enough air, and black spots danced across her field of vision. She could barely make out Doyle's face.

"Savard," Mac said urgently, his voice a harsh whisper. "Can you please get the commander out of here and see to her arm?"

Savard glanced once more in her superior's direction, assuring herself that he really was leaving, then turned toward the Secret Service agents. She gasped before she could stop herself when she saw the widening stain on Cameron Roberts's jacket. A rivulet of blood ran from under the end of her sleeve onto her hand and was in danger of dripping onto the floor.

"Right," she said, stepping quickly to Cam's side and putting one arm around her waist. "Come with me, Commander."

"I need to speak with Blair," Cam said, attempting to pull away. Her head was spinning, and she couldn't feel her hand, but she could still think. And *all* she could think was that Doyle wanted to put Blair out there so Loverboy could have another try at her. *I'll kill him for that.*

"I'll see to Ms. Powell," Mac said.

"No." Cam's voice was oddly flat. "She can't leave. Must talk to her. I...need Taylor's report. Want the FBI's..." She faltered, dizzy and in real danger of vomiting.

Savard tightened her grip as Cam swayed. She sent Mac a warning look.

"I'll see to that, Commander," Mac responded immediately. "Go on, Savard," he urged. He was afraid that Cam was about to pass out. He hated to see her in pain, and he knew that she'd be furious if any of the other agents saw her when she was physically compromised like this.

To his great relief, Cam finally let Savard lead her away. That crisis averted, he steeled himself for a meeting with Egret. Hopefully, she would not ask why *he* was briefing her instead of the commander. He had never been very good at subterfuge.

An open suitcase lay empty on the bed while Blair paced in front of it. The revelation that Loverboy had been intentionally targeting her security detail had shaken her badly. Learning that Jeremy Finch had been killed because of her—that Cam had almost died for the same reason—was unthinkable, beyond comprehension, and more frightening than the potential threat to her own life. She felt responsible, and guilty, and trapped by circumstances, and she wanted to pound something.

Doyle said I could go home. I should just go. I don't need her permission. Damn her.

It didn't help her irritable mood in the least that all she could think about was Cameron Roberts's forthright declaration of love. Because those few words had rocked her more than anything else that had happened, and *that* really scared her. Just when she thought she'd go stir crazy, a knock sounded on the door.

"Who is it?" she barked.

"Mac Phillips, Ms. Powell."

"Come in."

At his entry, she frowned in his direction and noticed that he looked vaguely uneasy. That was unusual for him. "What is it, Mac?"

"The commander requests that you remain here until we're completely briefed. SAC Doyle was...uh...premature in advising you that you could leave."

"Why doesn't she tell me herself?"

He hesitated. "She's unavailable."

"*Unavailable?*" Blair studied him, and for an instant he dropped his gaze. Her heart raced—something was wrong. "What's going on?"

"Nothing," he said quickly. "She's just...indisposed."

"Nothing indisposes *her* short of a nuclear meltdown. Where is she?"

Mac sighed and conceded defeat.

❖

Blair knocked softly, but she didn't wait for an answer. She pushed open the door to the bathroom adjoining Cam's bedroom and stepped into the small space. Savard knelt on the floor in front of the Secret Service chief, who was seated on the closed toilet, her shirt off and her head back, eyes closed. Cam's face was beaded with sweat, and her skin looked gray in the harsh fluorescent light.

Blair's stomach tightened. *God, I hate this.*

"What happened?" she asked sharply, moving around Savard to see what the FBI agent was doing. "Mac said she was indisposed."

Then she got her first look at the wound, and fell silent. *Indisposed. That's a pretty word for this horror.*

Savard held a gauze pad over a long, gaping laceration in Cam's forearm that steadily oozed dark blood. The surrounding burn was blistered and weeping, and her entire arm was swollen to twice its normal size.

"She tore open a bit of the burn here. The bleeding's almost stopped."

"Who did that?"

There was a dangerous tone in the first daughter's voice, and Savard chose not to answer.

"Let me see what's under that pad," Blair ordered, then bent over to look when Savard complied. It was obvious the wound had bled heavily. She didn't need to see the discarded pile of soaked sponges to tell that. All she had to do was look at Cam. "She needs a hospital."

Cam opened her eyes then and after a moment was able to focus on Blair's worried face. "I'm all right. Savard has it."

Blair's hands were shaking, and she knew her voice wasn't quite steady. *So much blood.*

"Renée," Blair said with as much force as she could muster, "either put her in a car and drive her, or I'll do it myself."

"Blair," Cam said softly, making an effort to straighten up. The movement sent her stomach roiling and, sinking back, she was forced to wait a second before continuing. "If I check into a hospital I'm likely to be relieved, at least temporarily."

"I don't care," Blair said more firmly, regaining her composure as the initial shock of Cam's injury began to subside. "Mac is here. He can take care of things." She edged closer to stroke her fingers over Cam's forehead, brushing a damp lock of hair away from her eyes. "You're cold," she murmured, struggling with the fist of anxiety in her gut.

"A little." Cam tried not to shiver. *Man, I do not want to vomit right now.*

Finally focusing on the fact that Cam was wearing only a thin sleeveless silk undershirt, Blair looked around for something to cover her. The dress shirt lying on the floor, rumpled and bloodstained, was useless. Eyes narrowing, she also regarded Savard kneeling on the floor, pressed tightly between Cam's outstretched legs. *I may have to kill Renée, but perhaps not just now.*

"There's a blanket at the foot of the bed," Savard remarked without looking up. She applied a topical antibiotic burn ointment to Cam's arm. "Sorry," she added when Cam winced.

"It's okay."

Blair was gone only for a few seconds. When she returned, Cam was sitting up a little straighter, obviously working hard to hide her discomfort.

"That's not going to work, Roberts," Blair commented darkly, covering Cam's upper body with the blanket. "You still need to go to a hospital."

"Ma'am"—Savard was efficiently wrapping a soft gauze bandage from Cam's palm to her biceps—"I'm certified as a physician's assistant as well as an EMT. They're not going to do anything for her at a hospital that I haven't already done."

Blair turned to her, an angry retort on her lips. Renée Savard met her eyes calmly, a soothing certainty in her gaze. "She'll be all right."

"You're sure?" Blair had moved back to Cam's side and, without realizing it, had rested her hand on the back of Cam's neck. She ran her fingers gently through the dark strands of hair, caressing her softly.

"Yes, ma'am, I am." If Savard noticed Blair's actions, she gave no sign of it.

"I just need to lie down for an hour or so," Cam insisted, feeling better now that the pain was starting to abate.

Blair removed her hand and took a step away. Her tone was dull with resignation. "Will you see that she does, please, Agent Savard?" She wanted to stay with her and knew that she couldn't. Not here, not under these circumstances. It was agony to leave her.

Savard's voice was gentle with sympathy, "I will, Ms. Powell. You needn't worry."

Blair studied Renée Savard closely for a moment, then looked at Cam. "For once, Commander, let someone take care of you."

Chapter Seventeen

Mac was on the sofa, looking exhausted, when Savard returned to the room. "Is she okay?"

"More or less." Savard sank down on the couch next to him and blew out a deep breath. "She's got to be hurting like hell, but it's nothing that won't heal."

They regarded one another cautiously, each trying to judge the other's frame of mind. They were on opposite teams, in a manner of speaking, and had only been working together a few days. A few days that felt like a century.

Since they had both seen the incident, Mac asked, "Do you have any idea what that was all about?"

Savard chose her words carefully. She was acutely aware of the fact that she was only on temporary loan to the Secret Service and that ultimately she would have to survive within the hierarchy of the FBI. On the other hand, she would never defend someone like Patrick Doyle, even if it did mean risking her career.

"Special Agent in Charge Doyle does not confide in me, Agent Phillips," she said. "However, speaking only as an observer, I would say the man has a hard-on for the commander."

Mac blinked, then grinned broadly. "Well then, he's going to wait a long time for a little relief."

"I'd say that's the truth." Savard grinned back.

Turning serious, Mac inquired, "Any idea why?"

Savard shrugged. "I don't know what's going on with him. At first, I thought it was just Bureau politics. You know how that goes—two chiefs together on the same case are like two pit bulls in a small pen.

But it seems like it's more than that, and I don't know him well enough to speculate."

"It's bad enough that we have to worry about Egret." Mac propped his feet up on the coffee table, suddenly aware of how very tired he was. "Now we have to worry about Doyle and the commander."

"I don't really think you have to worry about your commander," Savard responded. "She's a little torn up at the moment, but once she has her feet back under her, I'm sure she can handle him. She didn't get as far as she has by letting herself get pushed around by men who resent her position or her competence. I think we should all concentrate on catching Loverboy and let the commander handle Doyle herself."

Mac sighed in agreement. "Sounds like a plan to me."

"Have you seen Stark?" Savard asked.

"The last time I saw her she was talking to Lindsey Ryan in the kitchen."

Savard raised an eyebrow and stood. "Was she now?"

Mac watched her walk away and wondered why he felt as if he never really knew quite what was going on around him.

It was just after 0100 when Cam stepped into the darkened hallway. She closed her door noiselessly behind her and turned, meeting the eyes of Renée Savard, who stood night watch at the window nearby. The hallway was in shadow, but there was enough light coming from the lamps in the living room to illuminate their faces. They studied one another silently. Then, very deliberately, Savard turned her back to Cam and looked out the window into the night.

Cam crossed the few feet to the opposite side of the hall and opened the door to Blair Powell's bedroom. She stepped inside and stopped, waiting for her eyes to adjust.

"Is this an official visit, Commander?" Blair asked quietly from the darkness.

"No."

"Then I'll leave the lights off."

Cam made her way to the side of the bed and eased down on the edge, reaching for Blair's hand with her uninjured one. "I'm sorry about earlier. I didn't mean to worry you like that."

"How do you feel?"

"Better." She hesitated a beat but knew she had to tell her. "The damn thing hurts like hell, but I'm not dizzy and my stomach has settled. I'm okay."

"Did you come here to give me a personal medical report?" Blair asked, her tone sharp now. Relieved of some of her worry, she remembered how angry she was. She sat up against the pillows, acutely aware of the fact that she was naked under the light sheet. "Because if that's why you're here, you can consider your duty done and leave."

"No." Cam circled her thumb in the palm of Blair's hand. Even though Blair had opened the windows, the late July air hung hot around them. Cam was sweating in a sleeveless cotton T-shirt and a pair of sweatpants, and she brushed moisture from her eyes with her injured hand. "I came because I couldn't sleep. I kept thinking about you—in here. In bed."

Blair's pulse began to hammer, but she steadfastly ignored it. This was one time she was not going to let her body overrule her better judgment. "This isn't going to work, Cam."

A cold hand closed around Cam's heart, making it hard for her to breathe, but she answered calmly, "Why not?"

"You *know* why not. We've been all through this before, and nothing's changed. I can't stand caring about you and knowing that you might be hurt because of me. I can't do it. I don't want to risk feeling anything for you."

"If we were crossing the street," Cam said as if Blair had not just driven a knife into her depths, "and a car were about to hit me, would you push me out of the way even though you might be hurt yourself?"

"Yes, of course," Blair said softly. "But the odds of that happening are almost zero."

"I know." Cam moved her hand to Blair's shoulder, running her fingertips lightly along the ridge of Blair's collarbone. "And the odds of me dying to save you are just as slim. We've just had a run of lousy luck."

Blair laughed harshly, trapping Cam's hand in hers. The undeniable excitement that the mere brush of Cam's fingertips elicited was too damn distracting. "Well, I'm not trusting anything to luck. Either you resign from my detail, or I don't want anything to do with you beyond our daily briefings."

Cam leaned forward and brushed her lips over the tip of Blair's shoulder. "No," she said very softly.

Blair chose to ignore the swift stab of desire that raced through her. "I'm sorry?" she managed, forcing her voice cold.

"No," Cam repeated, moving her mouth a fraction of an inch closer to the base of Blair's neck. She was leaning over her now, breasts brushing lightly against Blair's bare arm. She felt her nipples stiffen beneath her T-shirt and knew that Blair could feel them, too.

"It's not about sex," Blair said harshly, all too aware of the fire burning hotter every second. She was shaking lightly, her skin alive to Cam's touch.

Cam took Blair's hand and pressed it to her own chest. Her heart pounded against Blair's palm. "Neither is this," she whispered. "I've tried so hard not to want you. I've tried so hard not to need you. I can't help it. I can't stop it. We didn't choose this, either of us." She lightly kissed Blair's fingers and placed them back on her heart. "I can't walk away from it. I can't walk away from loving you, and I can't walk away from doing what I know how to do to keep you safe. Please don't ask me to."

Don't do this to me. Blair turned her face away, struggling to resist the pull of Cam's words and the sweet seduction of her touch. "I don't want you to love me," she protested, her voice breaking.

Cam pressed her lips to the hollow of Blair's throat. "Yes," she said very softly as she reached under the sheet and gently cupped Blair's breast, "you do."

Unable to control the surge of desire, Blair moaned and arched her back. "Damn you, Cameron." But the fine edge of longing was clear in her voice.

"Blair," Cam murmured, nudging the sheet aside. She moved her lips over Blair's chest, found her nipple, and pulled it carefully between her lips. She sucked it slowly as it grew hard and tight, then bit lightly, making Blair groan.

She was hard, too, and wet, and a pulse pounded demandingly between her thighs. She sat back, gasping with sudden urgency.

"Help me get my clothes off."

Blair forced herself to focus through a haze of arousal and saw Cam struggling to pull the T-shirt off one-handed. "Here," she said quickly, sitting forward. "Let me do that."

She carefully worked the fabric down over the bandage on Cam's arm, then directed Cam to stand up, reaching for the ties on the sweatpants. After Cam kicked free of her clothes, Blair caught her uninjured hand and pulled her down to lie beside her on the bed. She ran her hand along the length of Cam's supine body—over her abdomen, down her thigh, and back up the inside of her leg.

"You're distracting me again." Cam lifted her hips, breathing rapidly.

"I like distracting you, remember?" Blair murmured. She ran her fingertips through the thick, wet heat between Cam's legs, her breath catching in her throat as her own body clenched in response.

Cam made an effort to move on top and gasped sharply as she pushed up on her injured arm.

"What is it?" Blair asked anxiously, sitting up.

"Just my arm," Cam replied, attempting to direct Blair back onto the pillows. The movement drew another groan.

"Lie back, Cam," Blair said firmly. As she spoke, she took Cam's shoulders gently and pushed her down. "Let me."

Cam did not protest. She was still tingling from Blair's brief caress, and she was more than ready for more.

"I actually enjoy being distracted," she confessed.

Laughing lightly, Blair fit herself between Cam's legs, then pressed her cheek to Cam's breast. She brushed her lips over a nipple, teasing a moan from her lover, before kissing her way slowly down the length of Cam's abdomen.

In response, Cam closed her eyes with a long, low sigh of surrender. She lifted her hips as Blair's palms pressed against her thighs, opening her; arched her back, muscles tightening, as Blair's lips closed on her; and caught back a groan, trembling, as Blair's tongue tormented her. Blair's tender, knowing touch banished the pain and the fatigue and the worry.

"You are so good," Cam whispered faintly, her fingers trailing through Blair's hair. She was very close and yet desperate not to come. "So good."

Blair answered by massaging the spot that made Cam's muscles quiver and quickened her pace, eliciting another sharp gasp. She felt Cam twitch under her tongue and knew she was there. Slipping an arm around Cam's hips, Blair pulled her close, knowing as she took her with her mouth, her hands, and her heart the clear and simple truth. She loved her.

There was no stopping, no turning back, for either of them. Not now. Not the next day. Not ever.

❖

The day shift had not yet come on duty when Cam left Blair's room just before dawn. Savard still stood watch at the window.

Cam walked over to her and stood by her side. Their eyes met as she asked, "Anything to report, Agent Savard?"

"No, ma'am. It was a very quiet night."

"Nothing out of the ordinary, then?" Cam asked again. She had a feeling that if Renée Savard had a problem, she'd deal with it out in the open, face-to-face, and not in some report sent to DC in a sealed folder. And if Renée Savard had a problem with her, Cam *wanted* it out in the open.

There was too much work to be done in the next few weeks that required her full attention, and she couldn't be worried about looking over her shoulder. Loverboy was not going to de-escalate. Not now. All of them needed to be sharp and focused if they were going to stop him without losing another of their number.

"Nothing you wish to discuss?"

"No problems that I'm aware of," Savard affirmed. "In fact, no activity whatsoever, Commander."

"Very well then. We'll brief at 0700, if you could inform your relief, please."

"Yes, ma'am." Savard returned her gaze to the first hints of a new day outside. If someone was going to make trouble about Cameron Roberts and Blair Powell caring for one another, it wasn't going to be her.

❖

Shortly after eight, Blair, carrying her second cup of coffee, crossed to a small patio table on the rear deck of the house and sat down. She'd consumed the first in between showering and pulling on a T-shirt and jeans. Stark came out close on her heels and walked down onto the lawn to take up her post there. The young agent leaned against the corner of the deck, apparently surveying the expanse of lawn and the river beyond.

A few minutes later, the sliding glass doors opened again and Cam walked out. It was the first time Blair had seen her since they'd parted in the dim predawn light. Blair smiled, enjoying the look of her in her fresh white shirt and tailored trousers. Even better, Cam looked rested and pain free, although Blair knew that she hadn't had much sleep. She also noticed the clean bandage on her hand and wondered fleetingly who had done that for her. It might have bothered her more if Cam hadn't been looking at her with such intensity that her skin tingled.

"Good morning, Commander," she called softly, her eyes warm with welcome.

"Ms. Powell." Cam's smile was equally intimate as she approached, a cup of coffee in her left hand. She sat down opposite, deposited her coffee cup on the small table, and rested one hand a fraction away from Blair's fingertips. "Good to see you again."

The words were as smooth as a caress, and Blair was instantly reminded of the last time they had touched, only hours before. It had been Cam's lips against her neck that had been smooth then, their arms around one another as they stood together by the door.

"I have to go," Cam whispered, her hands running lightly up and down Blair's back. She had pulled on her T-shirt and sweats. Blair was still naked. "I need to get back to work."

"I know."

"I'm sorry."

"Don't be," Blair murmured, her arms around Cam's waist, her lips against her neck. She kissed her softly, then a little harder as the stirring began again in the pit of her stomach.

"No fair," Cam protested, her voice husky.

"I know." Blair pulled away reluctantly. "Go on. Go. Go before I don't let you go."

"Blair, I lo–"

Blair stopped her, gentle fingers against her lips. Cam looked at her, puzzled.

"Don't make any promises, Commander. Just tell me you will come back."

"Yes," Cam had whispered, just as she kissed her.

"I'm sorry?" Blair said, realizing that Cam had been speaking to her.

Cam watched Blair's eyes swim into focus, just as they did after they made love and she slowly returned to herself. It was the sexiest thing she had ever seen, and she had to concentrate on her words to remember what she had been saying.

"Both the FBI and my team have independently cleared your building for re-occupancy. I'm satisfied."

Blair nodded. "I'd like to go home, then."

"I know."

"When do you think? Today?"

"I trust my team, and I don't believe that the situation will be any different unless we remain here indefinitely." Cam shrugged and admitted reluctantly, "I think another day won't matter. Today is fine."

"Thank you." Blair smiled, remembering the last two days and the few moments she had been able to have alone with Cam. Even that might be hard in New York. "There *is* something to be said for being locked up here with you, however."

"There is indeed." Cam's eyes darkened, and her grin was slow and easy.

Just in response to the husky familiarity in Cam's voice, Blair's heart rate doubled. Unfortunately, the rest of her responded, too, and as much as she enjoyed the sensation, she was all too aware that it might be some time before she could satisfy the pressure beginning to build inside. Flushing, she watched Cam's gaze fall to her breasts. The width of the table separated them, but she felt the glance as if Cam's hands were on her. Her nipples stiffened under the thin cotton.

"Don't do that," she said, her voice oddly breathy.

"What would that be, Ms. Powell?" Cam murmured, her fingers trembling with the desire to skim along the surface of the soft skin visible at the neck of Blair's shirt. *I'm in big trouble.*

"Don't look at me like that in public," Blair rejoined softly, "because in case you haven't noticed, self-control has never been my strong suit."

"Then I promise not to tease you..." Cam lifted eyes hazy with longing to Blair's. The wanting was a hard ache in her gut. Her chest tight, she whispered, "In public."

Unable to answer, Blair shivered lightly, like an animal run too hard in the hot sun. Her voice was gone, her blood burning. She had never expected this helplessness in the face of desire. If this was what loving Cameron would mean, she wasn't sure she would survive it.

"I must go," Cam said gently, because leaving her was the last thing she wanted at that moment.

"All right. For now," Blair murmured, following Cam with hungry eyes as the agent walked to the edge of the deck and leaned down toward Stark.

"Tell the team we'll be leaving for the Aerie at 1300 hours," Cam instructed.

Paula Stark, who appeared to be engrossed in the feeding habits of two fat robins on the lush green lawn, answered, "Yes, ma'am."

When Stark heard the patio door open and close, she glanced over her shoulder to ascertain that Blair Powell was still within visual range. Seeing that she was, she returned her gaze to the perimeter and her mind to the previous evening. She had been standing in almost this exact spot an hour after sundown when Renée Savard had walked down the patio stairs to her side.

"Everything quiet?" Savard had asked, leaning one shoulder against the deck support.

"Very," Stark answered, glad for the company. There was nothing quite so long or quite so lonely as the night shift.

"Agent Ryan leave yet?"

"About an hour ago. She left some files for the commander to review, but she said that she can do more from Quantico where she has better access to the data banks."

"She seems to know what she's doing."

Stark shifted her weight and automatically slid her hands into her pockets in an unconscious gesture similar to Cameron Roberts. "Yeah, she's very sharp. I'm glad the commander brought her up here today, because now I don't feel as if I'm chasing some phantom. At least I have a picture of him in my mind."

Savard nodded in agreement. "Well, I'd certainly rather work with her than some of the hotheads from violent crimes we usually get stuck with on something like this."

Stark laughed. "Boys with guns."

"Actually, I've always been partial to girls with guns." Savard gave a soft smile.

Stark was grateful for the darkness, because her blush would have been impossible to hide. Suddenly, the night seemed much warmer, and she was acutely aware of the way Renée Savard's voice sounded in the night—low and smooth and...sexy.

She swallowed and managed to answer steadily, "So am I."

"Well, that's nice to know," Savard responded. "When things quiet down a little on this detail, we should see what else we might have in common."

"Uh, that would be a...good," Stark mumbled, cursing herself for sounding like a dolt.

Savard smiled. "I don't think that Secret Service agents are supposed to be quite so sweet, Agent Stark. But on you...it's very nice."

Stark had been trying to think of a clever response when Savard brushed her fingers over the back of her hand and walked away. She'd been thinking about that fleeting touch ever since.

"Agent Stark?"

Stark jumped and turned quickly. The first daughter was leaning over the railing, a quizzical expression on her face.

"Ma'am?" Stark blushed again. *Damn it.*

"Would you let the commander know that I'm ready to go home as soon as she gives the word?"

"Yes, ma'am. I will." *Things should get interesting now.*

According to what Lindsey Ryan had told them the day before, once they left the relative sanctuary of this house, any and all of them were targets.

Chapter Eighteen

Mac swiveled in his seat at the comm desk and held out the phone, a perplexed expression on his face. "Commander? Egret wishes to speak to you."

Cam was bent over one of the nearby desks, replaying a segment of videotape taken in Central Park during Blair's speech, carefully studying the crowd in the general vicinity of Marcy Coleman. She searched each figure, looking for a slim twenty-five to thirty-year-old white male, approximately five-ten, a hundred and fifty pounds. That was the description Dr. Coleman had given them of the man who had handed her the envelope for Blair.

"I'll take it over here," Cam said immediately, surprised and concerned. Blair rarely contacted her for anything official. She reached for the receiver and picked it up the instant it rang, the only indication of her disquiet a faint line between her brows. "Yes?"

"Cameron, can you come up here, please?"

There was a hollowness in her tone that set Cam's heart racing with anxiety. "Right away. Are you—"

"I'm all right," Blair said, but there was a faint tremor in her voice.

"I'm on my way." Cam dropped the receiver into the cradle and headed swiftly toward the door, instructing Mac as she walked. "I want a voice check with every agent ASAP. Verify that all posts are manned and that no one has anything out of the ordinary to report. *Anything*, Mac."

"Yes, ma'am." Mac straightened and immediately turned to the monitors, simultaneously activating his transmitter.

Cam didn't hear his reply because she was already through the door and in the hallway, keying the elevator to Blair's penthouse. Thirty seconds later, she was at Blair's door when it swung open, Blair just inside, waiting, her face pale.

Cam took her shoulders in both her hands and looked intently into her face. "What is it?"

Blair managed a smile, but the smile was faint and her blue eyes were deeply troubled. She extended a white envelope toward Cam. "This came in the mail."

Grasping only the corner, Cam took it and studied the front. Blair's name and address were affixed with a common bulk-mailing label. The return address was for a well-known charity organization. It looked perfectly ordinary.

"I thought it was about a fundraiser," Blair said, barely audible.

Cam looked inside and the muscles in her stomach tightened. "Have you touched it?"

"Yes," Blair nodded. "I'm sorry. I wasn't thinking."

"Don't worry." Cam shook her head. "It doesn't matter. He's never left prints before. Still, we have to go through the motions." She looked around for something with which to tease out the white rectangle.

Blair crossed to her desk and retrieved a large paper clip. "Here, try this."

Cam hooked it over the corner of the photograph and slid it out. Then, with a sense of fury and dread, she silently regarded the image of Diane Bleeker standing in front of her Upper East Side apartment building. There was a familiar red circle with an X drawn through it centered over her chest. Cam turned over the Polaroid and saw another mailing label affixed to the back. Typed on it were the words: MEET ME OR SHE'S NEXT.

Carefully, Cam placed the photograph back into the envelope and slipped it into her inside jacket pocket. Then she walked directly to the wall phone in Blair's kitchen and rapidly punched in a series of numbers.

"Give me SAC Doyle immediately, please. This is Commander Cameron Roberts, Secret Service." She looked at Blair as she waited, smiling faintly as if to say it would be all right. Then, she said brusquely into the receiver, "Doyle, this is Roberts. I need you to send a team to Diane Bleeker's apartment at 88th and 5th Avenue, ASAP. She's his next target. I'll alert NYPD to get dogs and a bomb squad over there... Fine. I'll fill you in at Command Central."

"Thank you," Blair said quietly when Cam hung up after contacting the NYPD liaison. "I know you probably didn't enjoy making that call to the FBI."

Cam shrugged dismissively. "The problems between Doyle and me don't matter. Diane does."

"Something has to be done, Cam," Blair said vehemently, pacing in agitation. "I can't stand this any longer."

"Blair," Cam began gently, catching her arm and stilling her frantic motion, "it will be over soon."

"Not soon *enough*." Blair shook her head impatiently. "I don't care what it takes, Cam. I don't care what I need to do. I need this to be over."

"Soon. I promise." Cam put her arms around her and pulled her close, holding her tightly. "I know how hard this must be for you."

Although Blair did not resist the embrace, she was still stiff with fear and frustration. She didn't want sympathy—she wasn't the one being shot at or blown up. "I'm okay."

"I know you are," Cam murmured, resting her cheek against Blair's hair. "This is for me."

I need this, too. Blair relented, drawn into the comfort of her. She slipped her arms under Cam's jacket, sliding her hands up her back, pressing her face to Cam's shoulder. Her hands met the leather harness of Cam's shoulder holster, and she shuddered briefly. There had been too much loss, and it was draining her spirit.

Cam ran her hand lightly up and down Blair's back, caressing her softly. "Doyle's people and the police are on their way to Diane's right now. She'll be safe."

"Who will be next?" Blair's voice was muffled against Cam's body. "Will it be one of you? Will it be Marcy Coleman...or some poor random person who happens to be in the wrong place at the wrong time? I can't just stand by and watch it happen. I've got to *do* something."

"It isn't going to be anyone. We'll stop him." Cam's stomach knotted, but she smoothed her hand gently over Blair's hair and pressed her lips to her forehead. "I need you to trust me, Blair."

Blair said nothing, and Cam's heart pounded with sudden alarm. "Please, promise me that you won't do anything without discussing it with me. I *need* you to do that. Please."

Blair leaned back in the circle of Cam's arms and studied her face. There was something close to panic in her gray eyes. Blair had never seen her look that way before. Nothing ever scared her. "Cam," she whispered, slipping her hand to the back of her neck, stroking her. "Hey."

"I can't lose you," Cam rasped, her throat tight with the anguish, the edges of her mind still raw with old memories.

The unexpected haunted expression on her stoic lover's face tore at Blair's heart. She sighed and ran her fingers lightly over Cam's cheek. She could no more hurt her than she could stop loving her. "I promise. Just do something, please."

Cam kissed her, a kiss of thanks and tender possession. When she lifted her lips away, she whispered, "I will."

Cam walked into the conference room at Command Central and nodded to Patrick Doyle. As had become the custom, the FBI personnel were lined up on one side of the table and her team on the other. She and Doyle faced off once again from opposite ends.

"We have to assume an action from Loverboy is imminent," Doyle said without preamble, his preemptive attempt to take charge glaringly obvious.

Unperturbed by his attitude, Cam nodded her agreement as she sat down. She'd played these interagency power games before. "What's the status at Diane Bleeker's apartment building?"

"Our team and the bomb squad are there now," Doyle informed her. "She's been moved temporarily to a secure location."

Cam's face showed no sign of it, but she relaxed as some of her inner tension dissipated. *One disaster averted.* "I talked to Lindsey Ryan at Quantico and brought her up to date," she said. "She believes that this is a real threat, and if he can't access his primary target—Egret, or his designated substitute—Diane Bleeker—then he may choose someone else out of frustration or anger."

She looked around the table, knowing that she didn't need to repeat what Lindsey Ryan had already told them. Any of them could be next. No one voiced that obvious fact.

"Egret will remain sequestered here for the immediate future. She's agreed to temporarily postpone her plans for San Francisco, but we only have a two-and-a-half-week window until Paris. Canceling that trip is also an option, but not a very viable one. Ryan feels that if we change Egret's public itinerary so drastically, it concedes power to Loverboy, which in turn may make him bolder...and more dangerous. I agree. Despite the increased visibility, we'll have to travel."

Doyle waved a hand in dismissal. "It's unreasonable to keep her out of sight indefinitely." He carefully avoided the suggestion that Blair's visibility was one sure way to draw out their UNSUB. Unconsciously, he rubbed the fading abrasion on his neck. "On the other hand, offering Loverboy a meet is the best way to get him out in the open."

Both Mac and Stark stiffened, and Cam knew one or both of them was about to vehemently protest. She raised her left hand an inch off the table, and both of them settled back into their chairs, their faces set and angry.

Very evenly, her voice completely controlled, she said, "Special Agent in Charge Doyle, I am certain that you are not suggesting that we use the president's daughter as bait for a proven psychopathic killer."

"Of course not," Doyle answered woodenly, his jaw muscles bunching as he clenched his teeth.

"Then we needn't pursue that line of thought any further," Cam responded, leashing her own anger. "Egret continues to receive regular e-mail from him. He's using hacked IP numbers and routing messages through random computers, so he is still not traceable. As was previously decided, there has been no attempt to block his messages, because it's our only means of judging his state of mind and potentially predicting his moves."

"Well, *that's* been a royal failure," Doyle remarked harshly.

Cam ignored him and continued. "Agent Ryan suggests that we communicate with him via e-mail, as Egret, in an attempt to get more information about his plans. This seems logical. An agent with computer and electronics expertise will be joining my team later today. She can begin the exchange after Loverboy's next contact."

There was an uncomfortable silence as everyone realized that this new agent would be a replacement for Jeremy Finch.

Smiling smugly, Doyle broke the silence. "I talked with my director on the way here. He agrees with me that we need to be more proactive if we're going to resolve this situation."

Cam didn't move an inch although every muscle became rigid. "Meaning?"

"We're planning on initiating contact, just as you suggested, Roberts," Doyle stated with an unmistakable note of condescension. "But we're not interested in *dialoguing*. Our priority is to neutralize the threat."

"And how do you intend to do that?"

"We're going to set up a meet."

"A decoy operation?" Mac exclaimed in surprise. "This guy is a bomber. You can't send someone in undercover when she might be walking into a bomb."

"We assessed the risk to be acceptable," Doyle said brusquely. Straightening a pile of folders in front of him, he added, "We expect it will take several days to put things in place. We're bringing in our own person to establish electronic contact with him."

"It's a risky operation, Doyle," Cam said quietly. "There are other avenues we can pursue first."

"We've all waited long enough." Doyle's eyes bored into Cam, their expression accusatory. "Too long."

There was little Cam could say about an FBI operation. It wasn't what she would've done, but her primary concern was Blair's security, and she admitted to herself reluctantly that the FBI were well within their rights to attempt apprehension their own way.

"I'd appreciate it if you kept us informed of the timetable." She pushed back her chair, having registered her dissent. That was all she could do. "In the meantime, we'll continue to analyze the videos and photos from the park and monitor electronic contacts."

"No problem there, Roberts." This time, Doyle couldn't hide his triumphant grin. "You'll be informed since we're going to use one of your agents to work the decoy."

Cam placed both hands flat on the table and leaned forward, her body coiled with tension as if she might spring from her chair. Her voice dropped low, dangerously low. "No, Doyle, you are not. My agents are Secret Service agents. They are *not* decoys for the FBI."

"It's already been cleared." Doyle shrugged. "We need someone with firsthand knowledge of Egret in case we get into a situation where a verbal exchange with the UNSUB is necessary. I can't brief a new agent on the kinds of things he might ask. The decoy needs to be one of yours."

For a minute, Cam couldn't think through her fury. Doyle had gone behind her back and essentially conscripted one of her agents for a potentially lethal mission. She stood, struggling to maintain her composure. None of them had had much sleep in the last seventy-two hours, and she was riding the thin edge of control. She had lost one man already. She was not going to lose another.

"This is not going to happen, Doyle."

"It's not up to you," Doyle said, rising also. "It's been approved, and your agent has already accepted the assignment."

Cam glanced quickly at Stark, who shook her head almost imperceptibly. Clearly, she knew nothing of Doyle's plan.

"This meeting is over," Cam snapped as she turned and walked out the door. Another second and she would have had her hands on his throat. Again.

Cam stalked through the command room and barked, "Grant! With me."

Ellen Grant jumped to her feet and hurried to follow her tall commander as she pushed through the door into the outer hallway. The elevator ride down to the lobby was chillingly silent. As they approached the double glass doors, Grant felt compelled to explain.

"Commander, I—"

"In a minute, Grant." Cam was still working hard to quell her desire to punch Patrick Doyle in his arrogant face. Ellen Grant was *her* agent—hers to command, hers to protect. He had come between her and someone she was responsible for, and that was a serious miscalculation on his part. She could tolerate his personal affronts, but she would not tolerate anyone interfering with what was hers.

Grant set her jaw and prepared herself for a dressing-down. It would be hard to take coming from Roberts, because she respected her boss.

They crossed the street, and Cam unlocked the ornate park gates, stepping through with Grant on her heels. Once they were inside, Cam slowed so that Grant could walk by her side and finally looked at her. "Do you want to tell me what happened between you and SAC Doyle?"

"He contacted me this morning while you were on the phone with Washington." Grant stared straight ahead, her tone subdued. "He advised me he would need me for an undercover operation to apprehend Loverboy. I told him he should speak with you, but he informed me the decision had already been made in Washington. He said that he needed my answer then." She looked into Cam's face, her tone unapologetic. "I told him yes."

They had reached a secluded corner of the park, not far from the bench where Cam had sat with Blair only days before. They stood under the shade of a weeping willow, Cam with her hands balled into fists in the pockets of her trousers, Grant unconsciously at attention.

"I'm not going to let you do this, Grant," Cam said calmly, although her voice vibrated with tension. "You're a Secret Service agent, not FBI. This is an undercover decoy operation, and you're not trained for it."

Grant straightened even further, determination on her face. "Commander, I respectfully disagree. I was a cop before I joined the Service. I can do this."

Cam smiled slightly, expecting nothing less from the spit-and-polish Grant, who was a solid agent in every respect. Nevertheless, the operation spelled disaster from the outset.

There are too many people involved and not enough coordination. Especially when Doyle thinks you are expendable to his objectives. Janet was a trained undercover detective, too, and she died in an operation just like this. I am not about to lose anyone else.

"Agent Grant, I have never doubted your abilities. I value your contribution to this team, and I entrust Egret to your care. This is something altogether different, and it's *not* going to happen."

"Commander, you may not have anything to say about this." Grant met Cam's eyes and she spoke her mind. "I'm not certain that anyone can override SAC Doyle at this point. If I'm needed, and if I'm ordered, I'll do it. And do it willingly. I'm a good body double for her. Jeremy Finch is dead. You were almost killed."

She hesitated for a moment, and then said resolutely, "The next time, Commander, he may be too angry to settle for a substitute. The next time it might be Egret. Commander, I want this assignment."

Deep in thought, Cam looked past Grant's shoulder up to the penthouse of Blair's apartment building. *We can't keep her sequestered up there forever.*

In fact, she doubted they could keep her there even for a few days...nor did she really want to. Blair was suffering—from the guilt of others dying in her place and from the conflict of being at once exposed to countless strangers—and confined by them. It was a conflict that was suffocating her and one that would eventually destroy her strength. Cam could not bear to see that. She brought her eyes back to Ellen Grant's steady blue ones.

"If it comes to that, Grant, I want you to know that I'll be right behind you. You're not going into this alone."

Grant smiled softly and relaxed perceptibly. "Thank you, Commander. That makes me feel better."

Finally, Cam smiled, too. "And Ellen...thank you."

When they turned and walked side by side from the park, the silence between them was one of unspoken respect.

Blair answered the door at the first knock. "Is Diane all right?" she inquired urgently as Cam stepped into the loft.

Cam nodded and went directly to the phone. She disconnected the jack and inserted a small rectangular box between the wall and Blair's phone. An LCD readout blinked on the face of the metal device, showing a series of rapidly cycling ten-digit numbers. She depressed the receiver once to engage the scrambler, then handed the telephone to Blair.

"Why don't you call her yourself? 212-555-1950."

Blair raised an eyebrow and pushed the numbers. A few seconds later, she said, "I'd like to speak to Diane, please..." She whispered a *thank you* to Cam as she waited, then the first real smile in a long time lit her face. "Hey. How are you doing?"

Leaning against the breakfast counter that divided her kitchen from her work area, Blair reached for Cam's hand as she spoke and her smile became wry. "No, Diane, I don't think it's a good idea to try to seduce the FBI." She tugged Cam closer, and Cam slipped behind her to sit on one of the high stools lined up along the center island in the kitchen.

Situating herself, back to front, between Cam's legs, Blair ran her fingers up and down Cam's uninjured arm as she continued, "Yes, I know. They *do* seem to be criminally attractive, but I still think it might provoke an incident if you dragged one into the bedroom."

Cam shifted, spreading her legs so that she could pull Blair against her chest, slipping both arms loosely around Blair's waist from behind, cradling her softly in her arms. She rested her chin against the top of Blair's head and sighed, too faintly for Blair to hear. She hadn't held her for what seemed like days.

"I can't tell you very much. I don't know very much," Blair offered, placing her palm on the inside of Cam's thigh. Almost unconsciously, she trailed her fingers along the inside seam of Cam's trousers, listening to Diane tell her about the less-than-four-star accommodations to which she was being subjected.

Just hearing Diane's voice helped ease the ball of tension that had filled Blair's chest all morning. Beyond her relief, though, she was presently much more aware of the slight increase in Cam's breathing and the fine tension rippling through the muscles under her hand.

"She's here with me now...Yes, Diane," Blair said in mock exasperation. "I'm listening to her." She laughed and added, "I said I was *listening*. I didn't say I was necessarily following orders. I don't believe domestication is an immediate threat."

As Blair spoke, Cam fingered open the top two buttons of Blair's blouse and slipped her hand inside. Blair gave a slight start of surprise and automatically pressed her hips back into Cam's crotch.

"I'm sorry about this." Blair spoke as earnestly as she could, while trying valiantly to ignore the brush of Cam's fingers over her nipples. "I trust Cam, and she'll get you out of there as soon as it's possible." She reached behind and found the button on Cam's fly. A second later, she had it open and was tugging at the zipper. "I'll call again," she said, then listened briefly. "Yes. I'll be careful, I promise."

Before she said good-bye, her hand was inside Cam's trousers. She set down the phone and pressed the back of her head to Cam's shoulder—extending her neck, offering her flesh. Cam's lips were on her immediately, hot and hungry. Blair rubbed her fingers over Cam's briefs, smiling to herself as she found the heat she expected.

"Thank you for that," Blair said throatily, arching her back, pressing her breasts up into Cam's palms.

"What?" Cam asked dimly. She was focused on the way Blair's breasts filled her hands and the insistent pounding pressure between her legs that rose rapidly under Blair's fingertips.

"Letting me call her," Blair murmured, her eyes closed. She moved her hand back up to Cam's belly, aware of the faint growl of frustration from her lover. She smiled to herself, enjoying the power.

Slowly, she smoothed her palm over Cam's firm stomach and then quickly pushed her hand under the waistband of Cam's underwear, back down between trembling legs. She slipped a finger on either side of the firm prominence of Cam's clitoris, squeezing her slowly. Cam jerked against her, groaning softly.

Then Cam's lips were against her ear, her breath ragged, as she whispered, "Do that a little harder and you'll make me come."

"I intend to," Blair answered, a hungry edge to her voice. She moved her hand away and turned in Cam's arms until she faced her, still between her legs, her breasts exposed through her open blouse. She rubbed her hard nipples over Cam's shirtfront, gasping softly at the fine ripple of excitement that ran straight down to her own clitoris.

"Put your fingers back on me," Cam pleaded, her eyes hazy with need.

"Not here. Not just yet," Blair whispered, stepping away. She caught Cam's uninjured hand in hers and pulled her upright. "I want you slow."

"I don't have much time," Cam protested hoarsely, standing and following her nevertheless.

Blair glanced back, an enigmatic smile on her face. "You have enough time, Commander. The *only* advantage to our situation is that no one is going to question your presence up here."

She drew Cam around the corner of the partition into her sleeping alcove, then turned and reached for the buttons on Cam's shirt. "I've never yet made love with a woman in my own bed. Couldn't find one to pass the security inspection." She stopped long enough for a kiss, a deep languid kiss. She was having trouble keeping her hands from shaking she wanted her so badly, but she continued evenly, "Apparently, you're the one. Stand still."

Methodically, she opened each button as Cam submitted willingly to the slow torture, her hands clenched at her sides, shuddering with arousal. Blair stripped the shirt off and laid it carefully over a chair, mentioning almost as an afterthought, "It wouldn't do to get this too wrinkled."

When Blair began to pull off the tailored trousers, Cam's restraint wavered, and she hurriedly pushed them off herself. In a minute, she was naked. She reached for Blair, who stepped back quickly with a small shake of her head. Her eyes were laser bright and focused intently on Cam's body.

"No, you can't touch me," she said thickly. "I don't want to be distracted either." She drew Cam to the bed and urged her down on top of the covers.

Then, standing by the bed, she watched Cam watch her as she slowly removed her own clothing. She slid the sheer silk off her shoulders, let the blouse drop to the floor, and drew her fingers down her breasts—lingering on her nipples, tugging them lightly until the exquisite sensation became too much to bear. As she continued down to stroke her abdomen, teasing ever lower toward the curls at the base of her belly, Cam's eyes darkened, following hotly on her. Blair saw her lover's talented hands twitch where they lay on the covers, and Cam's reaction heightened her arousal more than her own caresses.

"I want to do that," Cam said urgently, watching as Blair's fingers slipped between her thighs. When Blair made a small whimpering sound, Cam was afraid that she might come herself. Hoarsely, she begged, "Blair, please."

Blair shuddered and pulled her hand away, knowing she was too close and not wanting it yet. Nevertheless, she needed contact, something to relieve the throbbing ache between her legs. Hurriedly, she moved onto the bed and straddled Cam's thigh, moaning softly as her swollen flesh rubbed against Cam's warm skin. She leaned forward, bracing herself on one arm, and brought the other between Cam's thighs. She entered her smoothly, all in one motion, knowing that Cam was ready for her.

Involuntarily, Cam's throat closed around a cry, and she heaved upward to meet Blair's thrust. The suddenness of it took her unawares, and a rolling wave of sensation followed fast upon the initial pleasure. Her eyes opened wide, and she stared at Blair, stunned and already lost.

"Close," she gasped.

With every ounce of her strength, Blair was holding back her own orgasm, but the feel of Cam contracting around her fingers and the tingling in her clitoris as she thrust herself along Cam's leg were too much to contain. She bore down, and as she felt herself begin to crest, she pressed her thumb hard along the length of Cam's clitoris.

At the first pounding spasm, Cam jolted upright and wrapped her arms around Blair. They pressed their bodies together, groaning softly in unison as they joined in surrender.

As the contractions subsided, they lay back, Blair curled up by Cam's side, her fingers still inside her. Cam's arm came lazily around her shoulder, and they rested together, breathing hard and drifting somewhere just behind the boundaries of reality.

On a breath, Cam finally whispered, "If we keep this up, it's all going to come out."

Blair pressed closer, moving her hand upward across Cam's stomach. She rested her fingers on Cam's breast, not in passion now but in contented possession. "Yes, I know."

"It will be complicated."

Blair pressed her lips to Cam's shoulder, kissing her lightly. "Yes, I know."

"We'll deal with it, somehow." Cam sighed, her lips soft on Blair's temple.

Blair closed her eyes, stealing a brief moment of peace, as she whispered, "Yes, I believe we will."

CHAPTER NINETEEN

Most of Cam's afternoon was spent enduring another meeting with Doyle while they hammered out their respective roles in the upcoming operation. She was forced to accept that the decision regarding Ellen Grant's participation was out of her hands. She let it go, choosing instead to focus her energy on assuring Grant's safety. If she needed to be on site twenty-four hours a day monitoring events to do so, then that's where she planned to be. Late that evening, Finch's replacement arrived, and the plan to engage Loverboy and draw him out into the open was set in motion.

It was close to 0400 when she finally headed across the square to her apartment. No one was about, and the night was very still. Acutely aware of being alone for the first time in days, she stopped at the corner and glanced back at Blair's building. A faint glow illuminated the double panes of glass in the penthouse apartment. She wondered if Blair was working and wished for a moment that she could be there—sitting nearby, quietly watching, as she used to watch her mother work when she was young.

It was the kind of memory that brought a longing for something she hadn't known she missed and couldn't afford to consider now. She shrugged it away and continued up to her small, impersonal apartment for a few hours of fitful sleep before the campaign truly began.

Four hours later, she was back at Command Central reviewing communications and reports from Washington, the New York field office, and the National Crime Information Center. Despite the current operation, she still had protocols to follow. She couldn't afford to let one threat to Blair's security obscure the potential for others. When the routine work was finished, she was ready for a status report on Loverboy. She refused to think of the operation by the truly asinine code name the Fibbies had come up with.

"Anything new?" Cam stood behind the two people seated in front of an array of computers, voice analyzers, video monitors, and other electronic tracking devices.

Both swiveled in their chairs, and both looked weary, but there was also an unmistakable sense of exhilaration about them, as if they were enjoying themselves immensely. The ebony-skinned woman, whose bearing was nothing short of regal, spoke first, her voice modulated by a slight accent that bespoke her European schooling.

"We've replied only twice since first contact twelve hours ago, Commander," Felicia Davis said. "As discussed, I've made no attempt to engage him in any way other than a few verbal probes—who are you, what do you want, why are you contacting me. Things Egret would already have said, but the kind of thing someone might ask if they were getting tired of the attention." A slight frown creased her sculpted features as she indicated the computers on the console in front of her. "I've tried to attach a tracking packet to my responses, but he's using some kind of anonymizer program that is preventing me from inserting any kind of bug into his machine. His point of origin is cloaked exceptionally well."

"If you could send a worm back with an e-mail message, would we be able to locate him?" Cam was impressed with her newest team member.

The woman who looked like she might have come directly from a Paris fashion runway shrugged, another small frown line darting quickly between her arched brows. "Theoretically, yes. With what I've been able to gather, though, the FBI's attempts to do the same thing have failed as well. My guess is even if we get a fix on his machine, it will show up somewhere in Romania or the like. He's rerouting his messages through a gateway...probably several. It's still worth trying, but if we get him this way, it will be pure luck."

"This could go on for quite some time," Cam observed. "The two of you are going to need a break."

Mac protested, "We're fine, Commander."

"Don't worry. You won't be replaced if you get a little sleep."

Cam appreciated that Mac wanted to protect his position as the communications coordinator in the unfolding operation that the FBI had cleverly named Love Bug. It had taken a call to Stewart Carlisle along with a threat to go over his head to the director before Cam could get Mac and her new computer expert, Felicia Davis, online with Loverboy to begin with. She had argued that her team could more easily and efficiently provide the kinds of information that an online encounter would require. Loverboy would expect to be speaking with Blair Powell, and Cam's team knew her best.

Carlisle had agreed with her and had pulled a few strings of his own.

So, despite Doyle's objections, Cam at least had her people in on the ground floor of the operation. Nevertheless, the FBI were hovering, and Cam had a feeling they were just waiting for the slightest excuse to take over. She couldn't afford to have her agents burning out in the first few days of what might be a protracted campaign.

"I wouldn't put anything past Doyle," Mac griped.

"Don't waste energy worrying about him." Cam edged a hip up onto the counter and leaned forward, meeting Mac's concerned eyes. "You need to be completely focused on your interactions with Loverboy. Remember what Lindsey Ryan told us. He's very astute, and in all likelihood, he's been studying Egret for years. Granted, there isn't all that much information of a personal nature available on her in the public domain, but, still, he'll be suspicious if 'she' begins to behave out of character. To date, Ms. Powell has been very reluctant to have any kind of dialogue with him, and we're changing that. Any further alteration in the pattern is going to tip him off."

Davis nodded in agreement. "Understood, Commander. We've been watching both the length of the exchange and the exact nature of our responses very carefully. Nevertheless, I don't want to miss an incoming."

"Agent Ryan should be here within the next hour, and I would like to conference as soon as she arrives," Cam said. "After that, you're both off for six hours. And I mean out-of-here off."

They barely acknowledged her order before they turned back to a stack of printouts, heads close together, intent on reviewing all of the previous communications from their intended contact. Cam knew she was going to have to force them out of the command room later.

"I'll be upstairs in the Aerie," she said as she passed by the agent who was monitoring the building surveillance cameras.

"Roger," he acknowledged without taking his eyes from the screen.

None of her agents had strayed far from Command Central for the last eighteen hours. Once they had decided to go forward with the FBI's plan to lure Loverboy into a public confrontation, Cam had put them all on twelve-hour shifts, but she noticed that no one was actually gone for more than a few hours at a time. Everyone considered they had a personal stake in catching the man who had cost them all a friend and colleague.

She glanced at her watch. It was 1030, and it had been twenty-four hours since she had last seen Blair.

Blair stood before the canvas, a fine sable brush in one hand, lost in the sensation of color and contour, not thinking of anything at all. It took her a few seconds to recognize the sound at her door as knocking. She put the brush down and glanced once more at the painting, knowing that when she returned, she would have it.

She crossed the polished wood floor, glancing at the clock, and was surprised to find that she had been working for several hours. *Amazing. I hadn't thought I could.*

In fact, she hadn't thought that she would be able to do anything at all except wonder what was happening downstairs. That and think about what she intended to do about being crazy in love with her security chief.

She glanced through the peephole out of habit, and, as it always did whenever she saw Cam, her heart rate seemed to triple. She pulled the door open and leaned against the door frame, regarding the tall, dark-haired woman in the immaculately tailored suit.

"You're early for the briefing, Commander," she commented, blocking the doorway. "We aren't scheduled until three o'clock."

Cam nodded gravely. "I'm aware of that, Ms. Powell. However, I have some pressing matters to discuss with you."

"Oh?" Blair moved aside to let Cam enter, then closed the door nonchalantly. When Cam turned, however, Blair had silently moved very close to her. "And what matters would those be?" She slid her fingers under the edge of Cam's jacket, her voice a husky murmur.

Very slowly, Cam put her hands on Blair's waist and drew her near. Captivated by the variations of blue in her eyes, she answered, "Personal matters."

Then she lowered her head and kissed her. It was a long, slow, thorough kiss that spoke of longing and desire and something else. Something beyond words, at once tender and yet heavy with need. When she lifted her mouth from Blair's, they stood silently, arms around one another, just feeling.

Finally, Blair stepped back, a crooked smile on her lips. "I'm glad you had them turn off the surveillance cameras in here."

"So am I." Cam grinned. "Although this wasn't what I had in mind at the time."

"How's your hand?"

"Better."

"Who bandaged it?"

"No one." Cam held it up for inspection. "Just a few areas to cover. I did it myself."

"Good." Blair pressed her palm to Cam's chest, stroking her gently. "Did you sleep?"

"Some. The operation's under way—I can't be away long."

"Can you talk about what's happening with...all of it?"

"Well, my attention is on something different at the moment." Cam laughed, trying to ignore the deep insistent throbbing. "I'd better have some coffee if you want me to think."

Blair took her arm and started to pull her toward the kitchen. Then she hesitated, turned, and grasped Cam's face with both hands. She pulled her head down and kissed her, hard and fierce. When she drew back, her knees felt weak, and Cam looked slightly stunned.

"Well," Blair gasped, running her hands over Cam's chest. "Now I guess I'd better have some of that coffee, too."

A few moments later they sat facing one another at the counter, their hands lightly touching.

"What's going on?" Blair asked.

Cam told her about Doyle and Grant and the operation.

Blair watched Cam's face while she talked, listening for the things that weren't said out loud. She had spent her life listening to her father and his associates discuss everything from foreign policy to armed intervention, and she knew something about strategy. She also recognized when some things were being glossed over or omitted altogether.

"You can't intend for Grant to take him on herself?" she asked when Cam finished outlining the basics of the plan.

"No." Cam shook her head. "No, not at all. Once we establish rapport and convince Loverboy that he really is speaking to you, we hope he'll reveal something to help us trace him. Some reference to location, some historical fact—something to give us a fix on his physical location."

"And if that doesn't work?"

"Then we'll set up a meet, under the pretext that you don't want anyone else endangered, and lay a trap for him that way."

"He might just lay a trap...for me," Blair said. *And he lays his with bombs.*

"He might," Cam allowed. "But we'll have dozens of agents securing the area, and if he's anywhere near the meet site, which Ryan assures us he will be, we'll have him."

"What about Grant?"

Cam's stomach tightened but her voice was sure. Uncertainty could not be entertained once an operation was in progress. "She'll be wired and armored, and hopefully he won't get close enough to her to be any real threat. Remember, she's a decoy—we just need her to leave here as you, in case he's watching the building, and to be visible approaching the meet location. Eventually, he has to expose himself."

Silent for a moment, Blair then asked, "Who's going with her as backup?"

"About thirty federal agents and twice that many Staties. We'll have people covering her like a blanket."

"I meant on the ground. Close in." Blair leaned back, putting a little distance between them, suddenly wary. "You can't risk him seeing an intercept team and getting spooked, right?"

"You're right. Two agents will go in with her."

"Who?"

"Savard." Cam met Blair's eyes, adding softly, "And me."

Blair stood abruptly and walked to the far side of the loft. Her back to the room, she looked out the tall windows toward the park.

Cam sat still for a moment, her good sense warring with an uncomfortable need to make Blair understand. She stared across the room at Blair's rigid back, telling herself that she should simply go back to work and do what needed to be done. But if she did that, she knew she would only be bringing part of herself to the job. The other part would be wondering about Blair, and that fact aggravated her almost as much as the cold silence in the room.

"Blair," Cam said quietly, crossing to stand behind her. As much as she wanted to, she did not touch her because the anger was nearly a palpable barrier between them.

Not turning, Blair held up a hand, her voice harsh and clipped. "Don't, Cam. Do *not* tell me it's safe or any other such fairy tale about the brilliant planning of our security agencies. I know the track records."

Cam did touch her then, because she had to. The distance between them was harder and harder to bear. She didn't want to think about what that might mean, particularly not now. She rested her hands very lightly on Blair's waist, stepping near but not trying to hold her.

"Everyone agrees that the risk is low."

Blair made a faint choking sound that might have been a laugh or a sob. She turned abruptly and faced Cam, pushing her hands away. "Just when did you start thinking that I was stupid, Cam? Before or after we fucked?"

"God damn it, Blair," Cam growled, trying hard to hold onto her temper. "I know damn well you aren't stupid. The risks *are* low."

"I suppose you thought that it wouldn't occur to me that Jeremy Finch is dead and this maniac almost killed you once already? Do you think I've forgotten that? Or do you think I've simply lost my mind?"

"If anyone has lost their mind, it's me," Cam snapped, her dark eyes flashing with fury. "And it *wasn't* when we fucked. It happened the first time I walked into this room and you had the arrogance to come on to me like I was some rookie you could lead around by my proverbial dick."

"Well, that didn't work very well, did it?" Blair seethed, looking pointedly at Cam's crotch and then back to her face. "And it has nothing to do with the particulars of your anatomy."

"Actually, it must have worked"—Cam was irritated, running a hand through her hair, tousling the dark locks into the disheveled look that Blair found so sexy—"because I haven't been able to make a single decision since that morning without worrying about you."

Blair stared at her, remembering their first meeting and her surprise at discovering that her new security chief not only wasn't intimidated by her but also actually seemed intent on working with her. "I never asked you to worry about me," she remarked, the sharp edges of her rage softening as she looked at her.

"I know that," Cam said, her voice intense, "but I do." She waited a beat, letting her temper cool, and then said more quietly, "I didn't want you to care about me."

"I know that," Blair whispered, and added even more softly, "but I do."

They both moved at once, closing the distance, slipping into one another's arms.

"I'll be careful..."

"Be careful..."

Cam kissed Blair's temple, murmuring, "I'll wear a vest, and I'll have Savard. She's good. We'll be in radio contact with Doyle's team. We'll have plenty of backup."

Blair pressed her lips to Cam's neck, feeling her blood pulse through the arteries just under the skin. So fragile. She took a deep breath, forcing the fear away, burying it deep inside.

"Savard'd better be as good as she looks," she threatened, "or I'll be forced to hurt her."

Chapter Twenty

Early the next morning, Cam leaned over an array of printouts on the table in the glass-walled conference room, talking to Patrick Doyle. She was working hard to ignore her intense dislike for the man.

Just get the job done and make sure Grant is well protected in the process. That's all that matters, she reminded herself.

When Doyle failed to respond to one of her questions, she glanced up from the transcript of the last communication with Loverboy and caught the FBI agent staring past her through the glass partition into the main area of the command center. The look on his face was a startling mixture of displeasure and something that looked very much like lust.

She turned and followed his gaze. When she saw that he was looking at Blair, her simmering anger flashed hotly into fury. The way he stared at her was an invasion.

"Do you have a problem of some kind, Doyle?" she demanded.

"You don't seem to have much control over her, Roberts," Doyle said derisively. "She shouldn't be down here."

"It's not my job to *control* her," Cam said as evenly as she could. "And there is absolutely no reason that she shouldn't go anywhere she likes."

He studied her as if she were some strange life form. "Civilians complicate matters, Roberts. Especially civilians with opinions…and friends in high places."

"I'm not concerned about anything that Ms. Powell might have to say to anyone about anything." Cam folded up her notebook and turned to leave.

"You might change your mind before this is all over," he called after her.

She closed the door without looking back and threaded her way through the desks and the mountains of monitoring equipment that seemed to grow in number and complexity every day. Their working space had previously been adequate for routine day-to-day matters. But now that Doyle's team had practically moved on site, Lindsey Ryan was staying to monitor the Internet communications with their UNSUB and the ATF bomb squad was coming and going with information about the latest analysis on the bomb fragments from the park. The room was crowded with people and makeshift workstations.

Nevertheless, the communications station at the far end of the room remained somewhat insulated from the rest of the activity. Everyone knew that Felicia Davis should not be distracted. Mac was with her most of the time, primarily to retrieve any data that she might need quickly in order to respond to Loverboy.

At the moment, though, Blair was leaning down and speaking to Davis. Both women appeared oblivious to the activity in the rest of the room.

It was the second full day of the operation, and there had only been sparse e-mail exchange between Davis, posing as Blair, and Loverboy. A temporal analysis of his previous communications revealed that he sent a message nearly every day. Frequently, it was only a few words or a single line.

Lindsey Ryan hypothesized that he not only needed to satisfy his compulsion to communicate with Blair but that he also wanted to demonstrate that he *could* reach her. His skills extended beyond bomb-making and marksmanship, and, despite all attempts to thwart him with shields and aliases and rerouting her mail servers, it never took him long to track her down.

Blair tolerated his messages because she refused to give up her own access to the Internet, and in an oddly understandable way, she had not wanted to be cut off from him either. She would not live in a cocoon as if nothing were happening. She wanted to *hear* his voice if he was threatening her.

As Cam drew near, she heard Blair say, "I'm the best one to do this."

Immediately, her stomach churned uneasily, because she had a feeling she knew what Blair was talking about. She had defended Blair's presence in the command center to Doyle, and she believed precisely what she had said. In point of fact, though, she hoped that Blair would stay away, if only because the tension and uncertainty were wearing for all of them, and she wished to spare her that. But in her heart, she had expected something like this.

Blair straightened and nodded to Cam, revealing none of the quick pleasure she took in seeing her. "Good morning, Commander."

"Ms. Powell," Cam said warmly, stopping behind the chairs occupied by Mac and Felicia Davis. "Is there some way I can be of service?"

Blair struggled not to smile, but she knew Cam could see the laughter in her eyes. She resisted the urge to make a clever comeback, only because she didn't trust her voice not to give her away. Being around Cam never failed to arouse her, and she knew it would show in the timbre of her voice. It was bad enough she could feel the liquid heat beginning between her legs.

"It occurred to me this morning, Commander, that I should be the one e-mailing Loverboy. There's no reason to use a go-between in this exchange."

Cam hesitated for a moment, needing the time to formulate an answer that would be both honest and convincing. She wouldn't lie to her, not only because she had never been able to but also because she could not bring herself even to try. On the other hand, the thought of Blair being involved so intimately with this man, even when there was no chance of physical connection between them, made her almost physically ill.

"The reason we're using an agent is because our people know how to manipulate the conversation to get the information we need. Plus, Agent Davis is aware of the things we need to know to secure the meeting site."

Blair listened, watching Cam's face carefully. Her security chief was very good at keeping her emotions completely compartmentalized. Her *lover*, however, was not. There was a flicker of worry in Cam's eyes—worry for *her*—and Blair saw it. She smiled in agreement.

"That makes perfect sense, Commander. However, I don't propose to start e-mailing him from my apartment. I would do everything right here with Mac and Agent Davis by my side. They could certainly coach me in any procedural things I might need to say much more easily than Agent Davis could pretend to be me. It seems to me there's far less likelihood that he would become suspicious if it actually *was* me."

Cam glanced at Mac, who raised an eyebrow slightly and nodded even more imperceptibly.

"You've caught me somewhat unprepared, Ms. Powell," Cam said, and this time Blair could read nothing in her eyes. "I need to discuss this with Agent Ryan and some others."

"I understand. Would you let me know what you think once you've done that?"

"Certainly."

Blair watched Cam walk away and wondered just how angry she really was.

❖

"You outflanked me down there," Cam said when she stepped into the loft.

Blair leaned against the arm of her leather sofa, regarding Cam carefully. She hadn't moved nearer once the door was closed, and her hands were in her pockets. She definitely had her game face on.

"You know," Blair said, "I haven't touched you in almost a day. I don't think I have the energy to fight."

Cam sighed and took her hands from her pockets. She shrugged out of her blazer and released the buckle on her shoulder harness, easing it off her still-sore right shoulder and placing it with her jacket. As she walked the few steps toward Blair, she pulled her shirt from beneath the waistband of her trousers. She didn't stop moving when she reached Blair, but put one thigh between Blair's legs and a hand behind her back, and then tumbled her over the arm of the plush leather sofa onto the seat.

Cam ended up on top and pushed herself up with her good arm so she could see Blair's face. No games between them, her voice was low and warm. "You can touch me now."

Blair slid both hands under the tail of Cam's shirt and raked her nails up Cam's sides, drawing a swift gasp. When she reached her breasts, she caressed them softly, tightening her fingers on the small, hard nipples.

Cam closed her eyes and groaned. Blair kept up the rhythm, squeeze and release, squeeze and release, until Cam was stiff with the pleasure-pain of it and trembling.

"That's good."

"Very good," Blair whispered.

Their legs entwined, and Blair felt Cam's heat against her thigh even as she felt her own arousal soaking into her jeans. When Cam caught the tender skin at the base of her neck between her teeth, Blair cried out once, sharply, and then managed to speak.

"Bedroom. Bed. I need you naked on me."

Vaguely, Cam could hear her, but the words weren't registering as she thrust her hips faster into Blair's. After they had been apart, it was always like this. She couldn't control the rocketing surge of excitement that brought her too high too fast, until she was teetering on the brink and ready to go off in seconds.

She was ready now, she could feel it curling in the base of her spine, tingling down her legs, cramping in her muscles. Oh yeah, she was going off soon.

Blair pushed Cam's hips away, breaking their contact, dragging Cam back from the edge. Cam gasped, lowering her forehead to Blair's chest, shuddering uncontrollably.

"I'm sorry," she groaned. "I can't hold it back."

One hand caressing the damp strands of hair at the back of Cam's neck, Blair eased away from her. "Yes, you can," she crooned softly. "Remember, you're a Secret Service agent."

Cam laughed shakily and sat up, her hands falling open by her sides. Her shirt was open, her body on fire and glistening with sweat. "I'm afraid I'm compromised."

"Just the way I like you." Blair held out her hand, her color high and her eyes blazing. "Let's go do that some more."

By the time they reached the bedroom, Cam had regained a slim thread of control. She managed to undress and lie down next to Blair. "Let me just touch you for a minute." Her voice was still unsteady. "I don't trust myself just yet, and I don't want to come right away."

"It's a tough order to follow, Commander, but I'll try," Blair said with a smile.

Cam started at Blair's shoulders and ran her hands down the toned body, watching in wonder as the fine muscles shimmered under her fingertips and the blood rose to warm the skin beneath her palms. Blair's breath came fast, and every now and then, a small sound of pleasure escaped her. When Cam trailed her fingers lightly up the inside of her thigh, Blair arched her hips and the fingers laced through Cam's hair trembled with urgency.

"You have the sweetest touch," Blair whispered, her voice choked with need.

Cam, too, was barely breathing. Every time they were together like this, the pleasure was so intense, she felt as if she was bleeding. She had never felt so vulnerable—or so helpless, or so blessed. It was almost more than she could tolerate.

She slid one finger between Blair's legs, tracing the delicate folds and swollen ridges. Blair's pulse raced against her fingertips, and when she brushed lightly along the underside of her clitoris, Blair jerked in her arms. She circled harder and put her mouth to Blair's, wanting her breath, wanting her blood, wanting all of her.

Blair wrapped her arms around Cam's shoulders, pressing her breasts to Cam's chest, clinging to her, desperate for the sweet release. She rocked her hips faster against Cam's hand, knowing she would come any second.

Feeling Blair's heart hammer against her own, Cam let loose her control, allowing the tension in her body to rise. When she knew Blair was there, she lifted her lips from Blair's and said softly against her ear, "Touch me now."

Ready to explode, Blair reached for her blindly. When she found her—hard and swollen and so ready—she couldn't stop her own momentum. Even as it began, wrenching through her, forcing her almost double with the clench of muscles deep inside, she pressed her fingers along Cam's length the way she knew Cam needed it.

Cam jerked and groaned and came with her.

Then they held one another and rested.

❖

Cam slept, her head on Blair's chest. Blair ran her fingers absently through Cam's hair, marveling at the sensation of being able to hold her. One floor below them, a dramatic tableau played out; but here, for the moment, all that mattered was the woman in her arms. It was unnerving, and more than a little terrifying.

She had spent most of her life surrounded by people, yet alone. She had learned to ignore the isolation and had discovered in her solitude the creative insight that inspired her art. Her work centered and defined her, and she would not change that. But each time she opened herself a little more to Cameron, she discovered another place in herself, another dimension of emotion. What frightened her most was the knowledge that without Cam those places would ache, empty and waiting—a deadly wound she would never be able to heal. She shivered and held Cam closer.

"Cold?" Cam murmured.

"No, not really." Blair's voice was still unsteady. Loving was a dangerous thing, the cost so high, and she struggled not to flee.

Cam moved her hand from Blair's thigh, where it had lain since she had fallen asleep, and brought it to Blair's breast, softly caressing the firm warm flesh. She moved her head an inch and lightly kissed the tight pink nipple.

"What is it, then?"

"Nothing," Blair said quietly.

Cam nuzzled her face against the side of Blair's neck and whispered, "Blair." She kissed the curve of her jaw. "I love you."

Blair caught her breath, trapped between need and a lifetime of denying it. "Cam," she breathed, amazed and still uncertain.

Pushing herself up on one elbow, Cam gently traced her fingers over Blair's face and down her neck, finding in her unguarded gaze what Blair could not put into words. "It's all right," she said gently.

"So you say," Blair whispered, wishing she could just keep her lover there, where it was safe.

"I should go." Cam was reluctant but moved away a little because the heat of Blair's skin was arousing her again. She kissed the tip of Blair's chin and then her mouth. "I'll be back."

"Good." Blair raised her head to claim Cam's mouth one last time.

A few moments later, she sat curled up on the sofa in nothing but an oversized T-shirt, watching Cam pull her clothes into order and strap on her weapon.

"Are you very angry about this morning?"

Cam stopped what she was doing and looked at Blair, who still wore a slightly bruised and hazy expression from their recent lovemaking. She wanted nothing in that moment as much as she wanted to touch her again.

"Probably," she said, reaching for her jacket.

"I thought you might be."

Fully clothed now, Cam regarded Blair steadily. "Then why did you do it?"

"Because I thought it was the right thing to do."

Cam blew out a breath and looked past Blair toward the wide, tall windows and the golden afternoon sun visible beyond. She forced herself to ignore her concerns and consider the facts. She tried not to think about Blair talking to him. She tried not to think about the fact that this nameless, faceless man wanted Blair, that he lay awake at night thinking about touching her, that during the day he set traps to destroy her.

She finally looked back to Blair. "You were right."

Cam turned and started for the door, and Blair rose quickly to follow. Just as Cam grasped the doorknob, she threaded her arms around Cam's waist from behind and lay her cheek against Cam's back. "I'll be down in a little while," she said softly.

"Yes."

"It wasn't my intention to make you angry."

Cam turned and gently lifted Blair's face in both hands. She looked into her deep blue eyes. "I know it wasn't, but I have a feeling that you would have done it no matter what."

Her voice completely serious, Blair asked, "Is that a problem, then?"

"Only when I'm not thinking with my head," Cam murmured, falling into those eyes.

Blair smiled, smoothing her hand down Cam's chest and hooking her fingers under the waistband of her trousers. She tugged lightly and replied, "Well then, hopefully we can count on that kind of problem fairly often."

"Apparently that would be the case," Cam said, resisting the urge to slip her hands under Blair's T-shirt. If she did that, she wouldn't stop until she had her again, right there on the spot. She kissed her once, hard and sure, and then pulled away. As she stepped through the door, she said briskly, "I'll see you shortly then, Ms. Powell."

"Certainly, Commander," Blair called after her, lingering just a moment to watch her walk down the hall. Then she closed the door and went to prepare herself.

❖

Blair sat at the long console table in loose cotton pants and an open-collared, pale blue linen shirt, flanked by Felicia Davis and Mac. Partially full Styrofoam cups of coffee, long cold, sat interspersed with keyboards, headsets, and monitors. She stretched and sighed.

"Tired?" a familiar deep voice asked from behind her.

So quickly she might have imagined it if her skin hadn't begun to tingle, Blair felt the fleeting brush of fingers across her arm. Slowly, she turned her chair and glanced up at Cam. She smiled softly. "A little."

"Why don't all of you take a break," Cam said to the three of them. "I'll have one of the FBI people watch the incomings for a few hours."

"What did Agent Ryan say our approach should be?" Blair asked, ignoring the suggestion to leave. She, Mac, and Felicia had been alternating breaks, and she was fine. "We should have contact any time. It's been almost twenty-four hours."

"She said it was time to push," Cam reported almost reluctantly.

What the profiler had in fact said was that they were running out of time. Ryan anticipated that Loverboy would make another strike imminently. His pattern suggested an extremely low restraint level that was rapidly deteriorating. Since Blair had not been outside the building in over seventy-two hours, he was completely cut off from her. If Blair didn't engage him verbally, he was very likely to take action, and Lindsey admitted that she had no idea what form that attack might take.

Cam studied Blair, acutely aware of the faint circles under her eyes and the weary set to her shoulders. She wanted to tell her to go upstairs and get some sleep. She wanted to tell her to stay away from all of this. She wanted to tell her that this was *her* job, and she would damn well handle it.

What she said was, "Lindsey said it's up to you. She said follow your instincts."

Blair straightened, staring at the monitor as if she could will a message to appear. "Well then, let's get down and dirty."

Three hours later, it began.

```
A001@worldnet.com: I've missed you,
    Blair. Are you hiding?
NYC1112@freemail.com: I got your message.
    Let's talk.
```

The four people watching the monitor held their collective breath. It was the first time that Egret had suggested a real-time chat. If it spooked him and he terminated all e-mail contact, they might lose their only conduit of communication at a time when information was critical.

"Come on, you prick, bite," Mac muttered. He rocked in his seat, his body so tense he vibrated. *God, I want this guy.*

Looking at Blair, who sat with her hands poised on the keyboard, focused and intent, Cam clenched her fists and shoved her hands into her pockets, torn between wanting him to answer and wishing he would disappear into the amorphous world of cyberspace.

Felicia Davis calmly readied the backup drives and prepared yet another worm to launch. "One of these times I'll get you," she said under her breath. He was out there, not so very far away; she could feel him on the line. Her fingers raced on the keys with the speed and sixth sense of an expert hacker.

Blair waited. She knew what none of the others understood. No matter what anyone said, this *was* about her—it had always been about her. She *was* the woman the cameras captured and the newspapers wrote about, just as she was the woman who painted late into the still night, and the woman who trembled helplessly in Cameron Roberts's arms. He simply wanted the woman that the world had made its own.

She breathed out slowly as the lines appeared.

```
A001@worldnet.com: Go to www.privatetalk.
    com, the game room.
```

```
NYC1112@freemail.com:   How  will  I  find
    you?
A001@worldnet.com: Don't worry. I'll find
    you.
```

Blair didn't hesitate.

```
NYC1112@freemail.com: I'll be waiting.
```

Chapter Twenty-one

Operation: Love Bug
0545

Lindsey Ryan sat alone in the conference room, a can of soda by her right hand and stacks of papers and folders scattered around her. She leaned her head in her left palm and drummed a pencil on the tabletop as she stared at a computer printout. Startled out of concentration, she jumped at the sound of the deep quiet voice from behind her.

"What do you think?"

Lindsey looked up as Cam approached, noticing the very fine lines of stress around her eyes. Other than that small sign, the security chief didn't appear to have a concern in the world. Except that Lindsey knew that the commander hadn't slept more than an hour or two in the last three days, unless she did it with her eyes open. She was rarely out of the command center.

"I think he's crazy as a loon."

"Me, too." Cam smiled grimly. "Will he show?"

Ryan sighed and looked back at the critical portion of the transcript for the hundredth time.

```
A001@worldnet.com: Why won't you believe
    me?
NYC1112@freemail.com: About what?
A001@worldnet.com: That I worship you.
    You're all I care about.
```

```
NYC1112@freemail.com:    Maybe    because
    you're  threatening  my  friends  and
    killing people.
A001@worldnet.com: You don't leave me any
    choice. You ignore me.
NYC1112@freemail.com:  I'm  not  ignoring
    you now.
A001@worldnet.com: This isn't enough.
NYC1112@freemail.com:  What  more  do  you
    want?
A001@worldnet.com: I want to see you. I
    want to make you understand.
NYC1112@freemail.com: Do you really love
    me?
A001@worldnet.com: I live for you.
NYC1112@freemail.com: If I meet you, will
    you stop the killing?
A001@worldnet.com: Yes.
NYC1112@freemail.com: Do you promise?
A001@worldnet.com:  I  have  been  patient
    long  enough.  You  know  what  I'll  do
    if you deny me. You'll have no one to
    blame but yourself.
```

Lindsey pointed to the last lines. "Here's the problem part. Until this point in the exchange, he's negotiating. But the minute Egret questions him, which, by the way, I'm glad she did—it's in character for her—he reverts to threats."

Cam's stomach clenched. "Is he threatening *her*?"

"Probably." Lindsey hesitated. "Yes...I think yes. He's had his fill of substitutes, I think. He wants her and no one else. If he can't have her now, I'd say that she'll become his target, and he won't stop until you catch him."

Rubbing her eyes, Cam pulled out the chair next to her and sat. "What does that mean for the operation? Will he show?"

"He's highly intelligent, so he must suspect a trap. On the other hand, he's arrogant and believes that he can't be caught. It depends on the balance between his ability to think rationally and his need to see her—to touch her—in the flesh. By now, he must be wild for her. So...

maybe."

"I need better than *maybe*, Ryan," Cam said adamantly. "I've got an agent going into that meet alone. And I've got Egret locked up in here and I can't keep her here forever." She repeated, "Will he be there?"

Lindsey considered the image of the man she had formed in her mind after spending dozens of hours reading his messages to Blair Powell. He was completely and totally obsessed with the president's daughter, and he spent every second of every day thinking about her. He fantasized about her returning his affections, about her fulfilling his needs. He had built an elaborate delusional system with her as his psychosexual center; he had resorted to violence to make her recognize his desires.

"He'll be there."

Cam stood, satisfied. They had less than a day to prepare, and even though Doyle was coordinating the teams, she was reviewing everything herself. Ellen Grant was going in with every bit of protection Cam could give her.

"Why is he doing this? Agreeing to this meet?" Cam asked finally. "He must know we'll be all over that place."

Lindsey shrugged. "Ms. Powell assured him that she would not reveal their plans. He *needs* to believe that, because he needs to believe that she desires him the way he desires her. The rational part of him will be suspicious, but the psychotic part desperately needs to believe that she is coming to him out of mutual love and desire."

"What if he discovers that she betrayed him?"

Lindsey Ryan said quietly, "Then he'll kill her...or anyone we send in her place."

1030

Stark found Savard in the workout room down the hall from the command center. The FBI agent was wearing black Lycra shorts and a sports bra, and she was punching the hell out of a heavy hanging bag. The sweat on her skin made its coffee color shine like bronze, and Stark felt her mouth go dry watching her. She'd looked like a gazelle running that day in the park—*Jesus, when was that—only six days ago?*

But now, with her muscles tensing under her smooth skin and the swift, even recoil of her limbs as she danced around the swinging bag, she looked more like a leopard running its prey to ground.

Savard looked over and saw Stark standing there, an expression on her face that would have surely made the Secret Service agent blush if she'd seen herself. Smiling, Savard thundered one last right hook into the leather. Then she wiped her forearm across her face, shook most of the sweat from her hair, and walked over to the other agent.

"Any news?"

Stark shook her head. "Still a green light for tonight."

"Good," Savard grunted, working at the laces on her right glove with her teeth. "It's time to put this bastard away."

"Here, let me get that," Stark said, reaching for the ties on the heavy boxing glove. Her hands were shaking. *God.*

"You okay?" Savard took a good look at her companion. The bruises had faded from around Stark's eyes, but the stitches were still there, a neat row of tiny black ants marching across her smooth pale forehead. Tenderly, she inquired, "Does your head still hurt?"

"No." Stark kept her head bent as she worked at the stubborn knot in the laces. "It's fine."

Savard raised the other glove until it rested under Paula Stark's chin and then gently pushed, forcing her head up, forcing Stark to look at her. "Do you want to tell me what's wrong?"

"It's going to get hectic later. I just..." Stark faltered, struggling to express emotions she scarcely understood herself. "I'll be in one of the backup cars. I probably won't see you alone again before you go."

Savard waited.

Stark swallowed. "I just wanted to remind you that we...uh...that later...when you get back..."

"I know. We have a date. I won't forget," Savard said warmly. She leaned forward and kissed her very lightly on the mouth. "You're brave, you know." She wasn't talking about the job.

"Not so very," Stark whispered, trembling in a place she had never trembled before.

"I'll see you when it's over," Savard murmured, then stepped around her and disappeared.

Stark closed her eyes, feeling the kiss still soft upon her lips. *Please just come back.*

1530

Cam stood in the rear of the room, listening while Doyle outlined the operation assignments to the FBI, ATF, tactical unit, and bomb squads. The state police were detailed to secure the perimeter with roadblocks, once the assault and capture teams were in place. So the sector captain was there, too.

Eight hours to go.

Cam was there because she wanted to know where everyone else would be if things started to go bad. Ellen Grant would not be caught in anybody's crossfire, because Cam intended to be right on her heels. She had been involved in the planning from the minute Loverboy took the bait and gave Blair the location—an abandoned amusement park. Doyle couldn't keep her out since he was using her agent.

Catching Grant's attention as Doyle wrapped up the briefing, Cam motioned with her head to the hallway outside.

"You okay?" she asked when they were out of earshot of the others.

Grant nodded. "Fine."

"Savard will wire you before you armor up," Cam reminded her. "I want to hear your voice every step. Everything you hear, everything you see, everything you *think* you see—I want to know about it."

"Yes, ma'am."

"You key on my voice. You do not engage, you do not intercept, unless you hear it from me."

Grant looked at her, a question in her eyes. SAC Doyle had said *he* would relay her orders from where he was stationed—a surveillance post on top of a warehouse five hundred yards from the contact point.

Cam saw her uncertainty. "I'll be on the ground with Savard, closer to you than anyone else. I'll hear the directives at the same time you do. And I'll have a better read on the situation than he will. You go when I confirm, understood?"

"Yes, ma'am, I understand. Thank you." Grant hesitated a second, then added, "Commander, my husband's on patrol tonight. I'll leave his number—"

"The only person," Cam interrupted firmly, "calling your husband tonight, Agent Grant, will be you when this action is over. Are we clear on that?"

"Yes, ma'am." Grant smiled gratefully. "Quite clear."

"Good, then go get some rest."

Cam watched her walk away and checked her watch. Then she went in search of Savard.

1730

Savard was laying out body armor and sorting rounds of ammunition in the small weapons room next to the main command center when Cam found her.

"Everything in order?"

She glanced up and nodded. "Yes, ma'am. Locked and loaded."

"Good," Cam leaned against the doorway, her arms folded over her chest. "About tonight..."

"Yes?" Savard noted the hard stillness in her eyes. There was a finality there that told her whatever was coming was not going to be negotiable.

"Ellen Grant is mine," Cam said quietly. "No one is going to order her into danger except me."

Savard thought hard about that, because she knew that Doyle expected to control Grant's movements. According to the book, she should go to the SAC now and inform him that there was a conflict in command. Roberts was giving her a choice. Which meant that she was also giving her the responsibility, and the accountability. Once they reached the rendezvous, there would just be the four of them—Grant, Roberts, her...and Loverboy. It came down to who she wanted to make the final call, and whose judgment she wanted to rely on in the heat of the moment.

"You'll be the senior agent in the field, Commander," she said quite clearly. "I have no problem with you making the call."

Cam nodded and straightened up. *Right. Now I still need to go over the comm links with Mac and then review the construction plans from the city planning office for the amusement park. I also need—*

"Commander?" Savard broke into her thoughts.

"Yes?"

"You'll need to be fresh, too, and you haven't had much sleep the last couple of days."

Cam raised an eyebrow, surprised by her frankness.

"There's still a few hours before we have to gear up," Savard added.

"I'll take that under advisement. Thank you, Agent."

Savard took one step forward, reached to touch her, then stopped. "We're all trained for this. It must be very difficult for someone who isn't—the uncertainty of it all." She hesitated, then added, "She'll need to hear that you'll be back."

Cam stared at her, expressionless for what seemed like an interminable length of time, before a grin lifted one corner of her mouth. "They certainly aren't making FBI agents the way they used to."

Savard grinned back. "No, ma'am, they're not."

1800

For the third time in as many days, Cam stood at Blair's door, knowing that when she crossed the threshold, her life would change. Each time she stepped outside of her comfortable world of regulations and routine to enter the uncertain arena of her relationship with Blair, she came away more deeply bound to her. It wasn't easy, but she couldn't deny that she wanted it. More than that, she couldn't deny that she needed it.

Blair opened the door and said softly, "Hi."

"Hi," Cam said, not yet moving to enter. Blair looked tired and that was unusual for her. There were smudges of fatigue under her eyes, and the smile she offered Cam was tinged with sadness. Reaching out, Cam ran her fingertips over Blair's cheek. "Have you slept?"

Blair shook her head. "I meant to, but I couldn't stop thinking."

"You should try," Cam said gently. "It's going to be a long night."

"I know," Blair answered.

She wanted to pull her inside. But she also knew that she wanted to *keep* her inside, away from the night, away from the danger, and that wasn't her choice to make. It hurt to think that Cam would not choose safety over responsibility, even for her. So she stood waiting, wondering what it was that Cam really wanted.

Finally she said, "I wasn't sure you would come."

"I'm sorry you didn't know that," Cam murmured, lifting her fingers to Blair's face again. "I'm sorry for the pain of all of this."

"No," Blair said quickly. "That's not your doing. It never has been."

"I could have done things differently," Cam said. "Between us."

Blair smiled at that, a faint fond smile. "Could you have?"

"No, I guess not." Cam shook her head regretfully. "But I *wish* that I could have, so as not to hurt you."

"That just might be enough," Blair admitted, because she couldn't imagine which part of Cam could be changed without destroying some essential element of her. She feared that to change her would be to lose her.

"Blair," Cam said urgently, "I want you to know—"

"Don't." Blair stopped her with her fingers on her lips. "You don't need to say anything else. Will you come in now?"

Cam kissed her fingertips. "Yes."

"Can you stay?" she asked again.

"For a little while."

"That won't always be enough," Blair warned, but there was no anger in her voice.

"I understand," Cam replied, stepping across the threshold. "But I won't always be leaving."

Then Cam was inside, and Blair closed the door, and they were alone. She raised her arms to Cam's shoulders and moved up against her, resting her face on Cam's shoulder. She sighed, and as she couldn't seem to do before, she let go of everything in her mind and floated in the certainty of Cam's embrace.

"Let's go to bed," she finally murmured. "I need to hold you."

"Yes," Cam answered quietly, her lips moving gently on Blair's ear. "I need to tell you things."

And then they were naked in one another's arms, face-to-face, covered only by a light cotton sheet. Slowly, they kissed, each exploring the other anew with gentle strokes and tender caresses. They didn't hurry but touched with absolute certainty, as if there had been no beginning and there would be no ending. Slowly, they stirred one another until they trembled together, breathless and poised on the precipice, ready to fall.

Blair brought one leg over Cam's hips, opening herself, as she stared into Cam's eyes.

"Come inside," she whispered.

Cam slid her hand between their bodies, her fingers parting the swollen flesh, gliding over Blair's clitoris, making her gasp and quiver.

"In a minute," she whispered back.

Their eyes locked as Cam held her tightly, drawing fingers lightly back and forth over the exposed, exquisitely sensitive tip. Blair's fingers dug into her arm, and Cam murmured, "There's no hurry. Let me have you."

Blair was barely breathing, her muscles clenched and begging for release, every cell focused on the overpowering pleasure rippling under Cam's fingertips.

"Oh please," she moaned at last. "Let me come."

Cam pressed harder, circling faster, each knowing stroke bringing her lover slowly but steadily to orgasm. She watched Blair's blue eyes darken to purple and lose focus.

"I love you," she whispered as Blair threw her head back and cried out sharply, pushing down hard against Cam's hand. She entered her then, prolonging the spasms with each thrust until Blair grew quiet and sagged against her.

"You wreck me," Blair gasped finally.

Cam wrapped both arms around her. "I meant to."

"Just give me a minute to catch my breath." Blair pressed her lips to Cam's shoulder, wondering if she would ever recover, not from the pleasure, but from the agony of loving her so much.

"I'm okay," Cam answered, kissing Blair's temple.

"Bullshit," Blair laughed softly. "I can feel you on my leg, and you're a long ways from being okay."

To prove her point, Blair pressed her thigh hard between Cam's legs, and Cam groaned at the rapid surge of blood into her clitoris.

"No fair," she gasped.

"Yes, fair," Blair said firmly, pushing Cam onto her back and rolling on top of her. "I told you I just needed a minute."

Cam looked up at her and grinned. "That's probably all I'll need, too."

"Oh no, Commander," Blair said. "I want much more than that from you."

And then Blair took her slowly, with her mouth and her hands and her tender caresses, drawing the fire from Cam's blood and the heat from her bones, igniting her nerves and scorching her senses, until all Cam knew was Blair, and all she could do was cry out her name.

They slept for an hour and awakened together, just on the other side of darkness. They lay side by side, hands clasped, their fingers entwined.

"What happens now?" Blair asked in the stillness.

Cam spoke quietly, her voice steady and calm. "At 2300 hours, Savard and I will leave for the rendezvous site. Thirty minutes later, Ellen Grant will walk out the front entrance and flag down a cab. Stark and Fielding will be in that cab. It will look like you have once again slipped by us and are on your way to him. We're assuming that Loverboy may be watching here to assure himself that you are really going to meet him, and that you're coming alone as you said that you would."

"So how will *he* get to the meeting site on time, if he's here when Grant leaves?"

"It's possible that he has someone else watching the building for him and relaying a message. Besides, he doesn't actually have to be there first, since he hasn't designated a precise rendezvous point. He's too smart for that—he just said the refreshment stand in the arcade. It's too general a location—he could be anywhere. Grant will have to wait for some sign from him."

"Why that site, do you think?"

"Lindsey Ryan speculates that he chose it some time ago, and I agree. He was prepared when you agreed to meet him. He named that place and time almost immediately. It may have just been his fantasy that you would someday come to him, but Ryan thinks he's actually been there, and may have already *readied* it for you."

"Readied it...how?" Blair shivered at the thought of someone creating these elaborate fantasies with her as the star. It made her feel as if someone had been touching her while she slept.

Cam slipped her arm around her shoulder and drew her near. "Blair, you don't need to hear all of this."

"No," Blair said quickly, her voice strong and determined. "I want to know. All of it."

"Okay," Cam continued with a sigh. "He'll either follow Grant to the site or use an alternate route to arrive before her. Since he's familiar with the area, we assume that he'll have planned a way into the arcade without detection. The snipers and the ground team will already be in place when she arrives."

"But she's not really going to meet him, is she?" Blair asked worriedly.

"No," Cam said. "Doyle's team and the TAC squad will have infrared heat-sensitive scopes that can pinpoint the location of any living thing bigger than a dumpster rat within a hundred yards of the meet site. They'll home in on him and take him out. Grant's only role is to leave here as you and get out of the cab at the entrance to the amusement park. She's not actually going to enter the arcade."

"And you and Savard?" Blair asked, her heart pounding.

Cam leaned up on one elbow so that she could look into Blair's eyes. The room lights were off, but the streetlights outside the loft windows were enough for them to see each other.

"We'll be there for ground support only, to assure that Grant is covered if any action takes place near her and to get her to the evacuation vehicle that will be nearby. Escort duty only."

"Is that all of it, Cam?"

"That's the plan, Blair." Cam held her gaze. "I won't tell you that unexpected things don't happen, but there will be a hundred agents right behind us and about that many state police watching the perimeter. It's as solid as these things get."

Blair ran her hand through Cam's hair, then tightened her fingers in the thick strands, pulling Cam's head down close to her face. "I can't take anyone else leaving me."

"I won't," Cam vowed. "I swear."

"Well, that's reassuring," Blair whispered, "because I know your word is good."

Then, in the last moment left to them, they sealed their promises, simply and surely, with a kiss.

CHAPTER TWENTY-TWO

At twenty minutes to midnight, Blair walked into the command center. She halted just inside the door, momentarily disoriented. The room was brightly lit yet eerily deserted. Monitors flickered with images that no one watched. Chairs stood askew in front of desks littered with coffee cups and food wrappers, as if abandoned in haste. Here and there a jacket or sweater lay forsaken on a counter. The atmosphere of control she was accustomed to had been replaced by a lingering sense of chaos that made her heart beat uneasily.

"Ms. Powell?" Lindsey Ryan approached with a cup of coffee in her hand and a question in her eyes.

Startled, Blair jumped. She turned toward the voice and smiled ruefully.

"I couldn't wait upstairs."

"I'm not surprised." Lindsey nodded sympathetically. "Would you like some coffee?"

Blair struggled to get a grip on her nerves. "I don't suppose you know who made it, do you? I've had the coffee some of these people make, and it's an adventure I'm not up to at the moment."

"Actually, I just made it myself," Ryan said with a laugh. "Mac and Felicia are both glued to the communication consoles, and they probably need it by now."

"I can imagine," Blair murmured, thinking of the twenty-four restless, anxious hours she had spent with them waiting for Loverboy to contact her. She stepped farther into the room and looked toward the far end where the communication equipment covered the entire wall and every surface within reach of the swivel chairs where Mac and Felicia

Davis still sat. She was certain that they hadn't moved in days.

"I'll take your word that it's safe, then," Blair said, indicating the coffee. "I could use it."

The two women walked back to the small alcove where the coffee machines and refrigerator were housed. Blair poured coffee, then raised the Styrofoam cup to her lips and sipped cautiously. Ryan was right; it wasn't bad. She settled her hips against the edge of the counter and regarded the redhead. "Is there any word?"

"Not yet. Mac has a direct line to Commander Roberts, but all we know is that she and Savard are on site." Lindsey hesitated, then added carefully, "Ms. Powell, we can only get a small piece of the picture from here, and sometimes an incomplete picture is worse than no picture at all."

"You expect trouble?" Blair recognized Ryan's delicate attempt to tell her to leave.

She hadn't come down earlier because she didn't want to distract Cam right before the team departed. Instead, she had forced herself to sit in her kitchen and wait. She had watched the clock approach eleven, imagining Cam putting on her protective gear and strapping on her weapons. As every minute passed, her anxiety had grown. She had wanted so badly to see Cam again before she left. Just to say...just to say what she hadn't said before. *I love you.*

Her throat dry, Blair asked again, "Is something wrong?"

"No," Lindsey said quickly. "But I've watched too many of these things not to know that sometimes what I *thought* was happening wasn't really what happened at all. It can be nerve-wracking when you're helpless to do anything."

"Agent Ryan, I doubt very much that anything will happen that I haven't already imagined." Blair laughed entirely without humor. "And believe me, knowing has got to be better than what I'm thinking. I won't get in anyone's way."

Ryan touched her arm briefly, a sympathetic gesture of understanding. "Come with me. We can wait this one out together."

0005

From her position atop an abandoned crane platform, Cam had a clear view of the entrance to the amusement park as well as the parking lot directly in front of the arched entryway. There were no functioning lights in the immediate vicinity, but the highway itself was not too far away, and there was enough illumination from passing cars and the bright summer moon for her to see without night vision goggles. She could discern the outline of a few buildings—windows shattered and doors hanging from deteriorating hinges—surrounded by the skeletal remains of broken-down amusement park rides. In the blue glow of moonlight, it looked like a graveyard of prehistoric creatures.

On the ground directly below her, Savard waited in the shadows. Cam had reluctantly agreed with Doyle that Savard should take the point position. While she looked for signs of an approaching vehicle or any evidence of movement in the park, Cam continuously scanned the multiple radio frequencies, listening to the usual pre-engagement checks from each position. All she heard was the occasional query from Doyle confirming the position and readiness of the intercept teams. It was possible that their exchanges could be monitored, but she doubted that Loverboy had had time to lock onto their communication frequencies yet, even if he was in the area already.

She checked her watch once again. Forty minutes had passed since Grant left Blair's building. She should be arriving any second.

Ellen Grant peered out the window into the deserted parking lot as the cab slowed to a halt. She could not see Stark, who was slouched down so that she would not be visible through the windows to anyone watching their arrival. Reaching for the door handle, she said, "Thanks for the ride, guys," and took a deep breath.

"Any time. Just holler, Cinderella, and we'll bring your coach."

"Roger that," Grant said as she stepped out into the night.

The cab pulled away, and Grant looked around, trying to get her bearings. Thirty feet to her left was the archway to the amusement park, its hinged metal gates standing partway open. Beyond that was only blackness. There was some construction equipment in the parking lot itself, but otherwise no sign of anyone.

A soft voice murmured in her ear, "We have you, Grant."

Her anxiety disappeared at the sound of Roberts's steady voice. "I copy."

"Proceed through the gates," Doyle's voice ordered. "You are clear to approach the rendezvous point."

Roberts's voice repeated the order, "Proceed through the gates *only*. Hold inside and give us a visual."

Grant spoke softly as she walked forward. "I can see into the arcade now," she advised as she pushed wide the tall iron gates and stepped through. "There are pieces of equipment all over the place. Most of them are large enough to hide someone."

She looked around the grounds for the building that Loverboy had designated as the place where they would meet. Sixty yards to her left, the refreshment stand sign hung askew over the boarded-up door. "No sign of activity."

"We have no hit on the thermal sensors. There is no evidence of occupation," Cam advised her. "Advance slowly but do not—I repeat—do *not* enter the building. Perimeter check only."

Scanning right and left, Grant moved forward, trying to ignore the cold stream of sweat that ran down between her shoulder blades and pooled at the base of her spine underneath the heavy vest. She was very aware of the fact that her head was unprotected and that the body armor she wore could be pierced by ammunition available to anyone over the Internet. She also knew that all the heavy metal and machinery was a good shield against the heat sensors, if Loverboy knew how to use it.

She had to trust that Doyle and his technicians had done a thorough sweep of the surrounding buildings and grounds, because she was a sitting duck. She pushed the thought from her mind and concentrated on the still, quiet night around her.

Nothing.

If it weren't for Cameron Roberts's voice in her ear, she might have thought she had awakened from a dream in an uninhabited world. She couldn't remember ever having felt so alone.

"Anything?" Doyle barked at one of the men next to him who searched the field below with night vision glasses and thermal sensing equipment. They had set up on top of a warehouse just beyond the amusement park. From there, Doyle could direct all the action.

"Nothing except the decoy," the agent grunted as he slowly panned the area. "Not even a stray cat."

"Somebody should radio the state boys and tell them that their perimeter is too close," someone else remarked. "I can see movement, and we've got state troopers almost on top of our people."

"Amateurs." Doyle laughed derisively. "They're just looking for a little piece of the glory. It must get pretty boring riding around in those bubble cars stopping speeders all day."

The men laughed.

"Well," Doyle remarked in disgust, "I guess we're going to have to sweeten the pot if this boy is going to stick his head out of whatever hole he's hiding in."

He checked his watch and then keyed his transmitter to Grant's frequency. "Five minutes, Grant. If he's still a no-show by then, I want you to find a way into that building. If he's around, he might be waiting for you to commit yourself."

Cam heard Doyle's order, and the hair on the back of her neck stood up. Something wasn't right. Lindsey Ryan had been certain that Loverboy would be here, because otherwise there was no point to any of this.

If he didn't want to establish physical contact with Blair, then this was all a ploy to get her out into the open where he could make an attempt on her life. The refreshment stand was the obvious place for him to have set a trap. If he wanted to kill her, that would be where he would do it. Either way, he would want to be able to watch.

He was here, and they were missing him. And Ellen Grant was already too exposed.

"Doyle," Cam said, transmitting on his private frequency. "If we don't have a position on him, you can't send Grant inside alone. We can't cover her from here, and that place could be rigged."

"He didn't bring her all the way out here just to kill her," Doyle said, making no attempt to hide his scorn. "He'll show once he's certain that she's really going to go through with it. I'm not debating this, Roberts. She goes in."

Cam heard the click in her ear and knew that he had switched off. He was doing what he had wanted to do since the beginning. He was baiting the trap, and he was using her people to do it.

"Grant," Cam ordered sharply, "proceed on my signal only. Do you copy? Grant? Grant!"

Blair stared at the blank computer screen, her mind miles away. She tried to imagine what it was like for Ellen Grant, walking alone into the darkness to face someone she knew had already killed with impunity. Despite her concern for Grant, in her heart, she hoped that Loverboy was waiting. She hoped that tonight would be the end of this nightmare.

She thought about Cam, watching Grant and working to protect her. If anything happened to someone else Cam was responsible for, Cam would never forgive herself. It would tear another hole in the fabric of her being and kill another piece of her heart.

Blair did not want that to happen, and most of her reasons were selfish. She was afraid that eventually, Cam would close off those parts of herself that bled for the wounds of others. And if that happened, Blair would lose the part of Cam that she needed the most. No one had ever been able to reach through the bars of her invisible prison to touch her the way that Cameron Roberts had. No one else had ever really seen her, not the way Cam did. She needed that, because without it, she was so hopelessly alone.

She did not know how long the words had been there on the screen before she noticed them. She gasped and pushed her chair back as if to escape from the reality of what she was seeing.

"Oh my God."

Instantly, Mac, Felicia Davis, and Lindsey Ryan turned toward her in concern.

"What is it?" Mac asked urgently.

Blair's voice shook as she responded, "I'm not sure. Look at what just came up on the screen."

The other three crowded behind her, peering over her shoulder to see the message.

`Egret. Are you there?`

"Is it him?" Blair asked breathlessly. "Could it be a timed message he sent earlier?"

Mac looked at Lindsey Ryan, whose face was a study in concentration. Mentally, she assessed everything she knew about him, furiously forming and discarding theories, trying to read his distorted mind.

"Maybe a stand-in?" Mac asked. "Someone helping him?"

"No, it's him," Ryan said with determination. "He'd never let anyone share in this."

"What should I do?" Blair questioned.

"If she answers, he'll know she isn't in the amusement park," Mac warned.

Lindsey stared at the question on the monitor, considering their options and trying to predict the consequences. It was almost impossible for a rational person to predict the irrational mind of someone like Loverboy. On the other hand, she, more than anyone else, had been trained to do just that. Her opinion was the best information they had to rely on.

"Lindsey?" Mac said. "I've got to advise the commander. It's your call."

She looked calmly at Blair. "Answer it."

Hands trembling, Blair typed, `Yes`

`I always knew you wouldn't come`

"Ask him where he is," Lindsey instructed, her eyes riveted to the screen.

Blair complied.

`I'm watching them look for me`

"Jesus Christ," Mac cursed. Immediately, he switched to Cam's frequency. "We have communication from the subject," he said sharply. "You are compromised—I repeat—you are compromised."

Cam didn't hesitate. "Grant, evacuate now. Repeat, evacuate now."

On Stark's frequency, she ordered, "Institute retrieval. Recover your package now."

Switching yet again, she said, "Doyle. We've been made. He has visual. We are evacuating."

No one answered. She frantically opened all frequencies and transmitted again.

Nothing.

She stepped to the edge of the platform and dropped to the ground. She landed a few feet from Savard. "Anything?"

Savard shook her head, her expression grim. "Commander, I don't see her. I'm getting no response on any channel. Comm links are all down."

"God damn it! Loverboy's jamming us," Cam snapped angrily. "Let's go get her."

For an instant, their eyes met. And then they turned, shoulder to shoulder, and raced through the gates of the decaying amusement park into the darkness beyond.

As they passed under the archway, Cam tried once more to reach Grant or Doyle. Her transmissions were met with silence. She looked ahead, but all she could see was the blue-black of the night sky broken by the silhouettes of the detritus of the abandoned park.

"Savard," Cam whispered as they rushed forward. "Swing right and cover our flank. If he's here, he's going to go after one of us. Let's not give him too many targets in one place."

Immediately, Savard melted away into the darkness.

The refreshment stand was fifty yards in front of her. She would be there in less than sixty seconds. Sixty seconds.

Jesus, where is Grant?

Cam looked to the high ground, which was where she would have positioned herself if she had wanted to command the battle. In this situation, the best vantage point was on top of a building, but the ones still standing in the arcade were in clear view of Doyle's men on the warehouse, and they hadn't seen him. Still, out of habit, she scanned the structures with a sightline to the refreshment stand. Nothing.

Where the fuck is he?

She was almost there. Still no sign of Grant. The night had grown eerily still, yet she couldn't hear anything except her own heart pounding in her throat. She ran, her skin prickling with apprehension. She thought she saw a figure moving in the shadows by the side of the building. She raised her gun, slowing minutely, struggling to see through the shifting shadows.

There! Coming closer.

She sighted, her finger depressing the trigger just short of the firing pressure, when another movement far off to her right caught her eye. She jerked her head around in time to see the top car on the Ferris wheel swinging lazily, seemingly suspended in midair with only shafts of moonlight to hold it aloft.

"Savard," she called into the dark, not bothering to lower her voice. She was fully exposed and, at this range, defenseless. If he was going to fire at her, there was nothing she could do. At least she could make sure he didn't get away.

"He's on the Ferris wheel. Go!"

Just then, Grant appeared out of the shadows in front of the refreshment stand, calling, "All clear here, Commander."

Cam's shout to take cover was lost to the night as the building disintegrated in a flash of orange flame and flying debris.

A rushing tornado of hot air hit Savard from behind, momentarily lifting her off the ground. She tucked her head and dove into a forward shoulder roll, letting the momentum of the blast carry her back onto her feet. Her gun was out and in her hand and, miraculously, she had managed to hold on to it. She refused to think about what had just happened. She couldn't think about Grant and Roberts now. She had only one thought.

Get him.

As she approached the Ferris wheel, she saw a thin shadow nimbly descending the exterior frame. She was fifty yards away, and at that range—in the dark—she wasn't certain she would be able to hit him. If he made it to the ground, he would quickly disappear amidst the jungle of twisted metal and tumbled-down structures.

She tried again to notify Doyle and the SWAT team of her location, but there was no response. Communications were still blacked out. They were probably converging, but they would never engage in time.

Running hard, she closed the distance and got a quick glimpse of the figure that had just reached the ground. For a split second, she hesitated. He was wearing a uniform.

Is he an advance lookout Doyle didn't brief us about? Or one of our own people who just wandered too far into the perimeter?

When he turned and fired, she realized her mistake, but that second of uncertainty cost her. By the time she registered the muzzle flash, she'd been hit and was already falling, a hot flash of pain spearing her left shoulder.

God damn. It was much worse than she ever imagined.

The force spun her around and knocked her flat on her back. For a second she couldn't breathe at all. When she finally got her air back, she had to swallow a scream. Then she blanked her mind of everything except the image of him turning and firing—at her.

Bastard.

The pain receded on the wave of anger. She was furious at him for shooting her, and even more furious at herself for letting him take her by surprise. Ignoring a swell of nausea, she rolled to her side and got her feet under her.

In the next second, she was moving again. Her left arm hung uselessly, but her gun hand still worked. She could see his back as he agilely vaulted a turnstile that had once been part of an admission booth. In another instant, he'd be gone. Her vision was starting to blur, and she was running out of time. Her arm was soaked with blood; she could feel it streaming off her fingers onto the ground.

She drew down and fired.

The second explosion was even larger than the first. And this time, the shock wave catapulted her into oblivion.

CHAPTER TWENTY-THREE

Mac worked furiously to reestablish contact, but no one was answering him.

"Commander? Stark?"

Blair continued to type queries to Loverboy, but there were no further responses.

"What's happening?" she asked urgently. The three agents looked grim, and the eerie quiet that hung in the air made Blair's blood run cold. She struggled for composure and lost. "What the hell is going on?"

"All our communication lines are down," Mac said grimly. "Loverboy was probably transmitting from a wireless connection at the rendezvous site. He's there, and he knows that you're not."

Blair got to her feet, her entire body trembling. "Someone better find out *right now* what's happening out there, or I'm going myself."

"Ms. Powell," Lindsey Ryan said calmly, putting her hand on Blair's arm very gently, almost as if she were afraid of startling her, "we'll get word here faster than anywhere else. Give Mac a minute."

Mac switched to the speakers and attempted to boost the signals. "Stark, come in please. Do you copy? Stark, God damn it! Do you hear me?"

A garbled, fitful transmission crackled through. At first, all Blair could make out were fragments of words, but what she could hear was enough to take her legs out from under her. She reached blindly for a chair and sat heavily.

"...explosion...shots fired...agents down..."

"Who?" Blair asked faintly, her eyes moving from one agent's face to the other, trying desperately to read their expressions. "Mac, ask her who."

"Can you clarify?" Mac asked woodenly, forcing down the quick surge of panic Stark's message produced. He clenched his fists and concentrated, straining for her words.

More static, then "...Evacuating injured...will advise."

Then there was only silence, a silence so profound that the three of them—impotent witnesses to a nightmare—stood numbly, not looking at one another. Blair closed her eyes and wondered how it was that she could still feel her heart beating, because something inside of her was dying.

The icy stillness was shattered by the ringing of the land-line. They all stared at it for a second, and then Mac snatched it up.

"Phillips."

Blair watched him anxiously, hoping for some sign that her fears were unfounded, but the grim set of his jaw never changed. He replaced the receiver and stood up.

"That was Fielding. Ambulances are en route with the injured to the trauma unit at Beth Israel."

"Who?" Blair asked quietly, prepared, she thought, to hear him say the words. She must be ready, because she was so cold inside. Frozen. "Please...who?"

"No ID yet," he answered, looking around for his blazer, "but Stark went with one of the ambulances, so I assume some of them are our people." He pulled his jacket on as he turned toward the door. "I'll call you as soon as I have any information, Ms. Powell."

"You can't be serious." Blair moved quickly, blocking his way, an incredulous look on her face. "I'm going with you."

Mac stopped short and, although it took effort, said as calmly as he could manage, "I'm afraid you can't do that, Ms. Powell. I don't have a full complement of agents available now, and I don't even know the status of the rest of the team. I can't provide security. I can't..."

"Mac," Blair said tightly, wondering how it was that she hadn't begun screaming, "either you take me or I get a cab. But there's no way I'm not going."

"He's right, Ms. Powell," Felicia Davis said emphatically. "We're shorthanded, and we don't even know if the UNSUB has been apprehended. It's not safe. The commander will have Mac's...uh...head if he takes you out there. It's going to be chaos."

Blair almost smiled, imagining Cam's expression, and thinking that Davis was probably right—her lover would be seriously annoyed. And then she realized she might never see Cam again, might never touch her again, and the cold dark place where she locked away her fears began to bleed. When she spoke, she couldn't quite hide the pain.

"I'll make sure Commander Roberts knows it was my doing."

Perhaps it was the way Blair's voice broke when she said Cam's name, or maybe it was just that Lindsey Ryan knew that the president's daughter was going to the hospital with or without protection, but she spoke up. In a voice not only calming, but also comforting, she said, "Agent Phillips, there are three of us here. We certainly should be adequate security for Ms. Powell's transport to the hospital. Once there, I assume there will be other members of your team available to assist."

Blair shot her a grateful look.

Mac relented, because he couldn't physically restrain the first daughter. And it was finally plain to him that she was going, one way or another.

"All right then, let's do it."

At first, all Blair could see through the Suburban's window as they approached the hospital was a plethora of emergency vehicles parked haphazardly in the small lot in front of the entrance. Light bars atop ambulances and police cars sent intersecting beams of red and blue strobing wildly into the night sky to reflect eerily off the double glass doors of the trauma bay.

Hospital personnel and law enforcement officers of all description rushed everywhere. She searched the crowd of state police, plainclothes federal agents, and SWAT team members in full riot gear, but the one unmistakable form she sought was absent.

God damn it, Cam, don't you dare do this. Don't you leave me now.

Blair realized that she wasn't breathing. She also realized that there would be reporters at the hospital by now. And photographers. By the time Felicia Davis held the door open for her and she stepped from the car, she had composed herself. When reporters caught sight of her and converged, she kept her head up and her eyes forward. She made no comment.

The federal agents triangulated on her in close formation—Mac on her right, Lindsey Ryan just behind her left shoulder, and Felicia Davis clearing the way in front. When they reached the sliding glass doors that marked the trauma entrance, a large, harried-looking hospital security guard blocked their way.

"Sorry. You folks can't go back there."

Mac extended his right hand with his badge, but the guard's attention shifted and he focused on Blair. His eyes widened slightly, and he said in a slightly awed tone, "Miss Powell! I...uh...I didn't recognize you...sorry...just one minute. I'll get a detachment to escort you."

"No," Mac said sharply. "That's not necessary." The last thing he wanted was a bunch of star-struck guards trying to be helpful and making his job more difficult. "We just need to get back to the triage area. Can you direct us?"

The security officer looked as if he were about to protest, but he must have seen something in Mac's face that made him change his mind. "Yes, sir. Straight on through, past the automatic doors at the end of the hall. It's a mess back there, though."

Quickly, they crossed the hall and stepped into the relative quiet of the main admitting region. No press had yet found their way back, but there were still scores of people, most of them looking like law enforcement personnel, clogging the hallway, and emergency carts and equipment were everywhere. Blair stared at the floor and realized that the congealing trails of crimson were blood.

"Oh God," she whispered faintly.

Lindsey looked at her in concern. "Why don't we find some place less public to wait while Mac finds the others?"

"This is still way too public out here. Let's get back to the treatment area, and I'll see what I can find out," Mac agreed. He was feeling a little overwhelmed. And worried. The fact that he hadn't heard anything else from his team members did not bode well.

He and Ellen Grant had worked together for several years, even before Egret's detail, and they were friends. He liked Renée Savard. And the commander—how he felt about her was too complicated to explain. He just knew he didn't want to think about *her* going down again.

When they stepped through the solid gray doors bearing the sign, "Trauma Admitting—Authorized Personnel Only," he was relieved to see a familiar figure braced in the doorway of one of the treatment cubicles.

"Stark!"

Blair and her entourage hurried toward her. Stark stared at them silently, her expression dazed. There was blood on her shirt and hands, and a darkening smear along the angle of her jaw. Before she could respond, she was forced to step aside as a transport team came out of the room behind her, pushing a stretcher bearing a portable respirator, bags of intravenous fluid and blood, and a cardiac defibrillator.

Barely recognizable in the midst of the equipment lay Renée Savard. Blair caught only a brief glance of Savard's pale, unresponsive face as the medical team rushed her down the hall toward the elevators.

Stark started after the stretcher, but a nurse gently took her arm and murmured something to her. A moment later, the elevator doors slid closed and Savard was gone. Stark's shoulders slumped, and she leaned heavily against the wall.

Mac reached for her arm. "Stark! What..."

"Just a minute, Mac," Blair said quickly. "Let me talk to her."

"Right, okay." He turned to Davis. "You have Egret. I'll go find someone who can tell me what's going on."

Blair stepped forward and put both hands on Stark's shoulders. She looked intently into her face. "Paula," she said gently, "are you hurt? You're covered in blood."

"It's hers," Stark said, her voice choked and low. Her gaze met Blair's, a world of agony swimming below the surface of her dark eyes. "There was so much of it. I tried...the best I could. It wouldn't stop."

"You're sure you're not hurt?"

Stark stared at the blood caked on her hands, turning them over, back and forth. "No."

"Where is Cam, Paula?" Blair asked, trying hard to keep calm. *Let her be here. Just let her be all right.* "Agent Stark?"

Stark was clearly in shock, but if someone didn't tell her something soon, Blair was afraid that she might start running up and down the halls screaming out Cam's name. She was about to come apart, and she was scared to death that she would never get the pieces together again.

"Paula," she whispered desperately, "please."

"I think...I think," Paula Stark began, then lost her thread.

She was having trouble thinking about anything except how pale Renée had looked and how much blood there had been on the ground and on her clothes and how cold Renée had felt in her arms. Stark had put her arms around the injured agent and held her until the evac team arrived.

She hesitated and swallowed, trying to get control of her racing heart and her shaking legs. Finally somewhat in focus, she cleared her throat and forced herself to straighten up. "Grant and the commander were caught in the blast. I didn't see either of them, but to the best of my knowledge they were both transported here, too. Grant went to the OR right away, I think. I'm not sure about the commander."

Caught in the blast. Blair closed her eyes, refusing to think what that meant. *No. She's alive. She must be alive. They wouldn't bring her here if she wasn't. Would they?*

"Thank you," Blair said softly after a moment. She looked over her shoulder and motioned to the two agents behind her.

"Agent Davis, would you please take Agent Stark someplace where she can lie down for a few minutes?"

"I'll do that," Lindsey Ryan said quickly to Davis. "You should stay with Ms. Powell until the situation is clarified." *And a few more Secret Service agents show up. Where the hell is everyone?*

As Lindsey put her arm around the unresisting dark-haired agent, she saw Mac approaching at a near run.

"I found Fielding," he announced breathlessly. "All he knows is that Savard's in the OR, listed as critical with a gunshot wound to the shoulder. Hit just where her vest stopped and she almost bled out. Goddamned lucky shot," he added bitterly. "Grant's unconscious with a skull fracture and a collapsed lung. She's in Critical Care. The commander is..." He stopped and Blair's heart stopped, too.

Don't say it, Mac. Don't say it. Don't say—

From behind her came one word. "Blair."

Blair spun around, her heart leaping. Cam stood just a few feet away. Blair didn't think about anything—not the federal agents, not the reporters, not the public—she just reached for her.

Cam opened her arms and pulled Blair close, holding her tightly. Blair was trembling. Lowering her head, Cam brushed her lips against her ear and said softly, "I'm all right. Do you hear me? I'm all right."

Not trusting herself to speak, Blair nodded. She pressed her lips to Cam's shoulder, wanting her mouth, but knowing she couldn't. Not right there, not with everyone right there. She hadn't lost that much of her mind, and the solid reassurance of Cam's body instantly calmed her.

Too soon, she forced herself to step away, although letting Cam go was the hardest thing she had ever done in her life. Her entire body ached for the feel of her lover in her arms. Her hands shook she wanted to touch Cam so badly, just to be sure that she was still there. Just to be sure that she hadn't lost her.

"Are you hurt?" Blair's eyes darted over her, trying to reassure herself that indeed Cam was in one piece. "You *are*, aren't you?"

Cam's face was white and her usually sharp, clear eyes were dull. She had shed her jacket and protective vest, and her shirt was soaked with sweat and grime and patches of something that looked a lot like blood. A hot flash of anger flared in Blair's depths. Not toward the woman, not even toward the job, but toward the relentless maniac that had tried to take Cam from her. She wanted to kill him herself.

"Cam? *Are you hurt?*"

Cam was careful not to shake her head, because she was dizzy, and the ringing in her ears affected her balance. She was afraid too much motion would make her vomit again.

"Not much. Scrapes and bruises. A bump on the head. I won't be hearing the high notes for a while."

"Just what exactly happened to you?" Blair was instantly suspicious because Cam wasn't moving, and she had that evasive look she thought Blair didn't recognize. Before the Secret Service agent could answer, Blair added, "And if you don't tell me the whole thing right now, I'll find the doctors and ask them myself."

"A minor concussion," Cam admitted with a sigh. She ran her fingers lightly down Blair's arm. "Nothing that time won't take care of."

"And they released you?" Blair persisted.

"Well, not exactly," Cam confessed. She didn't blame Blair for being angry with her. She was only grateful that Blair hadn't been there to witness the doctors trying to convince her to be admitted overnight for observation. Now *that* would have been messy. "I'm kind of on my own recognizance at the moment."

"Damn it, Cam," Blair seethed, keeping her voice low, aware that there were others nearby. "Don't do this to me."

"I have things I need to take care of," Cam continued urgently, taking her hand. "I have two badly injured people, Blair. I have families to contact, supervisors to inform. I have my agents to see to. I *have* to be here."

As much as she didn't want to, Blair let go of Cam's hand. She took a deep breath and counted to ten. "Will you promise me that if you start to feel ill you'll let the doctors look at you? Promise me that."

"I will," Cam said, her expression grateful. "I swear, Blair."

Blair nodded, relenting because that was the best she could get at the moment. And she trusted Cam not to lie to her.

"And the minute that you get things under control you'll get some rest?"

"Agreed," Cam said with a faint smile. "Will you let Mac take you home?"

"I'd like to stay until there's some word on Ellen and Renée."

Cam heard the true caring in her voice. She looked around, relieved to see her team reassembling.

"Of course. I'll have Fielding find a room where you can wait. I'll tell you the second I hear."

"Thank you," Blair said softly. "Take good care of yourself, Commander."

"I will," Cam murmured, losing herself for just an instant in her eyes. "I'm glad that you're here, you know."

"That's a good thing," Blair whispered, "because nothing could have kept me away."

Four hours later, Cam walked into the command center and regarded the remains of her team. Most of them had never gone home but instead had voluntarily taken turns rotating between there and the hospital. As she expected, Stark was among them. The young agent appeared pale and shaky, and she had that haunted look in her eyes that Cam knew would linger a long time.

"The conference room," she said as she walked through.

A few minutes later, she stood at the head of the table, as she had so many times before, and looked at each of them in turn. Finally, she said quietly, "While we were waiting to hear about our people, I've been making phone calls and Davis has been digging through the databases. I'll give you what I have. It's preliminary and unofficial until I'm formally debriefed. Clear?"

A quick rumble of assent as all eyes focused on her. She smiled then, a cold hard smile. "We got him."

The chorus of cheers was heavy with weariness, their triumph blunted by the injuries they'd sustained.

Grimly, she passed Mac a faxed page from a personnel file with a black-and-white photograph in the upper right-hand corner of a male in uniform. "State Trooper James Benjamin Harker. Ten years ago, he was detached to *Governor* Powell's personal security detail."

For a moment there was stunned silence, then Stark muttered vehemently, "Bastard."

"I can't believe it," Mac said, obviously distressed. He glanced at the picture, then passed the sheet to the person next to him. "Why weren't we onto this? Background checks should have turned up something."

"This information stays in this room," Cam said quietly. She had to work at keeping her own anger in check as she continued, "Apparently, the FBI task force ran background checks soon after Egret alerted them that she was receiving e-mail from Loverboy. That was before they saw fit to inform us. Supposedly they cleared everyone who had ever had anything to do with her security."

"Sure," Mac interrupted with a derisive laugh. "They checked all of *us* out."

"I haven't heard Doyle's take on this. He's been strangely unavailable for comment since things went sour at the amusement park." Cam continued grimly, "Apparently, it appears there was a breakdown in their internal communications, and the security officers assigned to Egret when her father was the governor were never checked. Harker, a.k.a. Loverboy, was one of them."

Fielding raised his head sharply. "Does that mean this nutcase was shadowing her for over ten years?"

"Lindsey Ryan says it's possible," Cam said, struggling to keep the loathing from her voice.

The fact that he would have killed Blair was only part of what made it so abhorrent. She was sickened by the very idea that this psychopath had probably watched Blair from the time she was a teenager. Worst of all, she knew this wasn't really the end. Blair would never be completely free from idle curiosity and might someday become the object of someone else's obsession. She shoved the thought away. She had to get through this, and then maybe she could lie down and the pounding in her head would stop.

"Whatever happened, the FBI will clean up their own mess."

"Yeah, right," Mac snarled. "Except we've had to pay the price for their foul-up. First you, then Jeremy, and now Grant."

"Update on the injured," Cam continued, ignoring Mac's remark, although privately she agreed with him.

From what she had learned during her initial call to Stewart Carlisle, SAC Doyle was getting all the credit for the takedown. She didn't begrudge the FBI that, because Savard had been the one to stop him. This was not about who got the glory, but about the fact that Blair was no longer in danger, at least for the moment. For that, she would always be grateful to Renée Savard. The fact that Doyle had nearly gotten Ellen Grant killed was another issue, and she would not soon forget that.

Her mind was wandering. She took a deep breath, trying to clear her head. "Grant is awake and says for none of you to touch her desk. Said she'll know if there's a pencil missing." Cam smiled faintly. "She'll be discharged in five or six days and back on duty in six weeks if the next CT scan is clear."

She glanced at Stark once, quickly, and then continued steadily, "Savard is out of surgery, but still unconscious in the intensive care unit. The surgeons are optimistic. She lost a lot of blood, but apparently no critical structures in her shoulder were involved. In the absence of any unforeseen complications, they're predicting a full recovery."

She looked pointedly at each person gathered around the table. "We owe her. She stepped up for us, and even after she was hit, she managed to get this guy. No one is exactly sure yet what happened, and it's going to take weeks for the final crime scene analysis. What we figure is that he was carrying another explosive device that he either hadn't had time to dispose of or that he was planning on planting somewhere else."

Several eyebrows rose.

"The ATF commander tells me that the shock waves from a bullet impacting anywhere near a high-order explosive can trigger it. Looks like Savard hit him, and his own bomb took him out. We're waiting for forensics to give us the final ID, but Harker was missing after the action and everything else fits."

"Too fucking good for him," Fielding grumbled.

A round of murmured assents followed.

"Davis ran a quick background check, and it turns out that Harker had applied to the Secret Service before he joined the Staties. He was denied for psychological reasons. I guess the state system never turned up that information with a computer check of his application. Not surprising, since none of our systems are interfaced."

Now came the hard part. "I just looked at the tapes from the explosion in Central Park. Harker was the trooper standing next to Jeremy's car. He probably placed the device right there."

The silence was heavy with sorrow and fury.

"He's also the one who pulled me away from the car that day. I don't know why."

Lindsey had told her that it might be something as simple as the fact that Harker didn't want anything or anyone to alter his plan—that he needed to be the one to determine who should live, and who should die...and when.

Mac slid Harker's sheet back to her, and Cam regarded it with a sense of finality. "I'll be flying to DC sometime later today or first thing tomorrow morning for the debriefing. Egret is due to leave for San Francisco in a few days. She's staying with Diane Bleeker until some of the publicity dies down and at the moment, her itinerary is in flux. I'll review her plans with you when I know them. Mac, would you set up the shifts, please. You'll head the detail until I return."

"Right," he said quietly.

She knew they needed to mourn Jeremy's loss. She also knew what else they needed. "I've arranged for a team from the local field office to cover the current shift. Everyone go home and get some rest. If there's news from the hospital, I'll see that you're notified. I need you all back here in twelve hours, and I need you to be sharp. We still have a job to do."

As the others in the room stood to leave, she added, "Stark, a moment, please."

Cam waited until the room had cleared, then she closed the door and said, "Take a couple days leave time, Stark. You look like hell."

"I'm fine, Commander," Stark's eyes flashed with anger. "I'll be ready to take the evening shift."

Cam smiled faintly and rested a hip against the corner of the table. She looked away for a second, and when she returned her gaze to Stark, she let the sadness show. "What happened out there is hard for everyone, Stark. Having friends and colleagues in danger, seeing them injured—it affects us all." She paused, not needing the memories to feel the terrible sense of helplessness, the horrible hopelessness. She'd never forget it. "It's much harder when it's someone you care about. I know."

Stark stared at her in surprise. Maybe it was the sympathy in Cam's voice or the shared sorrow that finally undid her, but she sat quickly and covered her face with her hands, hiding the tears that she couldn't hold back any longer. It took her a few minutes to get hold of herself, and then she sank back in the chair.

"I'm sorry. I think I'm just tired. I know she's going to be all right, but I can't stop thinking about the way she looked lying on that stretcher."

"Savard is tough, and she's going to be fine."

"She sure kicked some ass, didn't she?" Stark grinned, her spirits bolstered by the certainty in Cam's voice.

"That she did," Cam agreed.

Stark rose wearily. "Thank you, Commander. I think I will request a few days' personal time, just so I can...you know...visit the hospital and stuff."

Cam smiled. "A very good idea, Agent."

Waiting until the room had cleared, Cam then made her way slowly downstairs. She flagged down a cab and gave him the Upper East Side address. She was asleep before he pulled away from the curb.

Chapter Twenty-four

Well," Diane Bleeker said as she stood in the open doorway, "I've waited a long time to see *you* at my door, Commander."

"Sorry." Cam grinned tiredly.

"Don't be," Diane said with a laugh. "Some things are definitely worth waiting for."

Cam glanced at several suitcases standing by the door. "Going somewhere?"

"Just a three-day weekend," Diane said nonchalantly. Then she raised an eyebrow, a speculative look on her face. "Basically a spur-of-the-moment kind of thing."

"Thank you." Cam knew that Diane was leaving to give her and Blair a little time alone. "I appreciate it."

"Oh, believe me, Commander," Diane ran her fingers lightly down Cam's arm, lingering just a moment on her hand, "anything I can do to help."

"You might want to take your hands off her, Diane," Blair said softly from behind them. "I'm terribly short of patience at the moment."

Diane turned to smile at her old friend. "When did you lose your sense of humor, Blair?"

"Well..." Blair looked past Diane to Cam, who still stood waiting at the door, rumpled and pale and just about the best-looking thing she had ever seen. She ached to get her hands on her, her arms around her, her skin on her skin. Her voice was low, throaty with emotion, when she murmured, "I think it was along about the second time that maniac tried to kill her."

"Since that's the way it is, I'll just make myself scarce." Diane stepped aside. She had watched Blair pace and worry and stare out the window for the last few hours, restlessly waiting, and she could never remember seeing her so undone, and so clearly suffering. "The doorman's already called the cab. Try to behave for a day or so, you two."

"Thanks for everything." Blair touched Diane's shoulder briefly as her friend grasped her suitcases and left, but her eyes never moved from Cam's face. When they were alone, she came slowly forward and took Cam's hand. "Come with me."

Cam was too tired to question or protest. The dizziness had abated, but the headache persisted and probably would for days. Mostly, she was weary. There had been too much violence—too many injured and too many lost; she was worn down by it, body and soul. All she really wanted was to lie down next to Blair and close her eyes.

Blair led her through the apartment and into the bathroom, closing the door. She turned and began unbuttoning Cam's shirt. Cam lifted her hands to help, but Blair brushed her fingers away gently.

"No. Let me."

Tenderly, Blair undressed her, being careful to ease the clothing off the new patches of bruises and abrasions covering her back. She tried not to think of what had put them there, but she couldn't help imagining Cam flung to the ground, rocks and debris raining down on her during the blast.

Cam sensed her hesitate. "It isn't as bad—"

"Yes, I know, Commander. It isn't as bad as it looks." She put it from her mind for the moment.

When she had Cam naked, she took off her own clothes. She started the water in the shower and drew Cam in with her.

"Oh God," Cam groaned softly. "That feels so good."

"Mmm," Blair responded, she herself finally beginning to relax. She reached for the soap and worked the lather over Cam's body.

"And that feels even better," Cam whispered, her eyes closing. She was nearly asleep standing up. The hot steam and Blair's soft hands lulled her into a state of near torpor. By the time Blair was finished washing her hair, she wasn't sure she would be able to remain standing. "I'm not going to be much good for anything in another minute," she mumbled, her speech slurred with fatigue.

Blair wrapped her in a large towel and brushed the damp hair back from her forehead. She kissed her gently on the mouth. "Believe me, Commander, you are good for a great many things, which I'm sure you'll remember after a little sleep. If not," she added as she led the way to the bedroom, "I'll be sure to remind you."

❖

Renée Savard opened her eyes and tried to focus on the figure leaning over her. Finally, she succeeded. "Hi."

Stark smiled. "Hi yourself."

Carefully taking stock, Savard eventually assured herself that she could feel the bed covers touching each foot and each hand. Then she wiggled her fingers and toes, finally sighing with relief. "Apparently everything is working, yeah?"

"The doctors say you'll be fine," Stark said, a small catch in her voice.

"You want to give me a rundown of what *fine* means?"

"Uh, I guess the doctors should probably do that," Stark hedged.

"Paula," Savard said, and this time her voice trembled. "I'd prefer hearing it from you."

"Hey." Stark gently reached for her hand, cradling her fingers between her own palms. "You're okay, Renée, really. You took a bullet in the left shoulder. They said it pretty much severed the major vein from your arm. They sewed that up. But the nerves are okay—they think you'll have a little weakness for a few months." Stark gathered herself and worked on sounding optimistic.

"You bled like hell though, and they gave you transfusions for that. You've been out of it for a while because of the megadose of anesthesia and the shock. But you're going to be fine."

Savard closed her eyes for a few seconds, and when she opened them, her smile was stronger. "That doesn't sound too bad. A little rehab and I should be back in the field, right?"

"Don't see why not," Stark said positively, although at the moment she didn't want to think about that. She still couldn't shake the feeling of terror she'd had when she'd found her on the ground, lying so still, covered in blood.

"Did I get him?" Savard asked uncertainly.

This time, Stark's smile was brilliant, and her eyes flickered with something hard and edgy. "Oh yeah, you got him. You got him in about a million pieces. He took a little unexpected ride on his own rocket fuel. Straight to hell, I hope."

Stark forced back the rage. Later. There would be time to let it out later. "You're a hero, Renée. You deserve all the credit you get."

Savard shook her head. "I don't think so, Paula. Roberts was all over it out there. If it hadn't been for her..." She broke off abruptly and her eyes widened, more fear-filled than when she had first awakened and realized that she was in a hospital bed. "Oh God! Is she all right? Ellen Grant? What about Grant? There was an explosion—"

"They're both okay," Stark said quickly. "Grant will be in here a while, but the commander has already been released."

"Thank God." Savard closed her eyes for a few seconds. She was beginning to remember—running through the dark, the flash of the explosion, the tearing pain in her shoulder. *God, is it finally over, then?*

Stark frowned when she realized that Savard was trembling. "I should go. You need to rest."

Savard opened her eyes again. Softly, she said, "You look like you could use some, too."

"Yeah, maybe," Stark said with a sheepish grin. She was actually about to fall down she was so tired. But she couldn't leave just yet. "So...uh...Savard...just in case you have any memory problems, you know...from this little...uh, episode..."

Damn. It was easier when I rehearsed this.

"I...uh...wanted to remind you that we...you know...have a date. Right?"

Renée Savard smiled, and this time her eyes sparkled with their old vitality. "You don't need to worry, Agent Stark. It would take more than a bullet to make me forget that."

When Cam awoke, she was naked in bed and Blair was beside her. For a few moments, she lay quietly, simply luxuriating in the feel of Blair's arm possessively draped across her body. She liked the weight of it, the quiet reminder that she belonged here—with her.

"He's really dead, isn't he?" Blair said into the still room, part statement, part question.

"Yes." Cam reached for Blair's hand, interlacing her fingers with Blair's and squeezing gently. "We don't have a positive ID, but I expect that we will when the forensics people are finished."

"Who was he?"

Cam hesitated for a second and then said kindly, "He was a state trooper assigned to your security detail about ten years ago—when your father was still governor."

Blair rolled onto her side and pressed tightly against Cam's body, nestling her face against her uninjured shoulder. After a moment, she said, "I don't remember him. I don't remember any of them."

"There's no reason that you should." Cam's tone was gentle and her touch soothing as she brushed her fingers lightly over the curve of Blair's breast. Blair shivered in her arms. "We're not supposed to be memorable. We're supposed to do our job and keep out of your life."

There was an edge of bitterness in her voice that she couldn't quite hide. Harker had tarnished so many things she valued. Dishonoring his oath was the least of his sins. It enraged her every time she thought of him watching Blair with his fevered distorted longings all the time that he had been entrusted with her care.

"I seem to have quite a few pleasant memories of you though, Commander," Blair whispered softly, rubbing her palm lightly over Cam's chest, chasing away the demons.

Cam's swift intake of breath followed fast on the surge of excitement that rippled through her. She shifted so they were face-to-face, and she kissed her way along the edge of Blair's jaw to the corner of her mouth. "Let's make a few more."

Blair pushed Cam down and moved on top of her, straddling her hips. "Yes, let's."

"I love the way you look when you're on top of me," Cam murmured, reaching for the full breasts just inches away.

Blair leaned forward, catching her lower lip between her teeth as Cam's knowing fingers closed on her nipples, sending showers of excitement streaking low between her thighs. She rocked, slow easy strokes, teasing herself as well as her lover as her wetness coated Cam's stomach.

When the pressure began to peak and the tingling started on the insides of her thighs, she dropped her head and closed her eyes, bracing herself with her hands against the mattress on either side of Cam's shoulders. Her breath came in uneven sobs as she gave herself to the escalating urgency between her legs, pressing harder, faster. Soon, it would be impossible to stop.

She forced her eyes open and struggled to focus on Cam's face. "Should I wait?" she gasped.

"No," Cam rasped, barely able to force the words out her chest felt so tight. "You're so beautiful when you come."

She brought one hand down between them and slipped her fingers between Blair's legs, cupping her as she thrust.

"Oh, Cam," Blair moaned, riding hard on Cam's hand. She jerked once and then she was gone. As the spasms continued to bombard her, she collapsed against Cam's chest, groaning softly. "Sorry," she finally murmured. "I seem to be afflicted with terminal lust."

"Nice," Cam remarked, running her hands up and down her back. "Have I mentioned lately that I find you terminally sexy?"

Blair laughed, leaning up on one elbow and shaking the hair back from her face. "You think we're safe together?"

Cam stroked her face, then raised her head and kissed gently. "Oh yes. Quite safe."

"Are we free now?" Blair asked, suddenly serious.

"Yes."

But they both knew that wasn't quite true.

"I'd prefer that you not scare the hell out of me again for a while." Blair pressed her lips to Cam's bare shoulder, tasting the light tang of salt and feeling her desire rise again.

Cam brushed a kiss into silky blond hair. "I have no intention of scaring you again at *any* time. I know it's hard to believe at the moment, but these situations are extremely rare. I hope you'll be able to believe that someday."

"You're not resigning, are you?"

"I don't want to." Cam tightened her grip and held Blair closer when she felt her stiffen. "It's what I do, Blair, and it feels right to me. It lets me be with you more than I would be able to under any other circumstances. I don't want to see you for a night every couple of months. Not for the next seven years."

Blair tried hard to put her fear aside and listen to what Cam was telling her. She couldn't deny the reality of the situation, because if Cam were not part of her security detail, it would be very hard for them to be together. And with her as the security chief, it would still be hard for them to have a personal life, but that was not a new challenge for her. She had been working outside the system, in that regard, all her life. She sighed.

"I don't know if it will work, but I'm willing to try."

"If it doesn't work," Cam assured, "I'll do whatever I have to do. Blair, I love you."

Blair moved on top of Cam and looked intently into her face. "We'll both do whatever we need to do. Because I love you, too."

"Is that so?" Cam caught Blair's fingers and pressed a kiss to her palm. Then, she moved Blair's hand down her body. "Perhaps you could repeat that."

Blair laughed, watching Cam's eyes as she touched her. "As you wish, Commander."

About the Author

Radclyffe has written numerous best-selling lesbian romances (*Safe Harbor* and its sequels *Beyond the Breakwater* and *Distant Shores, Silent Thunder*; *Innocent Hearts*; *Love's Melody Lost*; *Love's Tender Warriors*; *Tomorrow's Promise*; *Passion's Bright Fury*; *Love's Masquerade*; *shadowland*; and *Fated Love*), two romance/intrigue series: the Honor series (*Above All, Honor*; *Honor Bound*; *Love & Honor*; *Honor Guards*; and *Honor Reclaimed*) and the Justice series (*Shield of Justice*; the prequel *A Matter of Trust*; *In Pursuit of Justice*; *Justice in the Shadows*; and *Justice Served*), and the Erotic Interlude series: *Change of Pace* and *Stolen Moments: Erotic Interludes 2* (ed. with Stacia Seaman). She also has selections in the anthologies *Call of the Dark* and *The Perfect Valentine* (Bella Books), *Best Lesbian Erotica 2006* (Cleis), and *First-Timers* (Alyson).

She is the recipient of the 2003 and 2004 Alice B. Readers' Award for her body of work and is a 2005 Golden Crown Literary Society Award winner in both the romance category (*Fated Love*) and the mystery/intrigue/action category (*Justice in the Shadows*). She is also the president of Bold Strokes Books, a lesbian publishing company. In 2005, she retired from the practice of surgery to write and publish full time. A member of the GCLS, Pink Ink, and the Romance Writers of America, she collects lesbian pulps, enjoys photographing scenes for her book covers, and shares her life with her partner, Lee, and assorted canines.

Her upcoming works include *Turn Back Time* (March 2006), *Lessons in Love: Erotic Interludes 3* ed. with Stacia Seaman (May 2006), and *Promising Hearts* (June 2006).

Look for information about these works at www.boldstrokesbooks.com.

Books Available From Bold Strokes Books

Grave Silence by Rose Beecham. Detective Jude Devine's investigation of a series of ritual murders is complicated by her torrid affair with the golden girl of Southwestern forensic pathology, Dr. Mercy Westmoreland. (1-933110-25-2)

Honor Reclaimed by Radclyffe. In the aftermath of 9/11, Secret Service Agent Cameron Roberts and Blair Powell close ranks with a trusted few to find the would-be assassins who nearly claimed Blair's life. (1-933110-18-X)

Honor Bound by Radclyffe. Secret Service Agent Cameron Roberts and Blair Powell face political intrigue, a clandestine threat to Blair's safety, and the seemingly irreconcilable personal differences that force them ever further apart. (1-933110-20-1)

Protector of the Realm: Supreme Constellations Book One by Gun Brooke. A space adventure filled with suspense and a daring intergalactic romance featuring Commodore Rae Jacelon and a stunning, but decidedly lethal Kellen O'Dal. (1-933110-26-0)

Innocent Hearts by Radclyffe. In a wild and unforgiving land, two women learn about love, passion, and the wonders of the heart. (1-933110-21-X)

The Temple at Landfall by Jane Fletcher. An imprinter, one of Celaeno's most revered servants of the Goddess, is also a prisoner to the faith—until a Ranger frees her by claiming her heart. (1-933110-27-9)

Force of Nature by Kim Baldwin. From tornados to forest fires, the forces of nature conspire to bring Gable McCoy and Erin Richards close to danger, and closer to each other. (1-933110-23-6)

In Too Deep by Ronica Black. Undercover homicide cop Erin McKenzie tracks a femme fatale who just might be a real killer…with love and danger hot on her heels. (1-933110-17-1)

Stolen Moments: Erotic Interludes 2 by Stacia Seaman and Radclyffe, eds. Love on the run, in the office, in the shadows…Fast, furious, and almost too hot to handle. (1-933110-16-3)

Course of Action by Gun Brooke. Actress Carolyn Black desperately wants the starring role in an upcoming film produced by Annelie Peterson. Just how far will she go for the dream part of a lifetime? (1-933110-22-8)

Rangers at Roadsend by Jane Fletcher. Sergeant Chip Coppelli has learned to spot trouble coming, and that is exactly what she sees in her new recruit, Katryn Nagata. The Celaeno series. (1-933110-28-7)

Justice Served by Radclyffe. Lieutenant Rebecca Frye and her lover, Dr. Catherine Rawlings, embark on a deadly game of hide-and-seek with an underworld kingpin who traffics in human souls. (1-933110-15-5)

Distant Shores, Silent Thunder by Radclyffe. Dr. Tory King—along with the women who love her—is forced to examine the boundaries of love, friendship, and the ties that transcend time. (1-933110-08-2)

Hunter's Pursuit by Kim Baldwin. A raging blizzard, a mountain hideaway, and a killer-for-hire set a scene for disaster—or desire—when Katarzyna Demetrious rescues a beautiful stranger. (1-933110-09-0)

The Walls of Westernfort by Jane Fletcher. All Temple Guard Natasha Ionadis wants is to serve the Goddess—until she falls in love with one of the rebels she is sworn to destroy. The Celaeno series. (1-933110-24-4)

Change Of Pace: Erotic Interludes by Radclyffe. Twenty-five hot-wired encounters guaranteed to spark more than just your imagination. Erotica as you've always dreamed of it. (1-933110-07-4)

Honor Guards by Radclyffe. In a wild flight for their lives, the president's daughter and those who are sworn to protect her wage a desperate struggle for survival. (1-933110-01-5)

Fated Love by Radclyffe. Amidst the chaos and drama of a busy emergency room, two women must contend not only with the fragile nature of life, but also with the irresistible forces of fate. (1-933110-05-8)

Justice in the Shadows by Radclyffe. In a shadow world of secrets and lies, Detective Sergeant Rebecca Frye and her lover, Dr. Catherine Rawlings, join forces in the elusive search for justice. (1-933110-03-1)

shadowland by Radclyffe. In a world on the far edge of desire, two women are drawn together by power, passion, and dark pleasures. An erotic romance. (1-933110-11-2)

Love's Masquerade by Radclyffe. Plunged into the indistinguishable realms of fiction, fantasy, and hidden desires, Auden Frost is forced to question all she believes about the nature of love. (1-933110-14-7)

Love & Honor by Radclyffe. The president's daughter and her lover are faced with difficult choices as they battle a tangled web of Washington intrigue for...love and honor. (1-933110-10-4)

Beyond the Breakwater by Radclyffe. One Provincetown summer three women learn the true meaning of love, friendship, and family. (1-933110-06-6)

Tomorrow's Promise by Radclyffe. One timeless summer, two very different women discover the power of passion to heal and the promise of hope that only love can bestow. (1-933110-12-0)

Love's Tender Warriors by Radclyffe. Two women who have accepted loneliness as a way of life learn that love is worth fighting for and a battle they cannot afford to lose. (1-933110-02-3)

Love's Melody Lost by Radclyffe. A secretive artist with a haunted past and a young woman escaping a life that has proved to be a lie find their destinies entwined. (1-933110-00-7)

Safe Harbor by Radclyffe. A mysterious newcomer, a reclusive doctor, and a troubled gay teenager learn about love, friendship, and trust during one tumultuous summer in Provincetown. (1-933110-13-9)

Above All, Honor by Radclyffe. Secret Service Agent Cameron Roberts fights her desire for the one woman she can't have—Blair Powell, the daughter of the president of the United States. (1-933110-04-X)